My Pet Werewolf

James Kaine

HORROR HOUSE PUBLISHING

For Jessica – Every book I write is dedicated to you because there is no me without you. You are the love of my life and my best friend and none of this is possible without you.

***

For James & Juliana – I am so blessed to be your dad and everything I do is for you, including writing these really messed up books. I love that you love the creepy stuff as much as I do, but no, you can't read this until you're MUCH older.

***

For Mom – Thank you for all your love and support over the years and for starting me on this journey when you bought me that copy of IT when I was 10 years old, even though it was in no way age appropriate.

PROLOGUE

One night, when I was ten years old, my dad asked me to take out the garbage. While that's not an unusual ask of a child learning to contribute to the household, we lived on a twenty-acre property, much of which was woods. So when I had to lug that garbage bag to the small shed about a hundred feet from our back door a good hour after the sun had gone down, my youthful mind concocted all types of scenarios as to the horrors that lay in wait for me as I approached their wooded lair.

This particular night was rainy, so I pulled on a hooded sweatshirt to give me some cover from the drops that had slowed from a torrential downpour to a steady drizzle. I slung the trash bag over my shoulder as I stepped off the deck onto the rain-softened ground below, making my way toward the ominous little structure no doubt hiding goblins, demons and ghosts.

As I got closer, my pace quickened, wanting to get the task over with and return to the safety of my house as soon as possible. When I was mere steps away, I stopped suddenly as I heard a crackle in the trees off to my left.

While that was nowhere near an uncommon sound and could have easily been a squirrel, when you're ten years old and it's dark in the woods, it's more likely to be the most horrific, vile creature you could imagine.

Yanking the door open to the shed I tossed the garbage bag at the bucket inside, not caring in the least when it clipped the side, knocking the receptacle over and spilling the other bags to the ground. The task complete, I slammed the door behind me, figuring I could easily go back out in the morning under the protection of sunlight and put everything back in place.

I started power walking back to the house, but after a few feet, I felt something behind me. Looking back on it now, it was probably nothing more than the ambient sounds of the forest, but to my youthful mind, it might as well have been every monster I'd ever seen on TV getting ready to grab me.

My walk turned into a full-fledged run. I made it to the deck unscathed, but as I hopped onto the rain-slicked boards, my footing immediately gave out and I slid all the way up to the back door, slamming my shin into the corner of the house as I came to an abrupt, unwelcome stop.

Lightning bolts of pain shot through my leg as I reached down to cup it. It felt wet, but I initially assumed it was the rain. As I writhed on the deck, my dad rushed out the back door, having been alerted by my screams which, more than likely, were louder than the situation called for.

Dad helped me up and into the house through the back door and into the kitchen. He sat me at the table and pulled a chair up next to me, lifting my leg up onto his thigh so he could get a better look at it.

"Brady, let me see," he said in his typically even tone.

I shook my head vehemently as I clasped my hands over my shin.

"Bud," he continued, "I can't help you if you don't let me see it."

I looked up at him, tears and rain streaking my face.

"You know I'd never do anything to hurt you, right?"

I nodded as I slowly lifted my hands off, instantly horrified when I saw the blood covering them. To my surprise, though, I gasped but didn't scream. Looking back, I think I may have wanted to seem tough in front of my dad. After all, he was the toughest guy I knew.

The wound looked awful. There was a wide-open gash separating the flesh of my shin. My leg was resting on top of Dad's thigh as he sat, angled to the right a bit, so the blood streamed down and dripped onto the tile floor. I'd never seen so much blood in my life.

"Liz!" Dad called for my mom, loud enough that she could hear, but by no means panicked. It impressed my young mind. I was on the verge of freaking out, yet Dad was cool, calm and collected.

My mom came into the kitchen and added a gasp of her own.

"Oh, my God! What happened?"

Dad remained calm. "Grab me those paper towels, please."

Even in crisis, the man had manners.

My mom did as he asked. He tore off four sheets and wiped away the blood, more spilling into the growing puddle on the tile as he did. When he removed the blood-soaked towel, I saw the ugly wound in its entirety. The gash was clean for a split second before blood started pouring out again. I felt nauseous. Almost like I was going to pass out.

"Honey, please go get the medical kit in the bathroom," he said to my mom before looking me in the eye. "Alright, sport, here's the deal. You're going to need stitches."

My body tensed up at the thought. I'd never had stitches before and the concept was terrifying to me.

Dad continued. "We're going to wrap this up, then I'm going to drive you to the emergency room while Mom stays here with Brandi."

Brandi, my baby sister. Well, baby sister by three and a half minutes that is, but I was still older than her. I teared up at the thought of her. Especially with everything that's happened these past few weeks? Months? Jesus Christ, I couldn't even remember how long it had been since this nightmare began.

I thought back again to that night when I was ten years old. Eight years ago, when I had never seen that much blood in one place.

That was nothing compared to what I was looking at now.

I lowered my shotgun, the barrel still smoking. I saw blood everywhere. And the bodies, ravaged and mangled. It wasn't supposed to go like this. I had just tried to help and now there was nothing but carnage and death surrounding me.

I had fucked up big time.

CHAPTER 1

TWO MONTHS EARLIER

I leveled my sight on the six-point buck just about fifty yards in front of me. I could probably hit it with my crossbow from my position in my blind—a kind of hunting tent for those of you unfamiliar with the term—but I didn't want to chance missing it, so I just observed it for the moment, trying to silently will it to get closer.

I had set up some lures loaded with gland attractant to get one of these horny bastards close. Mating season, the rut, was still a few weeks away, but I had gotten into the habit of setting a few lures early on to see if I could catch a straggler.

The buck sniffed around for a moment and then started toward me.

My heartbeat quickened. I had him. He wouldn't be the biggest deer I ever bagged—that honor belonged to a nine-pointer two years ago—but he would still be a nice one and we had been out of venison for a while, especially since my stepdad hurt his knee a few months back, leaving me the only active hunter in the house for the time being.

Stepdad. That still didn't feel right to me. The very thought brought me back in time seven years to the worst week of my life.

***

The tears began just as I reached the top of the tree. I fought them as long as I could, but as soon as I settled on the hefty branch twenty feet off the ground, the dam holding them back broke. Despite my attempts to wipe them away, they kept coming with each heaving sob.

The air was sharp and stinging as blasts of frigid wind smacked me in the face. If my emotions had been in check, I might have been concerned about the substantial gusts that might rock me enough to tumble to the ground below, but at that point I didn't care. The only thing that mattered in my world was that I had just come home from my father's funeral. He had died last week. And it was my fault.

The guilt bubbled back up and the sobs, which had subsided, returned full force. In my eleven years, I had never felt such a myriad of emotions all at once. It was like a battle royal was being contested between my stomach, my heart and my head.

Why didn't you just go with him? You stupid lazy piece of shit!

"Brady!"

The girl's voice came from below. I recognized it immediately, but I didn't answer. The last thing I wanted to do right now was talk to anyone, but I knew I couldn't hide from her. She knew exactly where I was.

"Brady Bennett, get down from there right now!"

I looked down to see Brandi standing on the frost-coated grass, looking up at me with that special annoyance reserved only for a sibling. Her brown hair was tied back in a ponytail and a pair of fluffy earmuffs shielded her ears from the cold. She wore a black dress and a heavy red peacoat, appropriate winter attire. My own was not as fitting. I was only wearing my now very wrinkled black suit with a plain white dress shirt that had become untucked during my ascent. I had discarded my solid black clip-on tie the moment we got back to the house. Although my garments were appropriate for a funeral, they did nothing to protect me from the elements.

I did my best to ignore my sister, but her presence brought me back from the nadir of my misery. My sobs subsided, leaving only a slight trickle of tears, rendering my efforts to wipe them from my bloodshot eyes simpler now. I wished I had run further into the woods behind our house. Living in a semi-rural area, it wasn't hard to make myself scarce, but I'd opted for the familiarity of my favorite climbing tree. I guess I shouldn't have been surprised it didn't take her long to find me.

"Brady!" she shouted, using a surprisingly stern tone of voice for an eleven-year-old.

I looked down again, this time making eye contact with her. She didn't verbalize it, but her eyes said *Get down here! Right now!*

I got the message and took a deep breath to compose myself, remaining seated for as long as I could without risking the further ire of my twin. Finally, I reached over and wrapped my arm around the trunk to grab the nearest branch. As soon as I had a grip, I raised my butt off the limb and lowered my foot onto the one below. I had discovered my penchant for tree climbing when I was five years old and I had climbed this tree more times than I could count. Every move during my descent came with confidence bred of familiarity.

When my feet landed on the ground, I dusted myself off, trying my best to avoid Brandi's glare.

"Here!" she said as I felt something weighty hit my chest. I instinctively brought my arms up to catch it. It was my winter coat—a thick blue and red hooded jacket emblazoned with the New York Giants logo. My sadness welled up again as I looked at the garment, thinking back to when the G-Men had beaten the Patriots in the 2012 Super Bowl. I hadn't really understood the game back then, but it didn't matter—I loved watching with Dad. Part of me wanted to root for the Patriots, given that I shared a name with their quarterback, but Dad was so into the Giants, it was hard for me not to be as well. I distinctly remembered one play where some guy named Mario—like in my video games—caught the ball barely in the lines. I didn't completely understand the significance of that sequence in relation to the overall game, but I remembered the referees looking at it for a long time and Dad jumping off the couch in jubilation when they confirmed the result of the play would stand. Dad had scooped me up in his arms and jumped around the room with me, the two of us laughing and cheering until we felt dizzy. When the game ended and the Giants were world champions, he had pulled out his phone and played Queen's seminal sports anthem, "We Are the Champions", all while bouncing around the room with me again as I laughed and clapped.

I clutched the jacket tightly, squeezing it as hard as I could, trying to keep my emotions in check. I'd never experience a moment like that again with my dad. Not to mention that the Giants had absolutely sucked since then. Ridiculous as it was, I silently cursed the team that my father's last memory of them was a horrendous overtime loss to the equally hapless New York Jets. On his birthday, no less.

"Put the jacket on, Brady." My sister's voice broke into

my thoughts.

While I wasn't necessarily concerned that Brandi was irritated with me—it wasn't the first time and wouldn't be the last—I agreed and slid the jacket on. The instant warmth it provided made me remember for the first time since I ran out of the house just how biting the New Jersey winter air could be.

"Did Mom send you?" I asked.

"No," she replied, "no one told me to come after you. I was worried, you jerk."

I didn't reply.

"Brady..." she started.

I fiddled with my sleeves.

"Brady!"

I looked my sister directly in her eye.

She softened a bit at the sight of the tears still drying on my cheeks. "Why did you run out of there?" she asked. "And why the heck would you be up in a tree of all places considering what happened to Daddy?"

"I... I just couldn't be in there anymore. They're all staring at me."

"Who?"

"Everyone!" I blurted out, angrier than I intended. "Everyone knows that it's my fault!"

"What the heck are you talking about, Brady? How is this your fault?"

I fought back more tears as I explained. "He wanted me

to go with him. He wanted me to go with him, but I just didn't feel like it! I wanted to sleep in and then play video games. I didn't want to spend the day in the woods in the cold."

"So he went by himself. What's the big deal? He went hunting all the time."

"Yeah, but if I went with him, we would have set up a blind. He wouldn't have gone up in that stupid old tree stand. He wouldn't have been up there and he wouldn't have fallen." I paused as the emotions resurfaced. "If I'd just gone with him, he wouldn't be dead!"

The last word choked off in my throat as the dam broke again. I tried to hold back but couldn't even though I really didn't want Brandi to see me like this. In a half-hearted attempt to mask my sorrow, I brought my hands up to my face and crouched down, lowering my head as I sobbed again, thinking about the night before he died.

Dad had asked me if I wanted to go out hunting with him the next day. He'd been teaching me for the past couple of years and, while I enjoyed spending time with my father, the actual rigmarole of getting up before the sun, trekking into the woods in the cold and then waiting for hours hoping a buck would come along was not my favorite thing. My grandpa had taught my dad to hunt and I know he had hoped I would take to it like he had, but I just didn't. It wasn't for me.

I didn't have the heart to tell him that, though, so I tentatively agreed. However, when he came into my room and tried to gently nudge me awake at 4:30 a.m., I just couldn't bring myself to get up, so I made an excuse about my stomach hurting. I know Dad was disappointed, but he tried not to show it. He simply kissed me on the forehead, tucked me back in and told me to "get some rest."

He never came back that evening and Mom got worried, especially when he didn't answer his phone. She ventured out to his tree stand, which is where she found him. An hour later, the cops were at the house and an ambulance was taking my father's body away. Mom's initial hysterics gave way to shock and my maternal grandparents tried to usher Brandi and me away so we wouldn't hear the particulars, but I already had.

Apparently, Dad's tree stand had somehow come loose and caused him to fall twenty feet to the ground below. He broke his neck in the fall and died. My heart sank when I heard this. Whenever he took me out with him, he set up a blind big enough for two that we sat in while we waited. But, with him going out on his own, he opted for his tree. The guilt was suffocating.

So now here we were, a week later. My dad was dead and I was devastated and plagued with guilt. I still couldn't bring myself to look up, and for a second, I thought Brandi had left. She hadn't responded and my sister not having something to say was rare, to say the least. But she confirmed she was still there, though not with her words. She simply crouched beside me and took me into her arms, her slight frame providing a surprising extra burst of warmth as I leaned into her and cried. She continued to hold me until the tears stopped.

It took a long time.

***

I remember everyone's eyes on me as we re-entered the house through the back door into the kitchen. Brandi went in first. She didn't say it, but I knew she was trying to shield me from the stares of the congregation of mourners who had witnessed my outburst. They were scattered about, mainly in the kitchen and living room. The conversation, which had been rather lively, descended to hushed whispers as we made our way through.

I found the whole thing to be odd and inappropriate. It felt like the minute we got back from the hospital, the parade of family, friends and acquaintances started filing through our door, carrying casseroles, deli trays, pastries and alcohol. Lots of alcohol. Everywhere I looked, someone was holding a glass of wine, a bottle of beer or a snifter of Scotch. It was like one big, depressing party. The weirdest part for me was hearing everyone's voices rise while their glasses drained, the somber tone growing gradually more jovial as the shock gave way to stories of my dad's life over the forty-three years between his birth and death.

The celebratory atmosphere didn't feel right to me. Not that I had any baseline as to what was proper in this type of situation. Grandpa explained to me it was not uncommon to hear laughter during the mourning period. He told me everyone grieves differently. Laughing and remembering the good times helps some people cope with their loss.

I guessed it made sense, but I didn't like it. My dad was gone and never coming back. The thought of laughing at anything ever again seemed alien to me.

So, as I made my way with Brandi through the kitchen and into the living room, I was glad that most people lowered their voices and stopped giggling at stupid stories about Dad. They were going to go home after this and go about their lives while Brandi, Mom and I would have to pick up the pieces of our own.

Where is Mom? I thought as I scanned the room.

She had been there when I had run out. Last I saw her, she was sitting in Dad's favorite recliner, clutching an old photo album. She wasn't crying or yelling or beating her chest. She sat there with a glazed-over look in her eyes, as if her tank had finally been completely drained.

But now the chair was empty and she was gone.

"Was Mom still here when you came out to get me?" I asked my sister.

Brandi shrugged and looked around. "I don't remember."

As I wondered which of the adults I wanted to actually engage to ask about my mother's whereabouts, my question was answered by someone behind me.

"She's lying down, buddy."

I turned to see Dennis McGill coming down the stairs. He was my father's best friend for as long as I could remember. I'd never had any type of serious, extended interaction with him beyond the typical pleasantries between kids and adults, but I remember him being around quite often. Dennis, like my dad, was about average size, but definitely in very good shape, which was not surprising, as they were both avid outdoorsmen. In fact, it struck me just then how similar they looked. Dad had chestnut-brown hair like Brandi and me and grew his beard out during the fall and winter, while Dennis sported blond hair and was always clean-shaven because of some corporate job he had. But despite that, I found the similarities remarkable.

Maybe it was the fact that he was coming from upstairs, a part of the house I felt was reserved for the people who actually lived here, but it definitely felt weird to think of Dennis being up there alone with my newly widowed mother. The only man I ever expected to see descend that staircase was my father, and that was a sight I would never see again. My pre-teen brain couldn't quite process why I was uncomfortable with it, but not knowing why didn't make it bother me any less.

Dennis stepped off the landing and knelt down in front of us. He put a hand on each of our shoulders and gave mine a gentle squeeze that I assume he replicated with Brandi.

"This ordeal has all been a little too much for her," he explained. "She took some medicine that will help her rest. Sleep is the best thing for her right now."

"How long is she going to sleep for?" Brandi asked.

"As long as she needs," he replied. "Your grandparents are going to be here for a while and I'm going to stick around to help out too. I'll be here as much as you all need."

That also bothered me for some unknown reason. It was a nice enough offer. There was nothing inherently wrong with it, but it just didn't seem like it was Dennis's place to be here in that way. I wanted everyone that wasn't my mom, sister or our grandparents to just go home, and the thought of Dennis sticking around longer than the rest just plain irked me.

I didn't vocalize that, though. It seemed like it would have been inappropriate and I had already come off as a petulant brat once that day.

If Dennis knew I was uncomfortable, he didn't let on. He simply continued talking.

"Your dad was like a brother to me. I can't even imagine what the two of you are feeling right now, but I want you to know that Uncle Dennis will always be here for you."

Never in our lives had we called him Uncle Dennis, but he sounded sincere enough. He pulled us both into an embrace and whispered, "It's going to be okay."

I caught a whiff of something familiar. He smelled like Dad. Did they use the same cologne? It was an odd thought, but one I couldn't help but ponder as he continued his attempt to comfort my sister and me.

Brandi hesitantly returned the embrace by placing her arm on his upper back and patting it in a half-hearted reciprocation.

I didn't do the same.

***

I was so lost in my reminiscence that I didn't realize the buck had gotten significantly closer. It was now less than fifty yards away. I had it.

Wanting a broadside shot, I lined up the crossbow's vertical reticle on the deer's front leg with the horizontal reticle about one third of the way up the deer's body. Dad taught me that a shot like this was ideal because there was a very good chance you would hit the heart and maybe even the lungs, killing it quickly. Not only did this save you time tracking the animal, it was also significantly more humane. A true hunter never wanted to make their prey suffer. They respected their kills.

With the shot lined up, I applied pressure to the trigger. But, just as I was about to take the shot, the buck thrust its head upward and pivoted, spooked by something in the distance, just like I had been all those years ago as I took out the trash. My reticle didn't move, but the deer's body did and when I pulled the trigger, my arrow caught it just underneath its front leg.

Damn it!

The buck squealed and ran off into the woods. My cover blown, I exited the blind as fast as I could and tried to line up another shot, but it was already among the trees.

I'd seen where the arrow had struck and knew that the deer wouldn't die, at least not any time soon. If I was going to get him today, I'd have to track him through the woods. I looked at my watch. It was 6:47 a.m. I was cutting it close to the start of school, but if I hurried, I might catch up to him in time.

I moved as quickly as I could through the trees without making too much noise. If I spooked it again, there was no way I'd have enough time. Hell, I probably didn't have enough time now, but fuck it.

There were occasional droplets of blood on the leaves. It was late September and a good number of leaves had fallen from the trees, making quiet movement difficult. After about 150 yards, I realized it was a lost cause. I sighed and slung my bow over my shoulder and looked at my watch.

7:12 a.m.

I really had to get a move on now. I turned and started back toward the house when something caught the corner of my eye. I unslung the crossbow and approached a shape lying in the shade of a large red oak tree. It looked like a coyote. The fact that it wasn't moving told me it was probably dead, but you can never be too careful.

As I got closer, I confirmed it was dead. As I brushed the leaves off of the body, I saw it was mangled, a large cavity ripped into its stomach, which appeared completely hollowed out. Something big had done this. A bear maybe? We got black bears in this area occasionally, but they were little more than nuisances that raided your trash.

Still, I figured I'd better give my family a heads-up to be careful when outside, especially at night. We still had our trash bins in the shed and there could still be danger back there, even if there was no such thing as monsters.

No such thing as monsters.

Thinking back, I wish I still believed that.

CHAPTER 2

I walked in through the back door and heard the sound of forks clanking on plates. I rounded the corner into the kitchen and saw my mom and Dennis sitting at the table, eating breakfast in silence. They both had fancy-looking omelets that were perfectly folded, with peppers, sausage and cheese stuffed inside. Their plates were topped off with bacon and fresh strawberries, a perfect shade of red. On the side of each plate were mugs filled with steaming-hot coffee. Mom's was light as she typically took hers with cream and sugar, while Dennis preferred his black.

Despite the Norman Rockwellesque portrait of wedded bliss, the lack of conversation between the two of them was a recent phenomenon. In fact, once they started dating a year after my dad died, they were practically nauseating with their displays of affection. She had displayed a giddiness with Dennis that I never recalled her having with my dad. Maybe I was too young when he died, or maybe it was just the difference between a fifteen-year relationship and a new one. So, while I wasn't too broken up to see them toning it down, there was definitely something off here. Some kind of unspoken tension.

Not that any of it surprised me. I tried my best to get along with Dennis, but he could be a prick. In fact, I often got the sense that he was putting on a show for all of us with his pleasantries. It was almost as if he wore a mask most of the time. He'd transitioned from "Uncle Dennis" to my stepfather, but over the past six years that he lived with us, I still felt like I didn't know the real person at all.

"Get anything?" he asked as I kicked off my boots and left them by the back door.

"No," I replied cordially. "Saw a decent buck and had a shot lined up, but something spooked it. I only managed to graze the underside."

"Too bad. You'll get him next time, champ."

Ugh. I hated his little nicknames. And that summed up our relationship perfectly. Nothing inherently wrong, but something just didn't click. Little harmless things like a nickname made me irrationally heated.

"You're going to be late for school if you don't hurry," Mom said, chiming in as if Dennis and I weren't even talking.

"I'll be fine, Mom," I replied. "I just gotta throw my clothes on."

"You've been in the woods all morning," Dennis noted. "You're not going to shower?"

"I'll do a hobo shower. Deodorant and body spray. No one will know the difference."

"And you wonder why you don't have a girlfriend."

Dennis's flippancy irked me. It may have been intended as lighthearted ribbing, but it came off as a dig. Maybe it was because Dennis was a hygiene nazi. He showered before and after work most days. In fact, it sometimes surprised me that he could tolerate hunting at all. Being in the woods when it was wet and cold, not to mention field dressing a kill, wasn't exactly for the squeamish.

He must have noticed my irritation, because he added, "Not trying to offend you, pal. If you're not interested in girls, that's okay. It is what it is."

It is what it is.

That comment, combined with looking at him sitting there dressed for work—he was a bigwig at one of the larger banks in the state—brought up some feelings on my part. He wore a navy suit, the jacket currently folded neatly over the back of one of the empty chairs as he ate, with a yellow tie and a crisp white dress shirt.

The sight of him in a dress shirt always brought me a few Christmases back to when Mom had bought him a number of brand-new shirts with various colors and patterns. He held them up with disgust on his face, as if someone had given him a bag of shit-stained underwear. I will never forget how he looked at them.

"I figured you could spice up your wardrobe a bit," Mom explained, her enthusiasm upon presenting him the gift morphing into a stuttering mix of apology and ham-handed explanation. I'm almost certain that I saw sweat bead on her forehead as she stammered.

Based on her reaction, I was legitimately scared Dennis was about to hit her or, at the very least, yell at her.

But he didn't. He calmly placed the shirts neatly, almost reverently, back in the box and handed it to her.

"Bankers wear white shirts," he told her. His voice was even, but goddamn if there wasn't a quiet menace in his words. "Hopefully, you still have the receipts."

She took the box from him, her anxiousness melting into crushing disappointment. "I'm... I'm sorry, Dennis," she said, on the verge of tears. "I don't have anything else for you."

Dennis got up and patted her on the shoulder. "It is what it is. Don't worry about it."

He had walked out of the room and left us to open the rest of our presents in silence.

So, yeah, there were moments like that where I felt Dennis was hiding a much darker side. But, even if that was true, he never let it out when Brandi or I could see it. Nevertheless, sometimes when I saw him with a pristine white dress shirt, I couldn't help but get a little pissed off, especially when he made comments like he had that day. And that wasn't the only thing he wore that did that to me. I felt the same way about the gold wedding band on his left ring finger. A piece of jewelry he'd worn ever since he'd married my mother.

***

It had been a little over a year since my dad died. Dennis had made good on his promise to "be there for us," although it didn't take long to realize that he was there for my mom more than for me or Brandi. I remember waking up early on Sunday morning because the Giants were playing in London that week and the international games started at 9:30 a.m. on the East Coast. Mom's mental state had been improving over the past few months, but it still wasn't uncommon for her to sleep in, especially on weekends when she didn't have to get us ready for school. She hadn't gone back to work either as, I later found out, my father had a rather robust life insurance policy that took care of all of her debt, including the mortgage and car payments, while still leaving enough for her to live on, especially when coupled with their savings and investments.

Brandi had preferred to flip on the TV in her room on weekends and just lie around for a few hours before getting out of bed, so I had no expectation of seeing anyone else in the house. When I smelled bacon as I descended the stairs, I was perplexed. It certainly wasn't my mother's style to cook a full breakfast on Sunday morning. She'd rather run down the road and pick up bagels and, if she were in a particularly good mood, a rarity over the past year, Dunkin' Donuts.

I remembered making my way into the kitchen to see Mom sitting at the table with a goofy ass grin on her face. She wore her pink fluffy robe and her hair was tousled as she sipped a cup of coffee. As I got older, I understood why she had been in such a jovial mood and, even now, I had to force myself to not to retch when thinking about it. Seeing her in anything but a stoic mood had been rare those days, but the more startling sight was seeing Dennis standing at the stove, scrambling eggs while the bacon snapped and sizzled on the griddle next to him.

"Hey, honey!" Mom said as soon as she noticed me, sitting upright in her chair and trying to pull her robe as tightly closed as she could. "Didn't realize you'd be up so early."

"The Giants are on at 9:30," I said, not taking my eyes off Dennis, who was the only one in the room that seemed unbothered.

"Hey, buddy!" he said, offering up another one of those irritating nicknames. "Want some eggs?"

"No thanks," I said, trying to use those two words to convey my actual sentiment, which was, *What the fuck are you doing here this early?*

"Don't know what you're missing, pal. Best you'll ever taste."

Mom smiled and tried to redirect. "The Giants are on this morning? They're playing in Dublin?"

"London," I replied with a smattering of sarcasm that I couldn't suppress. She hadn't even taken an interest in football when Dad was alive.

"That's great," Dennis had replied, brushing over my pre-teen attitude. "The game will be over by one so we can watch the Eagles."

"The Eagles suck," I said before I could stop myself. I hated nothing on this planet more than the Philadelphia Eagles, except maybe tree stands. And I was relatively confident Dennis knew that.

"Watch your mouth!" Mom said as Dennis snickered.

"So you're staying here all day?" I asked.

Mom and Dennis exchanged a look.

"Yes, Brady," Mom answered. "Dennis is going to be spending the day with us." She paused before adding, "There's something we want to talk to you and your sister about when she wakes up."

I felt a lump in my throat. I knew where this was going. Even at twelve, I wasn't an idiot and the signs had all been there, no matter how much I didn't want to acknowledge them. I knew exactly what they were going to tell us.

Thirty minutes later, Brandi had made her way downstairs and the four of us sat at the kitchen table as

Dennis confirmed that he and my mother were dating. Brandi just sat there and nodded, unsure of what to say. I was not so complacent.

"What?" I exclaimed. "Dad has only been dead a year and you're already replacing him?"

"Honey, I can never replace your father," Mom said.

"Well, you're trying your best to, aren't you?"

"Buddy, it's not like that," Dennis said.

"Fuck you!" I shouted, sprinting out of the house, knocking over my chair in the process.

For the rest of the morning, I wept in my tree, ending up missing the Giants game.

But that was years ago and now, like it or not, Dennis was my mom's husband. The worst part was, even though I thought he could be a sanctimonious prick, he did nothing that I thought justified my ire other than marrying my mom. Sure, there were incidents like the "bankers only wear white shirts," episode, but it wasn't like he flew off the handle or hit any of us. I knew in my heart that there was something that just didn't feel right about him, but none of it was actionable. My mom sure as shit wouldn't entertain any Dennis slander and Brandi was so aloof to life these days it was tough to know what she thought about anything.

So I did what I usually did and just played nice.

***

As I shook myself out of the memory, Dennis, Mom and I were still sharing an uncomfortable silence. Just when I thought things couldn't get any more awkward, Brandi walked into the kitchen, taking the focus away from me.

My cheeks flushed when I saw her. Now let's get this out of the way right now. This isn't some lusting after my sister porn-type bullshit. But anyone would be blind not to see that Brandi had adopted a very provocative style lately.

Her hair, once the same shade of brown as mine, was now platinum blond with raven-black tips. It was so long, it went down to the small of her back. Her makeup was dark and pronounced, not quite goth according to what little I knew of the style, but I imagined it was close. She wore a black skirt that barely extended to mid-thigh, with long fishnet stockings and high-heeled boots. She finished her look with a cropped band T-shirt, today's selection being *Bad Omens*. It was low cut, although the manufacturer had clearly not intended it to be that way. Brandi had just modified it to her liking. A shiny ring with a dangling black stone protruded from her exposed belly button, matching the multitude of rings in her ears and the stud in her nose. The early fall weather was still fairly tame, hovering in the mid-sixties, so she finished off her look with a light black hooded zip-up with the Vans logo on the back.

Why am I going into this much detail about what my sister was wearing? Because it had been very unlike her until recently. She'd been a true girly girl growing up—princesses and unicorns. The whole nine. Now she looked like she was ready to throw herself into a mosh pit. I'm not judging, I'm really not. I know people change as they figure out who they are, but it just seemed like one day she woke up and was a different person. Like she didn't want to be Brandi Bennett anymore.

If it was just her style that had changed, that would be one thing, but it was her entire demeanor. She was often quiet and withdrawn. It didn't seem like she cared about anything anymore. The little girl who'd sternly made me get down from the tree after my father's funeral, only to hold me until I stopped crying now would probably just step over me and keep walking if I fell.

Worst of all, she was getting a reputation at school as we started our senior year. I heard whispers—some that were intentionally loud enough for me to hear—that she had become quite promiscuous. I had no idea if it was true or not. Though I had seen her go out on the occasional date, she never brought guys home and we never discussed our respective love lives. Not that I had one to talk about. Still, if it was true, it didn't really matter. In the pecking order of high school life, once a rumor was out there, it was as good as true.

Everyone stayed quiet, probably silently judging her choice of attire. She seemed unbothered by the quiet as she moseyed over to the coffee maker and poured herself a cup. I caught a whiff of smoke clinging to her hoodie as she passed me. Couldn't place if it was cigarettes or weed. Probably both. I was sure Mom and Dennis could smell it too. I was also sure that Brandi didn't give a shit.

She sipped her drink and leaned against the counter, absent-mindedly scrolling on her phone.

Of course it was Dennis who broke the silence. "You think that outfit's appropriate for school?"

She looked up and met his gaze. "What's wrong with my outfit?"

Dennis frowned. "You know what's wrong with it. Boys your age have a lot of trouble keeping their hormones in check. You don't want to invite that kind of attention, now do you?"

Brandi smirked. "Boys my age are dipshits. Most of them would bust in their pants before they actually got a hand on me."

"Brandi!" my mother shouted.

Dennis remained unfazed. I think that was what bothered me the most about him. Mom could try to placate him, Brandi could bait him and I could lose my temper with him and he never so much as raised his voice. The bastard's pulse probably never even went up.

"You get out of this world what you put in, honey.

31

And that outfit is telling the boys that you're open for business."

"Maybe I am."

"That is enough," Mom said pointedly as she stood up. She brought her half-empty plate over to the kitchen sink, scraping the rest of her meal into the garbage disposal. Brandi snickered as she drained the last of her coffee. Mom alternated between the two of us with her sternest look. The one that still brought us back down from whatever high horse we were on at the moment. The smile left Brandi's face.

"I get that you two are teenagers, but you need to show Dennis more respect. He works very hard to provide for us and I'd say a little more appreciation is warranted, wouldn't you?"

It wasn't the first time she had rebuked us over how we'd acted toward Dennis, but this time, she sounded less resolved. Like she didn't even believe it.

I felt a little guilty now. Like I said, Dennis had never actually done anything to me other than marry my mom. Sure, he was annoying and more than a little pompous, but was he actually a bad guy? Didn't my mom deserve to be happy?

I looked over at Brandi, too ashamed at the moment to make eye contact with Mom or Dennis. However, it was clear that my sister did not feel the same sheepishness that I did. She practically scowled at them.

"It's your life, Mom," she said. "You do what you want."

"It's been seven years. I'd really like for us to become a family at some point," Dennis chimed in.

Brandi plopped her mug in the sink and made her way out of the kitchen, offering up one last dig before she did. "Then maybe you should start your own and leave us out of this."

A stunned silence blanketed the room. Dennis went back to his breakfast and Mom just stood there speechless.

It was Brandi who once again pierced the quiet.

"You coming, Brady?"

CHAPTER 3

Brandi rolled down the window of the gray 2015 Nissan Sentra and flicked her cigarette out the window, exhaling one last plume of smoke before rolling it back up.

"You know your clothes reek of smoke, right?" I observed.

"You know I really don't care," she retorted.

Brandi was whipping the small sedan around the curves of the back roads leading to school. I clung to the *oh shit* handle as she did. The roads were narrow in our town and it was often difficult to see what was around the bends. And it wasn't just cars you had to worry about. There were also plenty of deer and a good number of bicyclists obnoxiously crowding the lanes as if they would have any chance if a car swerved into their path.

The car was a gift from Mom and Dennis for our seventeenth birthday the June before last. It was meant for us to share, but as I had no job and not much social life, Brandi was the one who used it the most. Even though neither of us had been pestering our mom for a new car, she still felt she had to justify why we got a used one.

"This will be fine for your purposes while you're in school," she had said.

And she wasn't wrong. Besides, neither Brandi nor I wanted Dennis lording over us because he helped pay for a new car. The Sentra would do just fine.

Brandi smirked at me holding on to the handle. "Does my driving make you uncomfortable?" she asked knowing damn well that it did.

"Yeah," I shot back. "Among other things."

Her smile dropped in an instant. "What the hell is that supposed to mean?"

"I mean this," I said waving my hand up and down in front of her.

"My clothes? You going to give me shit about that too, now? Maybe Dennis isn't the only one who needs to realize he's not Daddy."

"No, I'm not. But I know he wouldn't like it either."

I noticed her grip on the steering wheel tighten. It also looked like a bit of moisture had gathered at the corner of her eye. "Yeah. well, he wouldn't have made me feel bad about it."

"No, but he would have let you know how he felt."

She took the next curve even harder than the last. I slid across the seat, thankful that I always dutifully wore my seatbelt. Brandi's silence stretched on, and I knew I had overstepped. As I contemplated how to make it right, she finally responded. "So, what? Just because I like to dress a little on the sexy side that makes me a bad person?"

"No! of course not! I just—"

"Just what? Spit it out, Brady."

"I just don't want guys to take advantage of you."

She let out a sarcastic laugh. "Brady, I'm more than capable of handling myself. But thank you for your concern."

"People talk, you know."

"Oh, I know," she said, pausing for a bit before looking at me. Her expression was softer, looking more hurt than angry now. "You believe them?"

"Should I?" I answered, regretting the words as soon as they came out of my mouth, especially upon seeing the hurt intensify in Brandi's expression.

"Oh, yeah, I fuck half the football team after lunch on Fridays."

"Okay, Brandi, that's—"

"I got an A in history last year because I sucked off Mr. Mathis."

"Jesus Christ! I get it!"

"Do you? Because don't even get me started on what I did with Heather Turner in the showers after gym class."

"Alright! Fucking hell, Brandi! I'm just looking out for you!"

"Look out for yourself, Brady," she snapped back at me.

"If you want to think I'm the Hillcrest High Whore, you go right ahead. Doesn't matter one fucking bit to me."

"I don't think that."

"Well, then you're in a pretty small club."

We drove in silence the rest of the way to school. When we got there, Brandi whipped around into the parking lot and drove quickly to the gravel lot on the side of the school where students parked—the front lot being reserved for faculty. She jammed the brake as she parked, jolting me against my seatbelt again.

"Goddamn it, Brandi," I said without looking at her.

I was ashamed that I had made her feel bad. But what was I going to do? She wasn't only my sister, she was my best friend. Or at least she used to be. I didn't want people to spread rumors about her. With Dad gone, we had always looked out for each other. Mom spent the first months after he died in a practically comatose state. Once she started dating Dennis, she was so far up his ass that she rarely saw when things were tough for the two of us. And we sure as shit weren't going to Dennis with our problems. No, it had always been Brady and Brandi against the world. But now it felt like it was just me.

Brandi killed the engine and turned to me. Her eyes were clearly watering now.

"I'm not a nun, Brady," she said and paused. "But I'm not some nympho sleeping my way around town. And even if I was—which again, I am totally fucking not—so what? Anything I do is my choice. Fuck anyone who has a problem with that."

"I'm just looking out for you."

"And I love you for it," she said. "But please know that I can take care of myself, okay?"

"Okay."

A moment of silence before, "Do you trust what I'm telling you?" Her eyes pleading for me to give the right answer.

"About the rumors being false or you being able to take care of yourself?"

"Either. Both."

"I believe you," I said definitively. "About both. I promise."

"Thank you." She nodded and took a second before her face widened into a grin. An actual one, not her usual sarcastic, screw-you smile. For the first time in a while, she actually looked like my sister again.

"You know, you should ask Arianna out."

I felt butterflies in my stomach. Arianna was one of my sister's few close friends. I found her to be drop-dead gorgeous, but I must have heard Brandi wrong. There was no way I'd ever have a shot with her.

"Yeah, right."

"I'm serious! You think I don't know you've been crushing on her since before you got your first boner? I wouldn't screw with you on this."

I squirmed. She was being raunchy just to mess with me now and it was working. Mostly because she was right.

"So, what does that mean to me? She's dating Trevor Wright."

Brandi's smile widened. "She *was* dating Trevor Wright."

I must have looked like a deer in headlights. "Was?"

She laughed. "Yep. They broke up last week."

"Why?"

"Well, let's just say that if you want to know who the Hillcrest High Whore actually is, it's Ari's now ex-boyfriend."

"What happened?"

"She thought he was cheating on her. I confirmed it."

"How'd you do that?"

"Let's just say that I put my *reputation* to good use. I made him think I was willing to hook up with him. I showed Ari the text messages and when he showed up to meet me, he found his pissed-off now ex-girlfriend. You wouldn't believe how she laid into him! I thought he actually might cry."

"Wow," was all I could say.

"Yeah. The fucking scumbag got what he deserved."

No arguments from me on that one. Trevor had been an asshole since middle school. And knowing that he would cheat on someone like Arianna, who was not only beautiful, but one of the coolest, nicest people I'd ever met—I mean she was always super-nice to me, so she had to be a good person considering I was a nonentity to most—really drove home what a prick he actually was.

My ruminations on the matter gave way to the crippling self-doubt that typically chased away my pleasant thoughts. My smile faded.

"So what? There's probably a million guys lined up wanting to date her. I wouldn't have a shot."

"Oh, sack the fuck up, Bennett! You want to be a lonely virgin forever?"

"I... I..." I didn't know how to respond.

"I'm just messing with you—I mean not about the virgin thing, that's kinda obvious, but it doesn't have to be."

"Oh, really?" I said, annoyed.

"Dude, you're a good-looking guy. I mean, you're my twin after all and I'm hot as hell." I shot her a look. She laughed. That hearty authentic laugh that I missed so much. It actually made a bit of my apprehension go away.

"You've got a pretty high opinion of yourself."

"Someone in this family has to have some confidence." She paused for a second and got more serious. "For real, bro. You're smart, you're in great shape from all that whatever it is you do in the woods. She's not the only friend of mine who's told me you're attractive. You'd have some game if you actually suited up once in a while. Ask her out. I can pretty much guarantee she'll say yes."

Pretty much guarantee wasn't the one-hundred-percent-no-doubt-about-it outcome I usually liked when making my decisions. Still, the chance to actually have a date with Arianna was probably worth the risk.

The morning bell interrupted my thoughts.

"Shit! We're late!" Brandi exclaimed as we exited the car in tandem and hurried for the entrance.

CHAPTER 4

Third-period science class was a nightmare. My teacher was nice enough, but he had the most boring, dry delivery I'd ever heard. He was going on about chemical compounds or some such nonsense, but I couldn't focus on this material on a normal day and today was not that type of day. I couldn't get what my sister had told me out of my head. Not just because of the idea she put in there, but because Arianna Kenton was sitting two desks up from me on the right.

In case I didn't emphasize it enough before, she was stunning. Her dad was Jamaican and her mom was Norwegian, a mix that gave her an exotic look that I had never seen before. Her skin was a smooth caramel tone and the loose curls of her dark hair cascaded down to the middle of her back. She didn't dress as provocatively as Brandi, but she didn't hide her figure either. Today's ensemble was pretty basic, but no less appealing to my hormone-fueled teenage mind.

She wore a pair of black leggings that contoured her lower body perfectly and a cropped gray T-shirt. If she were standing, it would cover her stomach, but as she sat at her desk, legs crossed and leaning over, it rode up, exposing the small of her back. It was one of those little actions that wasn't meant to be sexy, but was nonetheless.

Brandi was full of shit. There was no way she would be interested in me. I mean, I didn't think I was ugly by any stretch. I kinda knew that Brandi's description of me was accurate, but I wasn't popular. Come to think of it, I wasn't unpopular either. I was just sort of there. I went to school, did my work and went home, where I indulged in my hobbies like hunting, fishing or playing guitar. Despite having a limited social life, I never really felt lonely. Life was just what it was. I'd had dates. I'd even made out with a few girls, one time even being fortunate enough to get a hand job from Becky Summers in the very same Sentra we had driven to school that morning. All I really remembered was that it wasn't all it was cracked up to be. I mean, it wasn't bad by any means, but I could do that on my own and, to be honest, it was easier to get myself off. With Becky, it felt like it was taking forever and actually kinda got uncomfortable after a while.

So how the hell was I supposed to go from that to asking Arianna Kenton out?

The same Arianna Kenton who was looking right at me as I stared in her direction.

Fuck.

How long had I been looking? Was I being creepy? Had I blown it before I even had a shot with her? Fuck, I was being creepy.

She met my eyes and smiled at me.

A smile. My heart fluttered. I mean, I actually felt the motion in my chest. I didn't think shit like that really happened in the real world, but scout's honor, it happened to me in that moment. What should I do now? Brandi's voice invaded my mind. She wasn't in the same class, but it felt like some kind of twin telepathy.

Smile back, dummy.

So I did. I smiled and she turned back to her work.

Was my smile weird? Oh, shit, I'd blown it again. I'd skeeved her out. I fucking knew it. I'd had one shot and I'd totally fucked it up.

"Something on your mind, Mr. Bennett?"

"Huh?"

I looked away from Arianna and up at Mr. Liptak.

"You seem distracted, Brady. Anything you'd like to share with the class?"

"Um—"

The rest of the class turned and looked at me, including Arianna. I tried not to focus on her, but I couldn't help it. I caught her eye again and she giggled a bit, fully aware that she had flustered me. I had to act fast.

"May I use the restroom?"

***

I didn't really need to go, but I needed to get out of there to save some kind of face. As I made my way toward the bathroom, I peeked into the classrooms as I walked by. When I passed by Room 307, one student inside noticed me.

Trevor Wright.

I wanted to act like I didn't notice him, but he definitely noticed me, his face twisting with rage. Great. That was all I needed. We had long established that he was an asshole, but he and I had an *I don't fuck with you and you don't fuck with me* policy. From the look on his face, it seemed like that policy was null and void.

I put it aside for now and took advantage of the break. When I reached the restroom, I realized I needed to piss for real. After I went about my business, I zipped up and made my way over to the sink, washing my hands and splashing a little water on my face for good measure.

As I patted my face dry with a handful of paper towels the door burst open with a loud bang. I turned and saw Trevor barreling toward me. He stopped only inches in front of me. We were about the same height so he was practically nose to nose with me, close enough that I could feel his hot breath on my face. I wanted to take a step back, but I wasn't going to give him the satisfaction.

"Why is your fucking whore sister all up in my business?" he asked.

Any trepidation I may have had about an altercation with him went out the window. No one talks about my sister that way.

"Back the fuck off, Trevor."

"Or what, pussy? What's your little bitch ass going to do?" He did his best to shoot me his most intimidating look. It wasn't bad, but he didn't scare me. It's funny how experiencing tragedy at a young age makes you painfully aware of what is and isn't a dire situation. This certainly wasn't one, so I just smirked at him, knowing it would piss him off even more. I hadn't been in many fights in my life, but I could field dress and drag a 200-pound deer out of the woods, so I was pretty sure I could hold my own in a brawl with this prick.

I took a step closer, my nose now pressed against him. "Try me and find out, asshole."

Now Trevor took a step back. "What, you some kind of faggot? Trying to kiss me and shit? Maybe you want to suck my dick? Probably learned it from your sister. I hear she's pretty fucking good."

Seeing red, I clenched my fists, visualizing punching him in the mouth, wanting nothing more than to knock his fucking teeth out. It took everything I had to fight with my words and not my knuckles.

"Yeah, well, she didn't suck yours, now did she? And

now you don't even have a girlfriend anymore, so I guess you're just going to have to figure out how to suck your own."

"You motherfu—"

He was about to swing. I'm sure of it. But, fortunately—or unfortunately, depending on how you look at it—the door opened again and Mr. Garvin, the guidance counselor, walked in, immediately eyeing us with suspicion.

"There a problem here, gentlemen?"

I didn't take my eyes off of Trevor as I smirked.

"No, Mr. Garvin. All good. Just consoling Trevor here. He just had a nasty breakup."

Trevor's face turned so red I thought his head may very well explode, but he somehow held it together. Mr. Garvin didn't look like he bought it, but he couldn't disprove it either.

"Well if you're not using the facilities, I suggest you get back to class."

I held my gaze on Trevor for another moment before moving around him, patting him on the shoulder as I did. I could feel the tension in his muscles as I squeezed.

"Don't worry, champ. Plenty of fish in the sea."

I was more than a little pleased with myself as I went back to class.

CHAPTER 5

The bell sounded at 3:05 p.m., signaling a merciful ending to the school day. Between the silent flirting with Arianna in class and the altercation with Trevor, my adrenaline was pumping as I made my way to my locker. I thought about the best way to approach Arianna to ask her out as I rounded the corner. To my surprise, there she was. But she wasn't alone.

She was rifling through her locker, hastening to get her things packed up. The reason for her urgency was clear. Trevor.

He was standing next to her, practically breathing down her neck as he braced himself against the lockers. I couldn't hear what he was saying, but he was animated, making a lot of hand gestures as Ari did her best to ignore him. It looked like he was almost begging. I'd be lying if seeing the dickhead in such a pathetic state didn't bring me a little satisfaction, but more pressingly, it was obvious that he was making her uncomfortable. That was something I couldn't let stand.

I approached them quickly but quietly, not wanting to

draw attention to myself until the last possible minute. Trevor's whining became audible as I drew near.

"C'mon, babe. You know I'd never touch that skank."

That was clearly too much for Arianna as she stood up and looked directly at him for the first time since they caught my eye.

"First, asshole, that *skank* is my best friend. Two, I saw the texts. What exactly am I supposed to think about *I'm down, but Arianna can never find out?* Is that code for something less pervy?"

"She probably doctored them. I said she's a skank, I never said she was dumb."

"Whatever, dude," Arianna said, focusing on closing up her locker. "We're done. Just accept it."

She tried to walk away, but he grabbed her arm. It was time to make my move.

I sped up my pace and started like I was going to walk past them, but as I did, I hooked my arm in Arianna's free one and gently but firmly guided her away from her stunned ex-boyfriend.

She was definitely surprised, but she quickly played along as I stepped in front of her.

"So, Ari, I was thinking I'll pick you up at eight o'clock tonight. That work for you?"

Trevor's eyes bulged out. I thought they were going to explode in their sockets.

Ari flashed a smile at me. "That sounds perfect!" she

said, running her fingernails down my chest, sending a chill through my body that almost made me lose focus. "I can't wait!"

"What the fuck, Bennett?" Trevor said, apoplectic. "Is that what you and that slut sister of yours had planned? Set me up so you can swoop in and steal my girl?"

"I don't want to speak for the lady, but it seems to me like she ain't your girl anymore, bud."

Trevor seethed and stepped toward me. Ari turned and shoved him back, surprising both of us with her aggression.

"Back the fuck up, Trevor. Brady's right. You and me are done. Get that through your thick fucking skull."

Trevor tried to take another step forward. He obviously thought about pushing past Arianna, but even in his anger I think he realized a physical altercation with a female student would not be a good look for him, especially with teachers and admins roaming the halls, not to mention the security cameras watching all the goings-on at Hillcrest High.

For a few long seconds, I thought he actually might throw a punch, but he just stood there, fists and jaw clenched in tandem, hatred burning in his eyes. No attack came. He just looked at me and said, "You're dead, Bennett."

He stormed off down the hall, almost comically stomping around the corner and out of sight like a toddler who'd just had their tablet taken away.

Once he was gone, I looked back at Arianna, who was attacking me in her own right with that smile of hers.

"You okay?" I asked.

"I am now," she said, lightly brushing my forearm with her hands in a *thank you* gesture, eliciting another chill.

"Thank you for sticking up for Brandi."

"Of course, I love your sister. She doesn't deserve this shit."

"No, she doesn't. It's nice to know I'm not the only one looking out for her."

"I'll always have her back."

A silence fell between us. It wasn't so much awkward as anticipatory. I wondered if I should just make my move at this point. It seemed obvious, but, as I contemplated the best way to do it—which would have obviously been to just come right out and ask—the silence starting to drag out a bit too long. I had to come up with something so I blurted the first thing I could think of.

"I hope you didn't mind me pretending we had a date tonight."

"We don't?"

My heart skipped a beat. Her smile glinted with mischief as Brandi's voice invaded my thoughts again.

Say something quick, jackass!

"So, eight?" I was able to get out.

"Sounds perfect." She started to walk away, but after a

handful of steps turned back toward me to see if I was still looking, which I absolutely was. She smiled and said, "Don't keep me waiting."

CHAPTER 6

"I can't believe you actually pulled that off," Brandi said as she drove us home, lighting another cigarette as she navigated the wooded roads.

"Keep that shit on your side," I said as I brushed aside a plume of smoke.

"Don't change the subject, Brady! Where are you taking her?"

That was a hell of a good question. I was so caught up between the Trevor drama and actually getting the date that I hadn't stopped to consider what I was actually going to do on said date.

"I haven't gotten that far yet."

Brandi smirked as she took a long drag. She turned her head to make sure the smoke went out the driver's-side window, respecting my earlier request.

"You want a suggestion?"

"Definitely."

"Take her to Jester's Pub. You can get something to eat in the restaurant section."

"Why Jester's? Why not somewhere classier?"

Brandi rolled her eyes. "Dude. You don't have to go crazy on the first date. Ari's not that kind of chick. She wants to have fun. Just be a fucking gentleman. Ask her about herself. In fact, you should only do the bare minimum of talking. Ask her questions and take a genuine interest in getting to know her."

"That won't be a problem."

Brandi smiled again, a warm and knowing smile.

"Not only that, but The *Scene Kids* are playing tonight."

"No shit?"

"No shit."

The *Scene Kids* were a cover band that played songs from the post-emo 2000s music "scene"—hence the name. They covered everyone from Taking Back Sunday and Hawthorne Heights to We Came as Romans and Falling in Reverse. I'd been to a few of their shows and they were great. It was also a perfect show to take Arianna to because she, Brandi and I were all big fans of the genre.

Still, as my anticipation of the evening grew, a thought nagged at me a bit.

"So why now?" I asked.

"What do you mean?"

"You kinda hinted that she's been at least a little into me for a while. Why didn't she, I don't know, make a move or something?"

Brandi rolled her eyes a bit. "Because she was in a relationship. Granted it was one-sided and more than a little toxic, but she's not a cheater."

"So why not break up with him?"

"It's not always that easy. I've never been with anyone that long, but I do know there's a degree of comfort in having someone, even if they're not always great for you. Not to mention the high school status bullshit we all deal with. Everyone acts like they're above it and wouldn't give in to peer pressure to be cool or trendy or some other bullshit, but, until you're there, you don't know how hard it is to break the cycle."

I nodded. It made sense. Besides, none of it mattered. Arianna and I had a date tonight. My focus was forward not backward.

***

That evening, dinner was unusually awkward. Family meals always kind of were to a degree. That's just what happens when your mom marries your dad's best friend after he dies, but this meal felt more off than usual. Brandi didn't engage, but that part wasn't strange. Mom didn't say a word as Dennis unsurprisingly prattled on about Dennis things. Typically, Mom would smile and oversell how interesting whatever he was talking about was, but this time? Crickets.

I would have thought that would have irked Dennis,

but he was either oblivious or ambivalent. Mom was the first up from the table, dumping the untouched portion of her meal in the trash and placing her plate in the dishwasher before leaving the room without a word.

But, you know what? I didn't care because I had a date to get ready for. Politely excusing myself, I deposited my plate and utensils in the dishwasher and headed upstairs to get ready.

I showered, making damn sure to soap up and wash off multiple times to ensure peak cleanliness. Once I was dry, I grabbed my laundry basket of clean clothes and fished out a pair of underwear. Once we hit high school, Brandi and I started doing our own laundry. I was pretty diligent about keeping my clothes clean, a necessity for an outdoorsman, but I wasn't great at folding or putting them away. Fortunately, I had a few pairs of jeans hung up and wrinkle-free in my closet. I popped on a plain black T-shirt, figuring that would be good for dinner at a pub followed by a band.

Satisfied with my look, I popped back into the bathroom and styled my hair, which didn't take very long as I kept it short. I checked the time.

7:40 p.m.

Perfect. All I had to do was brush my teeth and then head out in plenty of time to make it to Arianna's by eight. I plopped the toothpaste on my brush and vigorously scrubbed my teeth. Unfortunately, it was a bit too vigorous, and a glop fell off and hit my shirt.

Goddamn it.

I had other shirts, but I really liked this one. I rushed downstairs to the laundry room to grab a stain stick to get the paste off before it settled in.

Making my way through the kitchen, I rounded the corner and stopped in my tracks when I saw Dennis standing in the laundry room. He must not have noticed me because he didn't turn around. Something made me hesitant to approach. Dennis *never* did laundry.

At first I thought maybe he needed a stain stick same as I did, but he was standing by the open dryer. He leaned over and rooted around in the piled clothes and produced one of the smaller garments. He held it up and I could see it was a lacy black thong. *Gross. Was that Mom's?* I really didn't need to see my stepdad fiddling with my mother's unmentionables.

I was about to look away in disgust when I noticed the shirt on top of the pile. It was the same *Bad Omens* shirt Brandi wore to school that day.

Oh, my God. That was Brandi's laundry. That was her underwear! What the fuck was Dennis doing?

I felt sick to my stomach, to the point where I actually thought I was going to throw up in my mouth. Dennis could be a condescending prick, but I had never pegged him as a pervert. Was there an actual good explanation for this? Should I sneak back out and up to my room before he sees me?

Too late.

Dennis turned and saw me, trying—and failing—to subtly toss the panties back in the dryer without me noticing. He tried to play the whole thing off.

"What's up, Brady?"

"Uh... nothing. Just need a stain stick in the cabinet."

Dennis looked up at the row of cabinets mounted over the washer and dryer. He pointed at the middle one. I shook my head. He pointed at the rightmost one and I nodded. He opened it, grabbed the pen-sized utensil and tossed it to me.

"Thanks." I said mutedly as I bobbled it before securing the catch.

"Going out?"

"Yes."

Dennis stared at me. I didn't look away. I could tell he was sizing me up. After what felt like an eternity, he broke the silence.

"Ask your sister to come get her laundry out of the dryer. Your mom isn't feeling well tonight so I'm helping out, but I can't do anything until the dryer is empty."

"Sure," I said.

I still didn't buy it. I'd seen my mother down and out with a cold or the flu plenty of times and never once did I remember Dennis lifting a finger to help. Still, there was a calm in his eyes. He certainly didn't appear frazzled by the fact that I had caught him examining my eighteen-year-old sister's underwear, but I had a hard time believing that it was just a simple misunderstanding.

We eyed each other for a moment. Not quite long enough to be too uncomfortable, but certainly long enough to know there was something unspoken between us.

I broke away and returned upstairs.

***

With my shirt salvaged, I pulled on a light jacket and shut my door, locking it behind me. As I made my way down the hall, I heard muffled music coming from Brandi's room. It was audible enough to let me know she was in there, but not so loud to draw my mother or Dennis's attention. I stopped in front of her door and debated whether I should knock.

Ultimately, I decided to, and gently rapped on her door.

"Yeah?" her slightly irritated voice came from the other side.

"It's me."

"Just a second," she said, her tone immediately relaxing.

The lock clicked on the other side and Brandi opened

the door. As she did, I heard a few notes of Ice Nine Kills's "Love Bites". She lowered the volume rather than turning it off completely, smiling when she saw me dressed up for my night out with her bestie.

"Looking sharp, bro. Simple but effective. Arianna will like it."

I didn't answer and her smile faded. She could read my face. She always could.

"What?"

"It's... probably nothing."

She sat at attention, her concern growing. "What?" she asked, more emphatically this time. It gave me a bit of a flashback to her scolding me in the tree on the day of Dad's funeral.

I sighed. "Dennis told me to ask you to come get your laundry out."

She looked confused. "Okay? I'll do it a bit. Why's that got your panties in a twist?"

Interesting turn of phrase.

"That's kind of it," I replied. "He was going through the dryer. The dryer with your clothes."

"He was *going through my clothes?*"

"I walked in on him holding a pair of your underwear."

"Ew!" she cried, backing up on her bed as if there were a giant spider in front of her. "What was he doing with them?"

"Nothing as far as I could tell. He was just... holding

them."

"What the actual fuck? What did you do?"

"Nothing, really. He saw me and dropped them back in. Played it off like he was just getting ready to do his own laundry."

"I've never seen him do laundry."

"Yeah. Me either. It was weird, Brandi."

"Did you tell Mom?"

"No. Even if I was going to, I'm not even sure where she is. I haven't seen her since dinner."

Brandi furrowed her brow.

I continued. "There's something really weird going on lately."

"No shit," she replied, irritation giving way to anger as she jumped up off the bed. "I'm going to go find him."

I put up a hand to stop her. "That's not a good idea."

"Why the fuck not?"

"Like I said. There's something weird going on. Mom is barely saying two words to any of us and Dennis—well, there's always been something off about him, but lately he's got this look that creeps me out. I can't describe it, but something doesn't feel right with him."

My sister scoffed. "The dude's a smacked ass, but I seriously doubt he's Patrick Bateman."

She went to move past me, but I stepped in front of her. She clearly saw my concern and took a step back, sitting down on her bed again.

"So what am I supposed to do with this information?"

"I don't know," I said, considering the situation for a moment. "Maybe it was nothing and we shouldn't sound the alarm. What if we just keep an eye out? Stay on guard?"

Brandi didn't reply, but slowly nodded, sharing my concern about the oddness that had been permeating our household of late.

"Okay," she finally agreed.

"You want me to stay home?" I asked. "I can reschedule."

She smiled at me. She tried not to make it look forced, but didn't succeed. "No, don't be stupid. You're lucky you got this opportunity in the first place."

"Fuck you."

"Fuck you too."

We laughed.

"Want to come with us?"

"Uh uh. I'm no cockblock. Despite the fact that you're not getting any tonight regardless."

"Understood," I said with a smirk.

"Seriously, dude. Like I told you - be a fucking gentleman."

"I always am," I said as I stepped into the hallway. "You sure you're okay?"

"I'm good, bro. Really. Have a good time and tell Ari I said hi."

I nodded and shut the door as the music blared back to life, louder this time.

***

As I exited the house and walked to the car, a wave of unease washed over me.

It wasn't just Dennis either. There was something about the night. It was too quiet. I looked back past my house to the tree line. There was no ambient sound. No branches cracking, no rustling in the brush. I couldn't recall a night so silent. Looking further up, I saw the bright light of the full moon, illuminating the stillness of the woods. There was barely even a breeze. It was as if all of nature was hiding from something out there.

I brushed off my paranoia, chalking it up to the weirdness with my stepfather. I checked my watch. 7:53 p.m. I had to boogie because I did not want to be late picking up Arianna.

Even though I tried to dismiss my unease, as I got in the car, I couldn't help but feel like I was being watched.

CHAPTER 7

I knocked at Arianna's door at 7:59 p.m. Her father, John Kenton, opened the door. He was a large, intimidating man with a bald head and broad shoulders. He wore a severe look on his face as he eyed me up and down.

"Hi, Mr. Kenton," I said, trying not to sound nervous.

"Brady Bennett," he addressed me in his thick accent. "I understand you're here to take my daughter on a date. Is that correct?"

"Um... yes?" I said, trying and failing not to make it sound like a question.

He didn't reply. We stood there for a few awkward moments, before a more pleasant, feminine voice interrupted.

"John, stop messing with him!"

John's facade broke and he let out a hearty laugh before patting me on the back and ushering me inside.

"You made it too easy, son," he said in between chuckles. "I could have knocked you over with a feather."

He led me into the living room where Arianna's mom Heidi was standing by a chair, an open book placed upside down on the end table next to her. She beamed a smile as she reached in and gave me a big hug.

"How are you, Brady?"

"I'm great, Mrs. Kenton. Um, how about you?"

"Oh, we're doing very well, thank you. Arianna will be down in just a second."

I don't think she meant literally, but, as if on cue, Arianna came bouncing down the stairs.

She looked amazing. Like me, she wasn't dressed overly fancy considering the choice of venue—which I had texted her to let her know of beforehand. She wore tight jeans and a black cropped *Escape the Fate* T-shirt. Like Brandi, she had made a few modifications to show a little more skin—not too much, but certainly enough to get my attention. A small leather jacket completed the look, perfect for a rock show.

I half expected her parents to give her shit about her outfit, but they simply ushered us out the door with a "Have a good time!"

As we made conversation while I drove, I noted that her parents seemed almost giddy at the prospect of us hanging out.

"They always liked you, Brady," she explained. "In fact, I heard it from them more than once when I was with Trevor."

"Oh, yeah?" I asked cocking an eyebrow.

"Why don't you go out with a nice boy, like Brady

Bennett?" she said, mimicking her father's accent flawlessly.

"Oof," I said half-jokingly. "Nice boy sounds like a one-way ticket to the friend zone."

She eyed me with a mischievous smile. "Well, you're just going to have to prove otherwise."

"Yeah, but wouldn't that just make me a dick like Trevor?" I asked, sort of regretting it as the words came out.

"If you take it too far, sure. Gotta find the right balance."

"Well, that sounds complicated."

"Tell me about it. I wouldn't want to be in your shoes right now."

***

We sat and ordered dinner. I'm not proud to say I agonized over the menu a bit, not wanting to have anything too heavy for fear of the latter half of the date being plagued by stomach issues. I also didn't want to get anything too messy. The buffalo wings here were fantastic, but there was really no graceful way to eat them.

"How about we split a pizza?" Arianna asked as if reading my mind.

"Sound great!" I replied. "Sausage and pepperoni?"

"Love it! Let's go for it."

We ordered and talked while we waited. It's funny. Arianna and my sister had been friends for years, but we never had anything beyond a surface-level conversation. Per Brandi's advice, I listened to her talk about her family—her dad was looking to retire in the next five years and he and her mom wanted to travel. That segued into Arianna's own love for and desire to see the world. She was enthusiastic and effusive in her description of wanting to go everywhere from the Amalfi coast of Italy to her father's family's hometown in Jamaica.

"How about you?" she asked. "Where do you see yourself after graduation?"

The question hit me harder than I expected. I had applied to a few local colleges, but I still didn't know what I wanted my major to be. For the first time I realized that true adulthood was creeping up fast and I would have to figure my shit out sooner rather than later.

"You know, I'm not really sure."

"Why does that bother you?"

"What makes you think it bothers me?

"Because you look bothered."

I couldn't help but chuckle. Arianna had this way of pointing out the obvious, but it wasn't mean spirited. Just observant. It was endearing.

"Well, I guess I feel like I should have it figured out.

Sometimes I'm a little embarrassed about not knowing."

"What are you passionate about?"

Oh, man, she was really asking the hard-hitting questions. I thought about it for really the first time.

"There's lots of things I like to do – hunting, fishing, watching movies, playing guitar. Stuff like that. If I'm being honest, I'm not mad at spending time with you right now..."

"Good one. You get a point."

We smiled at each other, but mine faded as my inner analysis spilled out.

"You know, after my dad died, I had this fear. If he could be taken from us in his early forties, leaving two kids and a wife behind, then any of us could go at any time."

Arianna's smile faded to match my serious tone. She didn't look away, though. She definitely had an interest in what I was saying as I continued.

"I just want to live my life and not think too far ahead right now. Just trying to, you know, go with the flow, I guess."

"I get that," she said with a nod. "We're only eighteen. People think we're supposed to have it figured out and know what the rest of our lives are going to look like, but if not, fuck it. Despite what everyone tells you, you do have time. Hell, I'm not even sure I'm going to go to college right away. I may take a year and do some traveling."

I nodded and lightened the tone. "Want some company?"

Her smile returned. "Maybe. We'll have to see how the rest of the night goes."

"Am I on the right track?"

"You're doing okay so far."

Our pizza came and we ate. It was a smaller, bar-style pie so it was just the right size that we could split it without feeling like crap afterward. I kept our conversation focused on her, figuring I had monopolized a little too much early on talking about my dad and my nonexistent college plans.

We weren't drinking. Jester's wasn't the type of place to serve underage patrons, but as our conversation went on, I felt a type of intoxication. Our conversation enthralled me. More than once, she reached across and touched my hand that rested on the table. Just a light brush to emphasize points in the conversation, but it was like a bolt of electricity shot through me on contact.

"I'm impressed, Brady."

"About?"

"You're actually listening to me. I don't even want to say his name, but let's just say my last boyfriend was a big fan of himself and was not shy about letting everyone know it."

"Well, that's why he's your ex, I guess."

69

"Yes. Among other reasons. Your sister really looked out for me on that one."

The mention of Brandi dampened my mood a bit. I had been so absorbed with talking to Arianna that I had put the strange incident with Dennis and Brandi's underwear out of my head. My distractedness wasn't lost on Ari.

"You okay?"

I shook it off.

"Yeah," I said, not wanting to divulge the incident to my date, so I pivoted. "It's just, Trevor had some fucked-up things to say about Brandi. I'll be honest, it took everything I had not to punch him."

"Well, you're better than that. Besides, that move you pulled, swooping in and getting a date in the process? Not gonna lie. Smooth as hell."

"Well, we all have our moments." I smiled but my thoughts went back to Brandi.

"Is it true what they say about her?"

Arianna sat back, contemplating. "What's truth anyway?"

"I don't know. I just hate that she has such a... reputation."

"So what if it was true, Brady? Does that change how you feel about her?"

"No! Of course not."

"So what does it matter?"

"It doesn't. I just don't want her to get hurt. I want to

protect her from it."

"You can't always protect people from the ugly in the world."

"I guess not, but we still have to look out for each other. After all, she looked out for you, didn't she?"

She smirked. "Touché. But there's gotta be balance. You have to trust her to take care of herself too."

I nodded. "Point taken."

We sat in silence for a few moments after that, not really knowing what to say next. Small talk was behind us and yet the silence was comfortable, neither of us breaking eye contact. As the saying goes, we were having a moment.

I was getting ready to say something—not entirely sure what, to be honest—when we heard the band starting their sound check from the other room. We silently acknowledged that it was time to move on to the next stage of the date, so I politely signaled to the server for our check.

***

I paid the bill. Arianna graciously offered to split it, but I insisted it was my treat. Once settled, we made our way down the ramp to the other section of the bar where the stage was located. A bouncer stood at the door. The restaurant area was separate because all ages were allowed. The bar–stage was eighteen to get in and twenty-one to drink. We showed the bouncer our IDs and he placed a red wristband on each of us, denying us the ability to purchase alcohol like those who had the green bands.

As soon as we crossed the threshold, Arianna got giddy and grabbed my hand, again sending tingling electricity shooting up my arm. I wondered if I would always feel that sensation at her touch. She effortlessly navigated through the decent-sized crowd to get us to the barricade in front of the stage.

The band was ready to go by the time we got settled. Arianna stood in front of me, leaning against the gate. I'm just under six feet, so there was a noticeable height difference from her five-foot-three frame, even though she her boots gave her a few extra inches.

The band walked out on stage to a decently loud applause and immediately started playing "Not Good Enough for Truth in Cliché" from the Ronnie Radke era of *Escape the Fate*. As soon as they got through the muted notes of the intro and transitioned into the main riff, Arianna started banging her head in rhythm to the music, looking damn fantastic as she did.

We talked little as the band continued, playing classics like "Misery Business" by *Paramore*, "Ohio is for Lovers" by *Hawthorne Heights* and "I'm Not Okay" by *My*

Chemical Romance. Arianna danced the whole time, moving perfectly in sync with each tempo and tone shift. It mesmerized me watching her move. I did my best to sway back and forth and bob my head at appropriate times, but dancing was definitely not my thing.

Ari looked back a few times, always offering a smile. Talking wasn't really an option due to the volume, but she still wanted to do an occasional check-in. Once they finished *Yellowcard's* "Ocean Avenue", the singer announced they would do one more before taking a break.

Arianna leaned back and said "Whew, I'm getting sweaty over here. We should grab some waters in between sets."

"Good idea," I confirmed.

She reached back and grabbed my hand again, giving it a squeeze. "I'm having a great time, Brady. Thank you."

"My pleasure."

We held each other's eyes until the band started playing "The Kill" by *30 Seconds to Mars*. Arianna lit up when she heard it and turned back to the stage.

"I *love* this song!" she shouted as she started swaying her hips, running her hands through her long hair as she did. Something about the way she was moving now seemed more seductive to me. Her perfume was so intoxicating that I didn't need alcohol. I was suddenly aware that she had backed up closer to me. Wanting nothing more than to put my arms around her, I stopped myself, thinking that it might be too forward, even though it sure seemed like she was giving me a signal.

While I over-thought it, she made it abundantly clear when she fully backed into me, her butt firmly pressed against my groin.

Oh, shit, I thought as I felt my body react, trying to will it not to. The old adage said to think about baseball, but that wasn't my thing. I tried thinking about the Giants coaching staff between Tom Coughlin and Brian Daboll, but to no avail. Even Ben McAdoo's goofy haircut and comically oversized play chart couldn't counteract Arianna's effect on me.

I was mortified. The way she pressed against me, there was no way she didn't notice that something was, um, different. I expected her to pull away as if branded with a hot poker, but she pushed back more, grinding into me in time with the beat of the music. At that point, the green light was clear, so I wrapped my arms around her waist as she continued to move. She threw her head back against my shoulder, her hair draping over it. I closed my eyes, lost in the moment. When I opened them again, she had turned her head into me, a look on her face I hadn't yet seen from her.

She kissed me. Just a peck, but it felt amazing.

Turning back, she continued to sway with the music as I held her. When the song concluded, the band thanked the audience, promising to be back in just a little bit. I gently turned Arianna to face me and she put her arms around my neck and I moved in for another kiss. This time, her lips parted and our tongues met.

Everything around me faded away. In that moment, it was just me and Arianna. Nothing else in the world mattered.

CHAPTER 8

I dropped Arianna off at her house after the show. We sat parked at the curb for quite a while, neither of us quite ready for the date to end. We alternated between continuing our conversation and making out some more. Finally, after we'd breathlessly broken away from each other, she smiled at me and said she had to go, but we made plans to hang out again during the weekend. She pulled me in for one last kiss to punctuate the evening and exited my car, bounding for her front door.

Not a drop of alcohol or anything else had entered my system that evening, but I was on an unbelievable high as I drove home. Although my past encounters with the opposite sex were limited, I didn't need a wealth of experience to understand that there was really something here. We just clicked in a way that I didn't think was possible. And I didn't have to be a body language expert to know that Arianna was feeling at least something similar.

I pulled into my driveway and killed the engine. It was late. Almost 2:30 in the morning. I pushed the door open carefully and shut it equally cautiously, clicking the lock on the door instead of the remote, sparing my sleeping family the abrupt beep of the horn.

I looked back into the woods behind the house as I headed toward the front porch. It was still weirdly silent. I felt a twinge of pain in my shin, right around the area of my scar from all those years ago. Since that night, I'd grown more than accustomed to the woods, but tonight, for the first time in a long time, they unsettled me. There was something off back there despite the night being clear as could be, the full moon providing better-than-average lighting.

Shaking my head, I quickly shrugged the feelings off. I wasn't going to let anything ruin what had probably been the best night of my life.

As I entered the foyer, I saw Dennis sitting in his recliner in the dark.

I jumped back, startled, as I didn't expect anyone to be there, let alone just sitting silently with no lights.

"Jesus, Dennis," I whispered trying to be aware that Mom and Brandi were probably asleep.

"Brady," he addressed me in the most formal of tones.

I was waiting for a follow-up, but he just sat there looking at me. I saw an empty snifter on the table next to him, behind which sat a mostly empty crystal decanter that had no doubt been filled with Oban 18, Dennis's Scotch of choice.

Fuck this. I wasn't going to engage. I moved toward the staircase.

"Goodnight, Dennis," I said as I passed.

"Brady."

Goddamn it.

"Yeah?"

He stood up out of the recliner and faced me.

"What did you tell your sister?"

"About what?"

He smirked. Something about it reminded me of the scenes where Christian Bale was trying to be cordial to his colleagues in *American Psycho* while simultaneously wanting to gut them for having nicer business cards. It brought me back to Brandi's quip that he wasn't the titular character from the movie.

"You know about what."

I did but I wouldn't give him the satisfaction.

"Dennis, it's late and I'm tired. Can you just be specific?"

"Did you tell her I was sniffing her underwear?"

"No." I said confidently. It was the truth. I told her he was holding them, but I never said anything about *sniffing* them. "Is that all?"

"Your sister said something to that effect to your mother. As you can imagine, my wife was not happy about that."

So much for my good mood. "You told me to tell her

to get her laundry. That's what I did."

"But you specified something about her panties."

Gross. The word *panties* coming from his mouth fouled me out, especially in reference to Brandi's.

"I told her to get her laundry out because you needed to do yours. I said you probably didn't want to move it yourself to respect her privacy."

Now I was lying, but I damn sure wasn't going to admit putting my sister on alert. It was probably the right choice given the fact that my guard was quickly rising.

Dennis eyed me for a few moments before saying anything. He didn't believe me.

"It seems that's not how Brandi interpreted it."

"Maybe it was Mom who didn't hear it right?" I deflected, being more protective of my sister than my mom. After all, Mom chose to be in this situation. Brandi and I just ended up here.

"So you're calling your mother a liar?"

"I wasn't here. I'm just saying maybe she misheard."

"By that rationale, maybe you think you saw something you didn't."

Where was he going with this?

"All I saw was you in the laundry room when I went to get a stain stick. You asked me to tell Brandi to move her clothes and I did. So what's the big deal?" I asked, knowing damn well what the big fucking deal was.

"The big deal, Brady, is that when you accuse someone

of something, that's not easily retracted."

I lolled my head back in frustration.

"I didn't accuse anybody of anything."

"That's the thing about the world we live in, son. Even the hint of an allegation can be enough to ruin someone. It can cost them their job, their friends, even their family."

As usual, his use of *son* to address me made my blood boil.

"I didn't accuse you of anything," I said again with confidence because, again, it wasn't a lie. There was no accusation; Just a statement of what I saw. What I knew damn well was exactly what it looked like.

"I hope not, Brady. That would be unfortunate. This misunderstanding alone has already caused a serious problem between your mother and I. If you were outright accusing me of wrongdoing, that could lead to even bigger problems in our family."

Our family. Son. He was trying to goad me and it was working. I tried not to clench my fists, avoiding even the subtlest movement to let him know how badly he was getting to me. This conversation needed to end now.

"Well, it's a good thing I didn't accuse you of anything then."

We stared at each other for a few more incredibly tense moments before Dennis broke the silence again.

"Good night, Brady," he said as he reclaimed his spot in the recliner and emptied the rest of the decanter into the glass before setting it down and taking a long, deliberate sip.

***

Quickly making my way upstairs, I saw that Brandi's door was shut as usual. It was silent on the other side. Tiptoeing over, I gently turned the knob, which only budged an inch before I felt the resistance of the lock. I had never really thought about whether she locked her door at night, but it was surprising just how relieved I was that her room was secure.

Making my way to my own room, I immediately locked the door behind me as well. I tried to put the weirdness with Dennis behind me and think about how amazing the night had been prior to the last few minutes. It was working as I recalled Arianna's smile, the smell of her perfume and the softness of her lips. We had done nothing but kiss but I was extremely aroused for much of the latter half of the evening, which, at eighteen, took little, so you could probably imagine how I was feeling considering what actually occurred.

As I undressed, fully intending to achieve release before going to bed, I found my mood dampened again, but this time by something outside. A sound. Something I had never heard in these woods before.

A howl.

What the hell? There were no wolves in New Jersey. At least not in the wild. I opened my window, which faced the rear of the property, and looked out.

It was silent again.

Had I actually heard that or did my mind, dulled by tiredness and horniness, just make it up?

Considering the latter, I was about to get in bed when I heard it again. Looking out the window, I saw birds hurriedly flying away from the trees, spooked by the inhuman sound.

It was closer than I was comfortable with.

Wide awake now and no longer thinking about Arianna, I quickly got dressed in my camo hunting pants and dark sweatshirt. I pulled the long hardshell case from under my bed and punched in the code, retrieving my father's Remington 870 Wingmaster shotgun. My mom had saved it after he died and I waited every day until I was old enough to claim it as my own.

Although it was technically bow season for hunting until December, it didn't matter since I was on my family's property and, if it actually was a wolf, there was no way I was going after it with my crossbow.

I loaded the gun and pocketed some extra shells. I also grabbed my Buck 113 Ranger hunting knife and attached the sheath to my belt. Prepared for the hunt, I made my way quietly down the back stairs, wanting to avoid

Dennis if he was still in the living room.

As I stepped off the last stair, I glanced down the hall toward the front of the house. No one was moving, but I heard the faint sound of snoring. The scotch had put Dennis to sleep.

Stepping out onto the deck, I slid the door shut quietly behind me. I stood there, looking out into the woods, which had once again fallen silent. A chill ran through me as the fictitious monsters that had chased me into the house and sliced up my shin all those years ago came back to life. Doing my best to shake off my anxiousness, I made my way to the tree line.

***

I kept my gun in front of me as I navigated the woods. It was hard to pinpoint where the howl had come from, so I listened for other sound cues to determine which way I should go. Among the trees, it wasn't as silent as it had been, but it was still quieter than usual. It felt like the woods themselves were trying to hide from something.

The trees and critters gave nothing up. There was no indication of which direction to go, so I had to wing it, constantly scanning the area to make sure nothing got the drop on me. I must have been crazy to go running off into the woods to track a wolf. It still didn't seem right to me that one would be out here, but I know what I heard. Maybe it escaped from a zoo or some kind of nature preserve? I wasn't aware of any nearby, but I couldn't be sure.

Either way, wolves were dangerous and there were a lot of homes spread out around here. Families with children who could easily fall prey to a vicious predator like that. If I found out that someone got hurt when I could have prevented it, I wouldn't be able to live with that guilt, a feeling I'd lived with since my father died. One I promised myself I would never live with again.

After almost thirty minutes of combing the woods, I'd had no luck. Ready to head back, I figured I would look into wolf tracking techniques and get back out here in the morning when I heard a different sound. One I was more familiar with.

It was a shrill bleating sound that I immediately recognized as the distress bawl of a deer.

I raised my shotgun and moved directly toward the sound. I heard it at irregular intervals. As I got closer, it was clear that the animal wasn't just in distress, it was wounded.

It didn't take long before I found it. It was the buck I had tracked earlier. As I got closer, I gasped.

I didn't know how the thing was still alive. Its entire stomach was ripped open, its entrails spilled out onto the ground below, resting in a pool of blood. It was as if the poor thing had been field dressed while still alive.

Lowering my shotgun, I approached the dying deer and saw that the wounds were jagged, with large claw marks on either side. Maybe a bear had done this, but if there was a wolf out here, it could have easily been that as well.

I looked around in all directions to make sure the buck's assailant wasn't close by. When I was satisfied that it was at least far enough away for me to retrieve my gun if needed, I slung it over my shoulder and knelt down beside the dying creature. I ran my hand over the fur on the back of its head, trying to comfort it even though I had no idea if that would help.

The deer made an awful gurgling noise and spat more blackened blood onto the pile of leaves in front of it. It was going to die, but it was taking too long. I had to put the thing out of its misery.

I retrieved my knife and thrust it into its neck. As its blood seeped out over my blade, I saw the remaining light in the bucks eyes go out as it mercifully expired.

I pulled the knife out of its neck and wiped it on the leaves to clean off the blood. I returned it to its sheath and unslung my shotgun. Just because whatever did this wasn't close didn't mean it wasn't still out here. Either way, there was nothing else I could do tonight. My body and mind were exhausted and I wouldn't be any good in a hunt right now. Best to get home to rest.

As I exited the woods and made my way back to the house, the night once again fell silent.

Until one last howl emanated from the trees.

CHAPTER 9

Even though I got little sleep that night, I woke up earlier than I expected the next morning. I was deeply unsettled, not only by the potential predator lurking in the woods behind my house, but also by my interactions with Dennis. I kept the second encounter to myself, not letting in Brandi or my mom, figuring it would just make things worse. When I talked to Brandi, it was mainly to get a sense of the vibe in the house after I had left for my date.

She confirmed she did tell Mom what I said about Dennis. She said Mom blew her off, insinuating that she was being ridiculous. Later on, however, Brandi heard her and Dennis having a very heated argument. She couldn't make out exactly what they were saying, but it was definitely one of the worst she'd ever heard between them.

We agreed it was best to just let this go for now. We had every intention of keeping our guard up, but there wasn't much we could do at the moment.

I went back into the woods a few times, looking for

the deer's assailant, but I had no luck. There wasn't even a hint of a fox or coyote, animals that were much more common to this area. Still, I'll admit I didn't spend as much time searching as I would have under normal circumstances. My priority was spending more time with Arianna.

There's a kind of unwritten rule that you don't call or text immediately after a date, not wanting to look desperate or some other such nonsense, but Arianna chucked those rules almost immediately.

My phone buzzed as I was heading out from my search as Saturday morning transitioned into afternoon. I had fully intended to break the rule myself but Ari beat me to it. My heartbeat immediately quickened before I even viewed the screen.

Arianna: Had a great time last night. Thank you.

I paused, trying to think of the right response, but I didn't want to delay too long.

Me: Me 2! I'd love to see you again soon.

I sort of regretted it as I hit send. I really never understood why we're expected to play it so cool instead of legitimately showing interest in another person. There's a fine line between enthusiastic and desperate, but the "too cool for school" act never really appealed to me.

The dots popped up on my screen, followed quickly by her reply.

Arianna: What R U doing today?

***

What I ended up doing was showering and picking her up again within the hour. We went to the movies. I offered Arianna her choice of flick, expecting it to be something serious and artsy, but she opted for a horror movie called *Barbarian*. I wasn't completely sure what it was about. The trailer indicated it was a suspense flick where two people end up renting the same Airbnb, but some creepy stuff happens. I thought I knew where it was going to go, but I was completely off. The film was batshit crazy and completely unlike anything I expected. (Don't worry, I won't spoil it for you.)

Ari reacted accordingly to the scary scenes. She jumped in her seat, giggled nervously in between and grabbed onto my arm more than once. On one of those occasions, I looked at her and smiled and she responded with a quick kiss, before turning her attention back to the screen. I loved sitting there with her. She was fully engrossed but made sure to do little check-ins like holding my hand or offering me popcorn.

Another make-out session followed in the car parked outside her house. This one a little more intense, our hands roaming over each other's clothed bodies. Nothing came off and it didn't move past just the kissing and some light fondling, but I was on cloud nine. There was nothing I wanted more than to finally experience sex and there was no one I'd rather experience it with than her, but I wasn't going to be pushy about it.

Still, I wasn't going to be the one to stop. She finally broke away, taking a second to catch her breath.

"I think we better stop or this is going to go further."

I tried to play it cool. "Yeah, um, sure. Would that be such a bad thing?"

Real cringe, dipshit. Nice one.

She smiled though, putting my mind at ease. "Oh, not at all. But not yet." She punctuated this sentence with a wink.

"Well, I'll be here when you're ready," I replied, wincing again at how goofy I sounded. I quickly spun into, "I've really had a great time the past two days. I know I'm supposed to be aloof and pretend I'm not as interested as I am, but that just isn't me. I can't wait to see you again."

Her smile widened before she moved in and kissed me again. I thought she was going to break away quickly, but she kept going. This time I was the one who broke it.

"Good night, Arianna."

"Good night, Brady."

***

I'd be lying if I told you I was a little disappointed when Arianna texted me the next morning to tell me she was going to visit her grandmother in Burlington County that day. We exchanged a few flirty texts, but, for the most part, I had the day to myself.

Grabbing my shotgun and crossbow, I headed back into the woods, figuring I'd try to see if I could snag a deer. Even though that was my primary objective, I wanted to make sure I was prepared if I ran into something more aggressive. I had no luck on either front, so I returned home just before the Giants game at 4 p.m. Dennis was sitting on the couch with a Scotch, watching the Eagles. Opting not to interact with him, I headed upstairs to watch the Giants in my room.

Around 5 p.m., Mom shouted up to let us know that she wasn't making dinner that evening and would order pizzas. They arrived forty-five minutes later. Brandi and I made our way downstairs to claim our slices before returning to our room. Mom was sitting at the table, her Kindle in her hand as she ate, barely nodding in our direction as we passed by. Dennis remained in his chair, not eating, near as I could tell. My sister and I exchanged a WTF look but said nothing. We simply took our food and retired to our rooms, where we spent the rest of our respective evenings.

***

If you counted pre-K, I'd been in some form of school or another for the past fourteen years and I can confidently say I'd never looked forward to stepping into an educational facility as much as I did that Monday.

As soon as I crossed the threshold of the building, I walked as fast I could, without looking silly, to C-hall, where Arianna's locker was located. I was thrilled to see that she was there, arranging her books for the day.

She looked fantastic as always. Today she wore light-blue jeans and a three-quarter-length black sweater that was cropped, much like her top from Friday, right at the waist. Her hair was tied back in a ponytail, showing off the row of small ringed piercings running up her ear from the lobe to the helix. Something about her hair tucked back behind her ears was incredibly sexy to me. But, then again, she would probably look sexy with a buzz cut.

I slowed my pace as I got closer to her locker, trying to see if I could catch her off guard.

"Nice try, Bennett," she said without turning around.

Damn it.

"How do you know it was me and not some creep?"

She turned and hit me with that smile of hers. "Who

says you're not both?"

"Ha ha," I said and leaned in for a kiss that she eagerly returned, keeping it PG to maintain decorum in these halls of learning.

Unfortunately, Arianna and I were the only ones in the vicinity thinking about decorum because, as soon as our lips separated, my head slammed into the adjacent locker. Stars sprang across my vision. I had always thought it was just an expression, but the second my cranium made contact, it was like I was looking at the night sky through a telescope.

As I crumpled to the ground, I tried to gather my wits enough to figure out exactly what had happened, dimly aware of Arianna yelling, although I couldn't discern if it was anger, fear, or both. It felt like I was hearing her while submerged in the deep end of the pool.

As I tried to make out what she was saying, everything went black.

***

The next thing I remembered was opening my eyes and immediately being blinded by an overhead light. I squeezed my eyelids tight and groaned.

"Where the hell am I?"

"You can open your eyes now," a familiar voice said.

I hesitantly opened one, then the other, discovering that the lights were out. Looking over to my left, I saw Brandi sitting in a chair next to the bed I was lying on. A hospital bed. The room was dark, but there was light coming from outside the room. A constant variety of beeps emanated from pretty much all around me.

"You're in the ER, bro," my sister said. "You remember your name?"

I looked at her, not sure if she was serious at first, but she certainly didn't look like she was joking.

"Eli Manning," I told her.

"For real, dickhead."

"Brady. Brady Bennett. Are you happy, Brandi Bennett, my twin sister?"

"Good," she replied, relief setting in. "You really couldn't spare too many more brain cells."

I laughed, but immediately regretted it because a sharp pain shot through my head, like I was being stabbed from the inside. I reached up and felt my forehead which I quickly found had a large piece of gauze, secured by medical tape.

"You needed a couple stitches. Your head smacked right into the grate on the locker next to Ari's. Gave you a pretty nasty gash. Kinda like the one on your shin from when you were a kid."

"How the fuck did I manage that?"

"You didn't," she replied.

I raised my eyebrows.

"Trevor," she confirmed.

"Motherfucker!" I yelled, louder than I intended, sending another lighting bolt across my cranium.

"Take it easy, Brady. You have a concussion."

Well, that certainly explained a few things.

"What happened?"

"I didn't see it myself, but apparently Trevor saw your little PDA with Arianna and flew off the fucking handle. He ran up behind you and slammed your head right into the locker."

I thought about it for a second.

"I remember kissing Arianna. Then I remember hitting my head, but after that, I got nothing. He knocked me out?"

"I don't think you actually lost consciousness, but you were definitely loopy. Like you were drunk or something."

That was odd, but I remembered back to my WWE-watching days—another favorite pastime with my father. It was Wrestlemania and my favorite wrestler of all time, The Undertaker, was fighting Brock Lesnar. At the time, The Undertaker was undefeated at Wrestlemania, having won all twenty-one of his matches. On this night, however, thirty minutes after the match started, The Undertaker was flat on his back and Lesnar had his hand raised in victory in front of the stunned audience, both in live attendance and in my living room.

The craziest thing I learned later on was that The Undertaker got a concussion in the opening minutes of the match, even though he appeared conscious throughout the whole thing. He later recounted that he woke up in the hospital the next morning and couldn't remember anything since about 3:30 p.m. the previous day, hours before the match actually started.

How long had I been out of it?

"Is it still Monday?" I asked.

"Yeah," Brandi replied.

That was a relief. I remembered everything up to and including getting hit, so I hoped that the concussion wasn't too severe. I tried to pick up the pieces as best I could.

"So what happened with Trevor?"

Brandi smiled wide, like the Cheshire cat. "He got suspended. Word is, he's probably getting expelled."

"No shit?"

"No shit. I think aggravated assault on another student more than qualifies. Mom is even talking about pressing charges."

Huh. I guess nothing like your son getting assaulted to bring your mother out of her funk. I looked around and confirmed that Brandi was the only one in the room.

"Where is Mom?"

"She went to go get coffee. We've been here about four

hours at this point."

I lay back and closed my eyes, the strain of keeping them open beginning to wear on me. "Trevor Wright got suspended and is probably getting kicked out of school?"

"Yes, he did. And got a black eye for his trouble."

My eyes popped open and I sat up a little too quickly, feeling like I might puke as I got stabbed from the inside of my skull again. "Huh?"

"Easy, champ," my twin said. "Right after you went down, Arianna pulled him back and punched him square in the face."

"No shit?" I asked again.

"No shit," Brandi parroted. "I'm so pissed I missed it, but Heather Turner told me it was spectacular."

"Jesus," I muttered laying back down again and shutting my eyes. "Knowing what a fucking scumbag he is, I'm surprised he didn't hit her back."

"He might have, but Mr. Garvin stepped in and broke it up."

"Good," I said, the thought of Trevor laying his hands on Ari making my blood boil. "Fuck him."

"Fuck him, indeed. Guess he's not going to be a problem for you anymore."

"Guess not."

If only that were true.

CHAPTER 10

Even though the initial symptoms were scary, my concussion was thankfully on the mild side. I didn't go to school the rest of the week, but that didn't break my heart. Still, it wasn't as fun as it sounded. I was stricken with a near-constant pounding in my head that went from a jackhammer inside my skull when untreated to a dull tap dance when I had my maximum dose of 800 milligrams of ibuprofen in me. Beyond that, I had to keep my room dark because of the light sensitivity. No TV. No video games. And forget about hunting. It was a great week for it, but I couldn't be out in the woods in this condition.

No, I mainly just had time to sit, sleep and think.

Brandi guessed correctly: Trevor was unceremoniously expelled from Hillcrest High School after a brief hearing later that week. She was also correct that my mother was furious. It was almost kind of nice to see her displaying actual human emotion instead of just zombieing around the house all night. The Wrights, to their credit, were incredibly apologetic and begged her not to press charges on their son. Ultimately, she left the decision up to me. I considered it but, to be fair, between Trevor's expulsion and my budding relationship with his ex-girlfriend, I figured he had been sufficiently punished. Maybe he'd use this incident to do some self-reflection and turn his life around.

Nah. Probably not, but it wasn't my problem anymore.

My saving grace that week was Arianna. Every day at 3:30, she accompanied Brandi home from school and came up and sat with me. She brought my homework and helped me transcribe my answers where she could so I wouldn't fall behind too much.

But mainly, we just talked. Sometimes for hours. We talked about nonsense like music and movies we liked, to heavier topics like life and religion. I was more agnostic, but Arianna's family was very religious. She and her mom were not as intense as her dad on the subject, but she believed in God, although admittedly wasn't sure exactly what God was. I couldn't remember ever talking to anyone on this level, not my family, my few friends, or even my sister. It was nice, it was interesting and, most importantly, it was easy. No matter what we discussed, I was never bored and the conversations always ended at a point where I would have been happy to keep going.

Of course, Ari being Ari, she teased me a bit, saying things like, "I'd totally make out with you right now, but I don't want to make your symptoms worse." She punctuated each quip with a knowing smirk.

I assured her I'd be fine, but she'd simply brush me off. "No, no. I'd hate to have a negative impact on your health."

As the week was coming to an end, we talked about the upcoming Halloween Dance at our school. Arianna told me she'd been waiting all week for me to ask her, but, since I was dragging my feet, she would formally ask me.

"Will you accompany me to the school dance, good sir?"

"It would be my honor, my lady."

It being a Halloween dance, we discussed what our costumes would be. Arianna refused to tell me what she was doing. She simply told me to pick something and she'd match it.

I hadn't put too much thought into it as I obviously hadn't been trick-or-treating in years and, up until Arianna asked me, I'd had every intention of skipping the dance. Looking around my room, I noted my Giants memorabilia.

"A football player," I announced.

"I can work with that," Arianna said with a wink.

***

By the night of the dance, my concussion symptoms were

completely gone and I was feeling like myself again. I had even managed to get back outdoors a few times in the previous week but had no luck either tracking deer or finding any sign of the "wolf" whose howl I hadn't heard since the night of my first date with Arianna. Whatever it was, I guess it had moved on. I just hoped no one got hurt.

The dance started at 7 p.m., so Brandi and I had enough time to suffer through another of our increasingly awkward family dinners. Mom was back to being a silent zombie, barely speaking more than a few sentences to us in a given day. Dennis, too. He only interacted when he absolutely had to. We ate in silence as Mom neglected her meatloaf in favor of substituting calories from several glasses of wine. Dennis wolfed his down as if it were a competition and dumped his plate in the sink before retiring to the living room without a word.

Brandi and I made small talk, both to break the silence where we could and, honestly, to irritate our mom and stepdad. If they wanted to act like miserable pricks, more power to them, but my sister and I weren't going to give them the satisfaction of thinking they'd got to us.

We finished our meals and cleared off our dishes, loading them, along with Dennis's inconsiderately discarded plate, into the dishwasher. We left mom at the table, her half-eaten dinner cooling in front of her while she poured her third glass of merlot.

***

After I showered, I quickly threw on a pair of shoulder pads I had purchased at Dick's Sporting Goods and covered them with my Victor Cruz number eighty jersey. I pulled on a pair of football pants that I had also purchased during the same trip. I knew I would never wear them again after tonight, but I didn't want Ari to think I wasn't putting any effort in.

I opted for regular sneakers, figuring cleats were a bridge too far for a high school dance. I completed the look by applying a line of eye black under each eye. Taking a quick look in the mirror, I was satisfied with what I had put together. I grabbed my replica Giants helmet, slung it under my arm and headed downstairs.

When I got there, Mom was gone, more than likely upstairs in her room. Dennis was sitting in his chair with his Scotch but didn't say a word to me. Come to think of it, I don't think he had said more than a handful of words to me since the night of the laundry incident.

Even if I cared, I didn't have too much time to think about it as I heard Brandi say "Let's go" as she bounded down the stairs.

I sighed when I saw her. She was wearing a goth clown costume that left very little to the imagination.

It was a black-and-white corset with red fuzzy buttons and a very short, similarly styled skirt. She wore red high heels and thigh-high stockings with white fuzzy rings around the upper thigh. The nylon strings of a garter emanated from her skirt to her stockings. Her hair was covered with a black-and-red wig styled into two high buns on either side of her head, with a small circus hat stuck in the middle of the tufts of hair. She completed her look with heavy black eyeliner with two streaks running down from her eyes to the bottom of her cheeks, punctuated with small rhinestones at the tips. Her lipstick was exaggerated and blood red.

"That's what you're going with?" I asked her, trying not to sound too dad-like.

"Not another fucking word, Brady."

I expected Dennis to chime in with some type of snarky, disapproving comment. I glanced in his direction and saw that his eyes were indeed on Brandi, but he said nothing. As soon as he noticed me looking at him, he stole another second to glance at her, but then returned his attention to the television, slowly sipping his Scotch as he did.

This weirdness permeating our household was getting to be too much. All I could think was that in less than a year, I'd be out of here. I'm sure Brandi was thinking the same thing.

"Let's go," my sister said impatiently.

"Yeah," I agreed, not taking my eyes off Dennis as we exited the house.

As we made our way to the car, I couldn't help but notice something felt different. It was the same feeling I had back on the night I had picked up Arianna for our first date. The woods were unusually quiet. Like that night, the moon was full and light was good, but the trees were still. Again, it was as if the denizens of the forest were all hiding from something. I half expected to hear that howl again, but I didn't.

Still, I couldn't shake the feeling that we were being watched.

CHAPTER 11

We pulled up to Arianna's house and Brandi jumped out to go get her. I saw Mr. Kenton's eyes go wide when he saw her, but it was definitely in an *I have a daughter your age and don't need to see you dressed like this* kinda way. His measured reaction made me even more uncomfortable with how Dennis had been acting.

Of course, all thoughts of Dennis fled my mind as soon as I saw Arianna exit the house, kissing her dad on the cheek as she did.

She looked utterly fantastic in a sexy referee costume. It consisted of a halter-style black-and-white top tied behind her neck and a short, but not too short, ruffled black skirt. She also wore black heels and stockings, but hers were knee high. Her hair was styled in twin pigtails and she finished the look with a whistle hanging around her neck. Compared to Brandi's outrageous costume choice, she was pretty conservative, but it was still sexy as all hell.

Brandi kindly got into the back seat to allow Arianna to sit next to me on the passenger side. She smiled and kissed me, telling me my costume looked great. I really appreciated the effort she put into making sure we looked like a couple.

That made me think. Were we? We had spent a lot of time together over the last month. I don't think she was seeing anybody else and I knew that I certainly wasn't. But still we hadn't put any labels on it. Honestly, I wasn't even sure how you go about something like that. Do you just say, "Hey, want to be my girlfriend?"

I must have been too lost in thought because I was jarred by the sound of Arianna blowing her whistle. I jumped in my seat and turned my attention to her. She pulled out a dyed yellow handkerchief and tossed it in my face.

"Fifteen-yard penalty for being a space cadet!" she told me in her best authoritative tone before busting into laughter along with Brandi.

"Yeah, yeah. I'm going," I said as I shifted the car into gear.

***

The three of us entered the school's gymnasium around 7:15 p.m. It was already packed with our classmates, all transformed into their characters for the evening. The room was appropriately decorated with cobwebs, skeletons and a large assortment of Halloween-themed snacks, and bowls of punch which would no doubt end up spiked by evening's end.

The DJ stood behind his table on the stage at the far end of the gym, dressed like the grim reaper, with a full hood and skeleton mask. A large plastic scythe rested against the wall to the left of him.

A giant projector screen was lowered above the DJ, showing clips from various classic Universal monster movies. Currently, Dracula and the Wolf Man were meeting for the first time. They muted the film in favor of the music, but it was a cool little touch to have the monsters looming over the crowd as they danced.

"I'm going to leave you two be," Brandi shouted over the music. "You don't need me being a third wheel."

Before Arianna or I could tell her that wasn't necessary, she was gone, heading for a mixed group of guys and girls, a few of whom I knew she was at least acquainted with. I guess with Trevor not here, she didn't have to worry too much about anyone else. At least not that I was aware of.

"C'mon, Brady," Arianna said, breaking my contemplations. "Let's see your dance moves."

***

As Arianna learned on our first date, I didn't have any

dance moves to speak of, but she didn't care. All I really had to do was sway side to side and occasionally throw my hands in the hair, at least pretending not to care. Ari was the real star. She knew exactly how to move to whatever type of music was playing. I was so entranced watching her I found myself not moving on more than one occasion. Each time, however, she was kind enough to grab my hand or waist to pull me back into some type of rhythm.

I focused most of my attention—rightly so—on my date, but every now and then I found my sister in the crowd. She was dancing with Ryan Marshall, a guy I was pretty sure she'd been seeing, at least casually. She was really putting on a show with her own dance moves, grinding up against him as he held her hips.

And she wonders why she has a reputation, I thought to myself, feeling a little shitty for the intrusive thought. She wasn't really doing anything wrong per se, I just felt weird seeing my twin flaunt her sexuality like that.

I put it out of my head. My sister was eighteen just like me and she could do whatever the hell she wanted. I knew she was more than smart and capable enough to take care of herself. I had to stop my bad habit of thinking I had to step into the role of our father.

Arianna threw her hands around my neck and pulled me close as the DJ announced, "We're going to slow it down for you now, give you a chance to catch your breath before we steal it back away! Muah huah huah!"

I rolled my eyes at the attempt at a sinister laugh and put my hands around Arianna's waist, clasping them together behind her back. It felt fantastic holding her this close. She smiled up at me, looking like she wanted to say something.

"What's on your mind?" I asked.

"Just thinking. We've been hanging out for a month now." She paused before adding, "Just wondering if you're getting bored yet."

I was a little surprised. Did she think I wasn't into her?

"Of course not!" I emphasized. "How could I possibly be bored with you?"

"Just checking."

I pulled her in closer for a hug. We stayed in that position as we moved along with the music. That song ended and another slow one began. I moved back so I could look at her again.

"So I guess you're not bored either."

"Not at all."

"I don't want to play any stupid, clichéd high school games with you. Not only am I not bored, you are the only girl I'm interested in. The only one I want to spend time with."

Her smile widened. "Brady Bennett, are you asking me to be your girlfriend?"

I returned the smile. "Yes, Arianna Kenton. I want you

to be my girlfriend."

She pulled me in for a kiss.

"I'll think about it."

Was she serious? I thought that was what she wanted too. I saw the glint of mischief in her eyes and realized she was messing with me.

I let go of her and pretended like I was going to walk away. She grasped my hand and pulled me back toward her. I didn't resist.

"I would be honored to be your girlfriend," she confirmed.

The DJ made an announcement: "One more slow one and then we're going to pick up the tempo again!"

As the next song started, we continued to hold each other. I was no longer aware of what Brandi was up to. In fact, in a room full of people, it felt like Arianna and I were the only ones in the world.

She pulled me close again, but this time brought her lips up to my ear where she whispered to me.

"Let's take a walk."

***

We slipped out of the gymnasium hand in hand. Thankfully there were no chaperones in sight as Ari led me down the hall and around the corner. About halfway down the next corridor, she stopped at the door that read *Prop Room*.

"What are we doing here?"

"Keep your voice down," she told me as she turned the knob and pushed the door open. I was surprised it was unlocked. "I forgot to lock it after school today," she said with a sly grin.

She pulled me inside and shut the door behind us, not *forgetting* to lock it this time. I knew Arianna was very into theater, having been in the school show each year. She had mentioned to me that she was hoping to get one of the leads roles in this year's production of *Into the Woods*.

The room was filled with clothing racks packed to the brim with all sorts of costumes. There were also several bins lining the walls with everything from hats to fake swords to different types of plastic food. It was kind of cool to see behind the scenes, but my prevailing thought was wondering just what Arianna was planning here.

"What are we—"

Before I could finish the question, she was on me, her lips pressed against mine for only a moment before her tongue slipped inside. I excitedly returned the kiss. We had made out a lot over the past month, but there was a new intensity now. This was next level.

She pushed my jersey up and over my head, rendering me shirtless, save for my shoulder pads. She ran her hands over my chest as she reached around and unclasped them on either side, never breaking the kiss until we loosened them enough to pull over my head. As the pads joined my jersey on the floor, Ari took a step back and removed her halter top, leaving her in only a neon-pink bra.

I was stunned at the events unfolding. Was this really happening?

She smiled at me as she took another step back.

"You like what you see?" she asked coyly.

I could only nod, hoping I didn't look like a fucking idiot.

Arianna reached behind her back and unclasped the bra, slowly pulling the straps down before tossing it on the growing pile of clothes, revealing her breasts to me. For the first time, there was a topless girl in front of me and she was stunning. Her dark nipples stood at attention as she moved back to me, grabbing my hands and guiding them up to her chest. I was in heaven as I caressed her, instinctively rolling the sensitive nubs between my fingers as we kissed again. Ari moaned into my mouth in approval.

As I focused on her breasts, she ran her hands back down my chest and over my stomach. She made her way to my waistline and loosened my pants, allowing her to reach inside. I can't recall my penis ever being so hard in my life and it took all my willpower not to explode as she wrapped her fingers around it and gently started stroking.

She continued to work me with one hand as she reached up with the other and pulled my right hand off her breast. Gripping my wrist, she moved it down over her tight stomach and past her skirt. She guided me up and under. My fingers felt the lacy material covering her sex. The panties felt damp as I rubbed her over the flimsy garment. She continued to stroke me as I pulled the fabric aside and inserted my index finger.

Ari's moans intensified as I fingered her while she ground her hips against my hand. She whispered in my ear again.

"Do you have a condom?"

"Yes," I answered. I had been carrying one for a few weeks now. I never wanted to presume that we would end up having sex, but I still wanted to be prepared should the opportunity arise. And—oh, man—was it arising right now. "In my pocket."

Arianna moved her hand away from my wrist and reached into my left pocket, pulling out the contraceptive. She released my aching member and placed her hands on either side of my pants, pushing them to the ground. As I wiggled my way out of them, she started moving backward toward a cot in the corner of the room. I wondered if she had set it up in anticipation of this evening's events.

When she reached the edge of the makeshift bed, she reached up under her skirt, pulling off her panties and stepping out of them, tossing them over my shoulder. She sat down and ripped the condom wrapper open with her teeth. She reached out and grabbed me again, pulling me toward her before slowly unrolling the rubber over my shaft.

With the protection in place, she reached behind my neck with one hand and pulled me on top of her, reaching between my legs with her free hand. She positioned me between her legs and guided me into her. Even with the barrier, it was the most incredible feeling I'd ever had. She gasped as I entered her.

Our eyes met; I saw the desire in hers, but there was something more to it. She looked at me lovingly. No matter where our relationship took us, I knew this first time was going to be special.

I leaned down and kissed her as I lost my virginity.

Thankfully, I was able to last a bit. My biggest fear about my first time is that it would be quick and disappointing for the girl. I honestly don't know if she had an orgasm, but she wrapped her arms around me and held me close for a while after we finished. I'd never been so happy in my life.

If I had known how brief that happiness would be, I never would have gotten off of that cot.

CHAPTER 12

We heard the commotion before we made it back to the gym. As we walked hand in hand to rejoin Brandi and the others at the dance, the music abruptly stopped, followed by confused chatter and gasps from within the gymnasium. Ari and I exchanged a brief WTF look and hurried inside.

I stopped dead in my tracks as I saw something on the huge LED screen above the DJ station. Something I never wanted to see.

There was a picture of Brandi on the screen. She was taking a selfie in the full body mirror in what I immediately recognized as her room. She was only wearing panties and a tight cropped tank top that was pulled down, exposing her breasts.

Before I could register my shock and turn away, another photo slid on-screen. It was a slideshow. The next picture looked to be taken soon after the previous one. This time, she had turned, displaying her backside, the skimpy underwear barely covering a damn thing. I looked down and saw the DJ furiously working to get the pictures off of the display.

I started toward him shouting, "Shut the whole fucking thing off!"

He heard me and looked at me dumbfounded as if it had never occurred to him. He turned back to his laptop and started slapping the keys in frustration.

"It's frozen!" he yelled. "Someone hacked it!"

The dumb fuck. I shoved my way through the crowd, seething at the giggles and gasps my classmates made at my sister's humiliation. Hopping on stage, I pulled all the wires out of the back of the laptop, looking up only to confirm that I had successfully killed the images, which I had.

"Hey! You fucked up my gear, dude."

I shoved the DJ. He stumbled back and landed on his ass on stage.

"You're lucky I don't fuck *you* up, asshole."

He tried to get up, but I pushed him down again, moving in and crouching over him. I grabbed his collar and pulled him up.

"Who the fuck did this?"

"I—I don't know, man. I'm just spinning these fucking tunes and suddenly that chick showed up on my screen. Like I said, someone must have hacked me."

"That chick is my sister, dickhead," I said, pulling him in closer. "How does someone hack your laptop?"

He held his hands up in a gesture of innocence. "I

don't know! Just because I can fuck around with sound equipment doesn't mean I'm Mr. Robot or some shit!"

I let go of his collar, letting him fall back on his head.

"Fuck dude!" he shouted as he reached up to rub his skull. I didn't give a shit. Turning toward the crowd, I looked for Brandi, finding her in the back corner of the room. Arianna was with her, trying to pull her off Ryan Marshall, who she had backed up against the wall. She was furiously pounding on his chest with balled-up fists.

I jumped off the stage and again pushed my way through the gawking crowd of teenagers who had all turned their attention to Brandi and Ryan. As I got closer, I heard her screaming.

"You asshole! How could you?"

Ryan had his hands up, trying to stop her assault, but she was apoplectic. I joined Arianna and our combined effort was enough to create some distance between them. Ryan had little time for relief though. As soon as Brandi was clear, I rushed him and grabbed him by the collar of his old-time gangster jacket. I shoved him hard into the wall.

"Why'd you do it, Ryan?"

"I didn't, Brady. For real."

Brandi shouted from behind me. "I only sent those pics to you, you piece of shit!"

I feigned letting him go, loosening my grip just enough for him to relax before I tightened it once again and shoved him back into the wall, harder this time.

"You better come clean with me right now, Ryan."

I saw tears in the corner of his eyes. "I didn't know he was going to do this, man. You gotta believe me."

"Who?" I yelled through gritted teeth.

"Trevor."

I should have known. I looked back at Brandi and Arianna. The betrayal in her face broke my heart. She leaned into Ari who held her tight as she buried her face in her shoulder, trying to hide her tears.

"How do he get those pics?" I asked Ryan.

"I don't—"

I punched him in the stomach. He doubled over ready to collapse, but I pushed him back upward.

"Don't fucking lie to me, Ryan."

He was actually crying now. I felt no sympathy. This scumbag was complicit in humiliating my sister in front of the entire school.

"He made me, okay? He knew Brandi and I were hooking up. I mentioned she sent me nudes now and then, you know, just guy-talk shit. But last week, he told me to send them to him."

"So you just did?"

"No! I told him no way, but then he threatened to tell my parents that I was selling molly. What was I supposed to do?"

"Give me your phone."

"What?"

"Give me your fucking phone."

He reached in and handed it to me. I held it up to his face to unlock it.

Filtering through his contacts, I found Trevor's name, texting the contact info to my own phone. I went to hand it back to him. As he reached to accept it, I smashed it against the wall behind him. He likely had everything backed up in the cloud, but I knew this would get my point across that he should delete any incriminating photos as soon as he got a new one.

I felt a hand on my shoulder and turned to see Mr. Garvin behind me. The chaperones had obviously sifted through the chaos enough to start getting things under control.

"Break it up!" he ordered.

I released Ryan's shirt and let him crumple against the wall. He held his stomach where I had hit him.

"Ryan was behind that stunt," I told the teacher. "Him and Trevor Wright."

Mr. Garvin took his hand off my shoulder and turned his focus to Ryan.

"Is this true, Mr. Marshall?"

Ryan nodded through his tears, knowing he would not get away with this one. I took the opportunity to make his night worse.

"By the way, Mr. Garvin, I hear Ryan's been selling

molly."

I heard him full-on sob as I turned to see Brandi and Arianna gone. I hurried out of the gym to see if they were in the hall, but as I got halfway to the exit, I got a text.

ARIANNA: I'm with Brandi. In the car.

ME: The keys r in Brandi's purse. Take her home. I have to take care of something.

ARIANNA: What?

ME: It's OK. Please, just get her home.

ARIANNA: OK.

I exited the building and saw the Sentra pulling out of the lot. Arianna would be the better option to comfort my sister at the moment. I had other things on my mind.

Scrolling back to my other recent messages, I found Trevor's contact info and clicked the message button.

ME: UR going to pay for this.

732-555-8632: New phone. Who dis?

He added a bunch of laughing emojis.

ME: U know who this is. I'm going to fucking kill u for this.

He sent a shocked face emoji. The bastard probably thought he'd got the better of me.

My next move was to order an Uber. Ten minutes later, it pulled into the school parking lot and I got into the car and confirmed my destination.

Trevor Wright was about to get his comeuppance.

CHAPTER 13

The Uber dropped me off across the street from Trevor's house. It was dark, but Trevor's car was in the driveway. I didn't see any others, so if his parents' vehicles weren't in the garage, they weren't home. I tried to suppress the rage I was feeling as I walked up the steps to the front door. If he answered, I knew I would punch him. Wouldn't even let him get a word out. I'd just lay him the fuck out. But, if one of his parents answered, I had to be calm and collected. It wouldn't be as satisfying as hitting him, but I'd tell them what he did. Maybe we'd even sue them. To be honest, I had no idea how I'd actually handle the situation once I was inside, but I would handle it. I could guarantee that.

I didn't bother with the doorbell. Instead, I pounded hard on the door a few times. After a minute or two, it was apparent no one was answering.

Was he out with his parents?

My fist slammed against the door again, harder this time.

"Trevor! Get the fuck out here, you piece of shit!"

No response.

I stepped back off the porch and looked up to the second story, seeing only the darkened windows. If he was there, he was ducking me. Probably a smart move on his part.

Frustrated, I went around the side of the house. There was no gate, so I could walk around back and examine the rear of the property. Like the front, there was nothing. No lights. No movement.

Goddamn it.

Returning to the front, I was about to just give up and order another Uber to take me home when I again noticed Trevor's BMW parked in the driveway. Despite the situation, I couldn't help but think of an old joke.

What's the difference between a porcupine and a BMW?

The porcupine has the pricks on the outside.

Very apropos. Trevor loved that fucking car. Thought he was hot shit rolling around in a Beemer while the rest of us peasants drove our Nissans and Hyundais. Well, if I couldn't take out my frustration on Trevor himself, at least I could fuck up his prized possession.

I'd given my keys to Arianna, so I couldn't key it. My hunting knife would have been good to slash the tires, but, as angry as I was, it was a good thing I didn't have it on me. I scanned around the immediate vicinity and saw a nice-sized tree branch across the front lawn. That would do just fine.

After retrieving the makeshift club, I went straight for the front of Trevor's car, selecting the front windshield for the first strike. I cocked the branch back and cursed myself as again Trevor got the best of me. In my rage, I hadn't seen him approach, but he speared me like Michael Strahan used to do to opposing quarterbacks. The wind left my body as I hit the ground, Trevor's full weight falling on top of me.

"You trying to fuck up my ride, pussy?"

He kicked me in the stomach to punctuate the question. I opened my mouth to take in air, but it was like there was an invisible barrier preventing me from catching my breath. I rolled on my stomach and he kicked me again, sending me tumbling onto my back.

He approached and crouched over me, cocking his head as he looked over his handiwork.

"First, your whore sister sticks her nose in my relationship."

He slapped me hard across the face. I tried to get up, but my body was not responding to my brain.

"Then, you move in on my girlfriend."

"She's... not... your girlfriend... anymore," I sputtered out as I recovered. My attempt to antagonize him was successful. He stood and stomped my chest, sending my upper body crashing back into the ground.

"And now you come after me, like I'm the one that

started this shit?"

He had a point. He was an asshole, but this whole thing started because Brandi dimed him out for cheating. She was looking out for her friend but, by trying to help, she created what was becoming a really bad situation.

"So now I have to fuck you up," Trevor continued. "And the best part is, I'm not even going to get in trouble. It was your stupid ass that came to my house looking for a fight. Hell, you even threatened to kill me over text. What? I'm not supposed to defend myself?"

He walked around his car and popped the trunk. Reaching inside, he retrieved an old wooden baseball bat. A classic Louisville Slugger. He held the grip hand over hand and squeezed as if he were heading into the batter's box. Which, I guess you could say he was.

"You tried to break in and attack me. So I had to whack you over the head with old Woody here. Too bad you weren't smart enough to stay out of my business."

Again, technically not wrong, but we were here now and I wasn't about to let him beat me to death in his back yard.

He raised the weapon over his head, a sick smile on his face. But before he could bring it crashing down on me, I quickly pulled back my leg and drove it as hard as I could into his knee. I felt it push back just a bit too far and he crumpled to the ground, dropping the bat and landing on his ass as he cupped his injured joint.

Using all of my willpower, I got off the ground before he recovered. Looking around, I saw the bat, but it was out of reach. The tree branch I was going to use on the car, however, was right at my feet. In one fluid motion, I snatched it off the ground and swung it into his chest, knocking him flat.

At that moment, I had a decision to make. This had gone way too far. If we kept fighting, one of us was going to get seriously hurt. Maybe even killed. As angry as I was at him for what he had done to my sister, this wasn't worth either of our lives.

Trevor tried to sit up, but I kicked him in the chest, pulling the blow so it was just hard enough to knock him back down.

"This is done, Trevor. Stay the fuck away from me, my sister and my girlfriend."

Despite my instinct to de-escalate, I couldn't stop myself from twisting the metaphorical knife by calling Arianna my girlfriend. That was the wrong move.

Trevor grabbed the bat and swung wildly as he sat up, I managed to dodge, but he clearly had no intention of stopping the brawl.

"I'll fucking kill you!" he roared.

He moved toward me, but his hyper-extended knee slowed him down. He swung again, but I was out of reach. At this point, I knew the only way to stop this was for me to get out of there. He was blocking my path to the front of the house, so I did the only thing I could.

I ran back into the woods.

CHAPTER 14

Because of Trevor's injury, I was able to put some decent distance between us as I navigated my way through the trees. I knew my property line was about half a mile east, so I headed that way. I thought about calling someone, maybe even the cops, but Trevor was right. What he had done was essentially a really nasty prank. I came to his house looking to assault him. I was the one who was going to be in trouble this time.

But that was a problem for later. My focus now was making it back to my house. My mom and Dennis should be home and Brandi probably was too. Hopefully that many people would deter him from pursuing me further.

That was easier said than done. Trevor was hobbled, but my own injuries were slowing me down. I had gotten my breath back, but my lungs still burned as I ran. Every time I thought I'd gotten far enough ahead, I heard him shouting behind me.

"Get back here, Bennett! You're a fucking dead man!"

I felt myself slowing while Trevor's footsteps grew louder. I'd messed up his knee pretty good, but he must have been running on pure hatred at this point.

Still, I kept moving. I recognized where I was. I could tell I was on the edge of our property. There was a small cave over to my right that I used as a landmark. There were lots of those in the area. The opening was big enough for an average size man to enter, but I was happier not knowing if anything was actually in there, so I had never looked inside when I'd been out this way.

What I was looking at now was the large tree off to the left. I'd scoped it out a few months back with a view to possibly putting in a tree stand. It had a pretty good view of the area and would be ideal for hunting. I'd even climbed it, the branch alignment making it relatively easy.

And just like that, an idea came to me.

Without thinking too hard on it, I grasped the branch and started making my way up. Every step brought burning agony into my rib cage, but I found the strength to keep moving. In less than a minute, I was perched high in the branches. Many of the leaves had fallen, but there was still a decent amount of foliage in place. Plus, it was dark, so I hoped that would be more than enough to camouflage me until Trevor gave up looking for me. Once he turned back, I would get down and go home. After that, I'd figure out how to deal with the consequences of everything that had gone down tonight.

A few minutes later, Trevor came limping into view.

He looked like he was slowing, but he also kept pushing himself to keep going. He made it a few steps away from the tree when he stopped, bracing himself on the bat as if it were a cane as he scanned the area.

"Where the fuck are you, Bennett?"

I tried to breathe shallowly, my lungs screaming at me as I held the air in. I felt a pain in my hip from the way I was sitting. It ran up to the small of my back and I felt a tear escape my eye as I tried not to react to the pain.

C'mon. Go the fuck away.

"Trying to hide? Okay, I see."

Fuck!

Did he know I was up here? He wasn't looking at me.

I saw him lift the bat off the ground, but he still didn't look up. Instead he started making his way to his right. He was moving toward the cave.

This was good. If he went inside to look for me, I'd be able to climb down and get home. I'd had a few minutes to rest, so I should be able to push the rest of the way while he was distracted.

Sure enough, he moved toward the entrance. He braced himself on the rock as he bent over and peered inside, waving the bat ahead of him into the darkness like a blind person uses their cane to find their path.

"You in there, Bennett?" he called, his voice echoing off the inner walls. "I swear I just wanna talk. Come on out and we'll squash this whole thing."

Yeah, nice try.

He stood there for a little while longer. For a moment, I didn't think he was going to actually go in. My hip screamed at me again. I felt like if I didn't move soon I was going to fall out of this damn tree. I could feel the sweat beading up on my forehead as I tried to hold my position.

"Okay, bitch. I gave you a chance. Now I'm going to beat the fuck out of you."

He moved into the cave. As soon as he disappeared into the darkness, I started my descent. I moved quickly but cautiously. Above all else, I was trying not to make any noise. The pain in my hip subsided enough to become a dull ache. Adrenaline was still pumping, so it wasn't too bad, but I knew I would feel it in the morning.

When my feet hit the ground, I moved slowly in the opposite direction of the cave. I didn't want to take my eyes off of it in case Trevor emerged before I was far enough away.

It was right when I felt confident enough to turn and run that I heard it.

A feral growl came from inside the cave, followed by Trevor's scream.

What the hell was that? The wolf I tried tracking a few weeks ago?

The growl escalated into a roar; Trevor screamed again.

He was in trouble and I had an out; I could run right now. I didn't owe him anything. No one had told him to cheat on his girlfriend. Or to leak lewd pics of my sister. Or to chase me through the woods with a goddamn baseball bat. Fuck him.

Yeah, that was all well in good, but if Trevor Wright died in the woods tonight, I wouldn't be able to live with the guilt. He was a piece of shit, but he had parents. He had people who loved him. People who would be devastated if something happened to him.

I rushed toward the cave.

**

Trevor's screams didn't stop as I entered the hole. The small entryway contradicted the actual size because the inside was bigger than I thought. It was also pitch black. Even though I couldn't see, I still heard Trevor crying. He was begging for help in between screams and sobs. I also heard the snarl. It was low. The aggressive rumble of an angry animal.

I took out my cell phone and turned on the flashlight, pointing it toward the turmoil. Nothing could have prepared me for what I saw.

The first thing I noticed was Trevor. All hatred in his eyes was gone, substituted with pure terror. His face bore a fresh set of slashes. Three parallel lines ran from the right side of his forehead to the bottom of his left cheek, a flap of skin exposing his molars. His entire face was smeared with blood.

"Brady," he pleaded. "Help me."

His voice was weak and peppered with desperation. I didn't immediately know what had happened to him, but my first clue was when a large clawed hand, bigger than any man's I'd ever seen and covered with dark black fur, reached around and gripped Trevor's stomach, the razor-sharp nails digging into his T-shirt, puncturing first the fabric, then his flesh.

The bully screamed, but the high-pitched noise became a gurgle as blood filled his throat. I moved the flashlight up and over his shoulder and saw the assailant.

It was large, towering a foot over Trevor, who was about the same height as me at five foot eleven. The physical features were wolf-like. No doubt. Its face was covered with the same dark fur and its ears were large and pointed, sticking straight up on either side of its head. An elongated snout jutted from the center of its face, its mouth wide open and lined with razor-sharp teeth. Reddish fluid poured from its mouth, a mixture of blood and saliva.

But the most disturbing thing were its eyes. They were bright yellow and glowed in the darkness. They displayed an intelligence that, while not quite human, was greater than any animal I'd ever observed.

It looked right at me, almost as if Trevor wasn't there. Fear paralyzed me. I wanted to help Trevor, but how could I? What could I possibly do?

As the beast stared into my soul, I noticed a thick steel collar around its neck. The restraint was held by a heavy chain that was presumably attached to something in the darkness behind it. Was this thing being kept here intentionally? What the fuck?

Before I could think too hard about it, the wolf roared and yanked back the arm that was embedded in Trevor's stomach and ripped his midsection open like a piece of tissue paper. His insides slid out of his ruined torso and piled on the ground in front of him. He couldn't even scream anymore as his eyes rolled back in his head.

As Trevor died, the monster took its eyes off of me and reared back its head, unleashing another primal growl before bringing its mouth down on the bottom of Trevor's neck where it met his shoulder. As it sank its teeth in, an arterial spray shot out and blasted me in the face. I recoiled and tried to spit out the blood that had landed in my mouth, the coppery taste making me want to vomit.

I fell backward and dropped my phone. Frantically I searched for it. It only took me a few seconds to find it, spotting the light that was still on. I picked it up and again shined it on the creature.

Trevor's body was on the ground, obviously dead considering his eyes were wide open and his insides were on the outside. The wolf had crouched over him and its snout was now digging into the cavity in his stomach. I watched as it pulled a meaty-looking piece of the boy's innards out and chewed.

The light got the monster's attention and it roared at me, attempting to lunge but thankfully unable to reach me thanks to the restraint collar. It growled, angry at its captivity, but apparently resigned to not being able to get to me. It turned its focus back to feasting on Trevor's corpse.

I thought briefly about taking a video, just to have evidence of what I was actually witnessing, but it was eating my classmate so I couldn't bring myself to do it. Instead, I did the only thing I could: I climbed out of the cave and ran home as fast as I could.

CHAPTER 15

I approached my house from the back. It was completely dark inside, a fact for which I was grateful. I didn't have a mirror on me, but I could only imagine what I looked like. My face felt wet and sticky, no doubt still covered in Trevor's blood.

Jesus Christ. Had this actually happened?

Trying to be as quiet as possible, I opened the back door and stepped inside. As suspected, there was no one in the immediate vicinity. Dennis may very well have been in his chair, but it was dark in the den so, if he was, he was likely passed out again.

I made my way upstairs as quickly as I could without making too much noise. As I got to the top of the stairs, I saw all doors were closed and the place was silent. There wasn't even music coming from Brandi's room.

While I was still concerned for my sister's mental state, there were more pressing matters at hand. I skipped my room and made my way straight for the bathroom, locking the door behind me immediately after entering. I flicked on the light and forced myself to look at the mirror.

My God.

It was even worse as I thought. My face and my clothes were completely covered in Trevor's blood. What the hell was I going to do? I had to call the cops, right? That was the right thing to do. There was no other option.

I pulled out my phone and unlocked it. Before I could dial 911, something made me stop. I saw all the notifications. There were texts and missed calls from Arianna. But that wasn't what gave me pause. The one thing that made me think better of calling the cops.

Trevor's reaction GIF to my last text was on the screen. I knew what it said but pulled it up, despite my stomach sinking at my stupidity.

I'm going to fucking kill u for this.

That comment was out there. In writing. Forever. Even if I deleted it, I'm sure they could retrieve it fairly easily. That and my Uber account would show a trip to Trevor's house tonight. I played out an imaginary conversation in my head.

So, you threatened the victim, then took an Uber to his house. Now he's dead.

No, officer, I swear. It was a werewolf!

My next vision was of myself in a straitjacket in a padded cell in a mental hospital. Maybe the old, abandoned hospital a couple miles away if it ever reopened.

I couldn't call the cops. Not right now. I had to think hard about my next move.

Unsure of how to proceed, I looked at my other notifications.

There were three missed calls from Arianna. And a bunch of texts.

Where R U?

Did u go to Trevor's? Please don't.

Please call me. I'm worried.

????

I took a deep breath. It still pained me, the result of my battered ribs. How could this night have gone from me losing my virginity to the most amazing girl I'd ever met to being an accessory to a werewolf attack? Was that even a thing? Was it an actual werewolf? Could it have been a bear?

No fucking way. I'd been hunting for years. I knew what a damn bear looked like. That was a fucking seven-foot-tall wolf on two legs.

My phone buzzed, breaking me from my thoughts. Arianna again.

Brady, if you don't answer me I'm driving over there. I'll wake your entire house if I have to.

Shit. I couldn't have her come here. Not until I knew what to do.

ME: I'm OK.

ARIANNA: Did u go 2 Trevor's?

ME: Yea. He wasn't home. Probably 4 the best.

I felt terrible lying to her, but I was not involving her in this any more than she already was. There was a long pause as the three dots at the bottom of the phone appeared than disappeared. Finally, she wrote back.

ARIANNA: R U OK?

ME: Yea. I just need some sleep.

ME: How was Brandi? She was locked in her room when I got home.

ARIANNA: Not good. She's devastated.

I felt rage boil inside again. For a moment, I thought Trevor had gotten what he deserved. But, after remembering the look on his face as a monster disemboweled him, I knew in my heart that no one deserved a fate like that. I wrote back.

ME: Thank u 4 taking care of her.

ME: I'm sorry I left u like that. I just wanted to make it better. Guess I really can't.

ARIANNA: I know u want 2 protect her. But this wasn't your fault. Trevor is a scumbag.

Was, I thought. Now he's a lifeless husk in a cave in the woods.

I glimpsed myself in the mirror again. I had to wrap this up and get myself cleaned up quick, so I sent one last text.

ME: We should get some sleep. I'll talk 2 Brandi and call u in the a.m., ok?

138

ARIANNA: Ok. Good night, Brady.

She added a kissy face emoji. It was a small, silly gesture but, despite everything, it made me feel good. Sure, I had this minor matter of a dead body on my property, but somehow knowing that Ari and I were okay made me feel a little better. I certainly didn't need any compounding problems at the moment.

Placing my phone down, I stripped off my bloody clothes, tossing them in the tub. The shower was hot, but the water felt good on my skin as the aches settled into my body while my adrenaline waned.

Dirt and blood cascaded off of me and swirled down the drain. Once the water pooling at my feet became clear, I picked up my clothes and rinsed them under the stream, and the same filthy mixture flowed downward again. I continually moved the garments around, wringing them out occasionally until they also stopped leaking the incriminating fluid.

Even though I had cleaned them, I decided the best thing would be to get rid of them. The thought of ditching my Victor Cruz jersey, especially considering it was one of the last Christmas gifts my father had given me, was sad, but I couldn't keep anything that could link me to Trevor's death. Despite my attempt to clean it, there were deep-red stains embedded in the white number eighty and the NY logo on the front.

I dried myself off and took another towel to wrap the

clothing in. I'd have to dispose of it as well. Hopefully, my mom wouldn't notice it was missing. Given her recent state of drunken apathy, I figured she wouldn't miss it.

I turned off the light before opening the door, continuing my attempt not to draw attention to myself. Creeping out into the hallway, I made my way to my room, taking a second to stop outside Brandi's. I thought about trying the knob, but knowing she kept it locked under normal circumstances, there was no way it was open now.

This whole thing was so fucked up. I pressed my ear up against the door. I couldn't be sure, but it sounded like she may have been quietly crying to herself.

My poor sister.

Leaning my forehead against her door, I tried to will her some good thoughts or something like that, if that was even possible. I was exhausted, sad, and downright fucking terrified.

Pulling my head away from the door, I entered my room and locked it behind me.

Reaching under my bed, I pulled out my shotgun. I contemplated going back now and blowing the monster's head off, but I didn't know if I even could. That thing was a giant wolf. A werewolf? I didn't believe in werewolves, but I also didn't think I believed in whatever the fuck I just saw in the woods. If that thing was a werewolf, would it follow the same rules as the movies?

One of my dad's favorite movies that he showed me from when he was a kid was called *The Monster Squad*. It was about a group of kids with a monster club who ended up encountering real life versions of Dracula, Frankenstein, the Wolf Man, the Mummy and the Creature from the Black Lagoon. In one part of the movie, one member argues that silver is the only way to kill a werewolf, but others argue that there are alternate methods.

Later in the movie, they blow up the Wolf Man with a stick of dynamite, but he pulls himself back together to attack again. At that point, the kid proved his theory right by shooting it him dead with a silver bullet.

Told you. There's only one way to kill a werewolf.

So, if that thing *was* a werewolf and the lore *was* true, I needed silver. My shotgun shells wouldn't do the trick.

But then again, who says it wouldn't? Just because the movies and books said one thing doesn't mean that was actually the case.

It wasn't just that, though. I was tired and physically less than a hundred percent. If that thing somehow got out of its restraints, I wouldn't be any match for it in the dark.

If that thing somehow got out of its restraints.

A chill ran through my body at the thought. It was wearing a collar, sure. And it couldn't get to me. But the creature was massive. Who's to say it couldn't break free, especially agitated like it was? It could be heading this way right now. Besides that, who had chained him up in that cave? Was it a prisoner? A pet?

I loaded the gun and looked out my window. The woods were still and silent. I had a good view of the tree line from my vantage. If the wolf escaped, I should be able to see it coming.

Rolling my desk chair over to the window, I sat down and laid the gun on my lap. Despite my fear and my sickness at the night's events, I could have easily gone to sleep right then. But I had to stay awake.

I had to make sure the wolf wasn't coming for me.

CHAPTER 16

4:23 a.m.

That's what the clock said when I stole a second to check the time. It was still dark, but the sun would be up soon. I'd stood sentry for hours, but there was no sign of the wolf.

Just when I thought I was in the clear, I heard it.

The howl.

A blood-curdling animal noise, the same one I'd heard weeks ago, only this time it was different.

It was closer.

I grabbed my gun and pushed the window and screen open, resting on the windowsill, training the barrel on the tree line which was about fifty yards away. I'd hit targets from further distances—my shotgun had a range between seventy and eighty yards when loaded with slugs—so I was sure I could make the shot. The question was, would it have an effect?

Terror washed over me as I heard the growl in the distance. There was no doubt it was the wolf. Should I run? Grab my family and get the hell out of here?

It was too late.

The yellow eyes were the first thing I saw as the creature emerged from the woods.

I pumped the shotgun without hesitation and took the shot.

I missed. Goddamn it!

The creature snarled as it looked up in the gunfire's direction. In my direction. It lumbered toward the house.

I pumped again and pulled the trigger. Nothing happened. It was jammed.

What the hell? This gun had never jammed before. I tried again, still nothing.

The wolf was just below my window now. It stepped onto the front porch as I tried again. Still nothing. Dropping the shotgun, I retrieved the lockbox from under my bed and pulled out my father's old Glock 17 checking to make sure it was loaded. I didn't know if it could take that monster down, but I didn't have a better option with my shotgun malfunctioning.

As I went back to the window, I heard a loud crash downstairs. I looked down and saw that the wolf was gone from view, but I knew exactly where it was.

It was in the house.

I ran to my door and unlocked it. I turned the knob, but it wouldn't budge. The door was stuck. I rattled it with no luck, so I thrust my shoulder hard against it. As I tried to slam open the door, I heard thunderous footfalls making their way up the stairs.

"Brandi!" I shouted as I threw all my weight against the door again. "Barricade your door! Hurry!"

I heard the inhuman snarl in the hallway as the creature drew near. I kept shoving myself against the door, trying futilely to break through before it could get to my sister. My insides twisted when I heard a door open in the hall.

"Brady?" my twin called a moment before letting out a terrified scream.

"Brandi! No!"

My sister screamed as the wolf growled. I took three steps back and ran at the door with everything I had. The wood splintered and the door collapsed as it fell with me into the hall.

When I got up, I saw the wolf. It was hovering over Brandi, who was sprawled out on her stomach, covered in blood.

The wolf roared at me, its hideous mouth agape.

Brandi looked up. Her face was clawed like Trevor's. She tried to pull herself toward me, her fingernails scraping against the hardwood floor. I raised the gun and fired, emptying the clip into the wolf's chest, each bullet finding its home as pockets of blood exploded with each impact.

It didn't faze the creature. It stood tall, a low rumble emanating from its throat as it stared me down.

I continued to pull the trigger even as the gun clicked

empty. I chucked the useless weapon at the beast. It bounced harmlessly off its shoulder.

As Brandi pulled herself up, the wolf took a step forward and straddled her back. It reached down and covered the top of her head with its mammoth hand, thrusting its clawed fingers into the top of her mouth.

"Brandi!" I shouted as it took its other hand and inserted it into the bottom of her mouth. I tried to rush it, knowing it was a death sentence, but it might give Brandi a chance to escape. The effort was futile as I froze in place. My body once again betrayed me, rendering me unable to move.

The wolf looked at me and unleashed another primal roar as it pulled its hands apart, separating the top of Brandi's head from her jaw. Blood erupted like a geyser from her ruined dome as her tongue rolled out of what was left of her mouth.

I screamed in a way I hadn't thought possible when I saw my sister die. The wolf stood upright and tossed the top of her head at my feet. I looked down and saw Brandi's dead eyes looking back at me. Still unable to move, I screamed in anguish.

As I sobbed, I smelled the fetid stench of the wolf's breath. I looked up and saw it was right in front of me, practically nose to nose as it hunched down to my level.

The last thing I saw was the beast's mouth open wide before it came down on my skull.

***

I snapped up in the chair, dropping the shotgun to the floor. My hands instinctively went to my cranium to make sure it was still intact. Where did the wolf go?

Turning to the window, I saw the sun was up. I looked at the clock.

6:46 a.m.

As I tried to slow my rapid breathing, I turned to my door. It was still shut, not broken down like I remembered.

I took a deep breath, realizing I had fallen asleep and had had one hell of a fucked-up nightmare.

Cautiously opening the door, I observed the hallway. Thankfully, there were no signs of damage and, more importantly, there was no dead body. I went over to Brandi's door and listened in but I heard nothing.

I didn't want to bother her, because she wasn't a morning person under the best of circumstances and I'm sure she hadn't had the best sleep. Lord knows I hadn't.

But, as tired as I was, I had a mess to clean up.

CHAPTER 17

It was Saturday morning, so I could get my gun and head into the woods without anyone questioning it. They would just think I was going hunting. I pocketed some extra ammo wondering again if a run-of-the-mill shotgun shell would take down the wolf if needed.

I mean, yeah, it looked like what I would picture a werewolf to be, but I had no idea if any of the lore was accurate. It could have been some fucked-up science experiment gone wrong for all I knew. Say that was the case. Silver aside, would a regular slug be powerful enough to take down something that big? Christ, that thing was bigger than a grizzly bear.

Also, I didn't know quite what would be waiting for me in there. Let's say the werewolf theory proved accurate... When I got there would it still be a wolf? Or would it be a human? I had no clue what I was going to find. My heart was pounding as I prepped.

I inserted my dad's Glock into the worn leather holster he kept for it. I attached it to my belt, along with my knife and put on my coat which, thankfully, was long enough to cover it. Dennis was a hunter too and if he noticed I was more heavily armed than usual, it may raise some questions that I had no interest in answering.

There was one more item I needed. I retrieved the long-handled flashlight from the top of my closet and slid it into my pocket. Once out of sight of the house, I would attach it to the gun so I could see once I entered the darkness of the cave.

Before I left, I shoved my clothes from the night before into my bag. I didn't exactly want to leave them on the curb in a trash bag. After I figured out what to do about the wolf and Trevor, I'd burn them or bury them.

Was I really doing this?

I answered my own rhetorical question by gathering my gear and heading downstairs.

***

A short time later, I found myself in front of the cave. I checked my watch. It was 7:18 a.m. I approached the threshold and leaned over, trying to listen, but I heard nothing inside. Every fiber of my being was screaming at me to turn and run back home, but I ignored my trepidation and raised my shotgun. I flicked on the flashlight and entered the cave.

The first thing I noticed once inside was the stench.

It was like a mixture of wet fur and rotting meat. I felt vomit rise in my throat but I suppressed it, doing my best to keep my nerves steady as I made my way through.

My light first hit the pool of blood. There was so much of it puddled on the ground. I followed the trail and shined the beam on what was left of Trevor.

The gaping wound in his stomach had been ripped further open, encompassing the entirety of his torso. Broken ribs jutted out of the hole like a fence surrounding a construction site. The inside was hollow, as far as I could tell. There weren't any organs remaining, at least on the interior. There were still a few ropes of chewed intestines lying on the floor next to the body.

His face was mostly intact, save for the large claw marks and ripped-open jaw. His eyes remained open, but his formerly blue irises had morphed into a milky gray.

As much as I hated him, as much as I thought I'd wanted to kill him myself the night before, I could only feel sorrow at the fate that had befallen him. No matter what he had done, he didn't deserve this.

"Did you know him?"

The voice startled me, and I jumped backward, almost tripping over myself. I recovered quickly and shined my light toward the sound.

My beam illuminated a man sitting on the ground against the back wall of the cave. The first, and most obvious, thing I noticed about him was that he was naked. He sat with his knees drawn into his chest with his arms resting on top. He seemed to have no concern over his state of undress.

His hair was long and dark, the same as the wolf's fur. It hung down over his eyes, which were actually a light blue, not the glowing yellow of the monster that had murdered Trevor. I don't know why that surprised me. He had a bushy, unkempt beard that matched his hair.

As if it wasn't obvious enough that this was the wolf's human form, the steel collar around his neck cemented it. It hung down slightly, looser than the tight fit it had on his lupine form, but it wasn't big enough that he could slip over his head. Had he done this to himself? I'd seen movies where a werewolf would chain himself up while in human form to prevent himself from attacking others when he turned. Was that the case here? Or was someone holding him captive? Every new thing I learned only raised more questions.

"Who are you?" I asked.

The man looked up at me, sadness in his eyes, but no panic, despite being chained in a cave with a teenager training a shotgun on him.

"Nobody," he said.

"Are you a... werewolf?" I asked, not believing it was a serious question I had actually posed out loud to another human being, but I figured I may as well cut right to the chase.

The man laughed.

"What's so funny?"

"Kid, the way my life has gone, the only thing left to do is laugh."

I shined the light on Trevor's mutilated corpse.

"Is that fucking funny?"

"No," the man replied pointedly. "It is definitely not fucking funny."

"What are you doing in here?"

"Trying to avoid what happened last night."

"You remember?"

The man nodded, silently answering my question.

"So why did you do it?"

"Just because I know something is happening, doesn't mean I can do anything about it."

"So, like, you're aware when you're in wolf form, but can't control yourself?"

"This isn't *Werewolf 101*, kid. I don't have a lot of answers for you."

Well, I guess that confirmed that he was a werewolf. Now that we had that cleared up, I wondered how much of what I knew from movies and books would actually apply here. I still had no idea if silver bullets would actually work.

I kind of felt like an idiot, but he was right. This wasn't the time for questions anyway—I had to figure out what to do.

"You want to help me find the keys to this collar?" the man asked breaking into my thought process.

So he was the one who locked himself in here.

"You don't have them?"

"I did. They were tucked behind a rock over here so I could reach them in the morning, but they must have gotten lost in the commotion."

I scanned the ground using my light. I didn't see them. But even if I did, could I really set him free?

"So, I'm just supposed to let you go so you can kill again?" I asked, shining the beam back on him.

He barely flinched when it shone in his eyes. "I wasn't trying to kill anyone. That's why I chained myself up in here. Your friend came in here and got too close."

"He's not my friend," I snapped without really thinking about it.

The man cocked an eyebrow.

I wasn't going to say any more about it. Anything else could incriminate me.

"Why didn't you call the cops?" the man asked.

Damn it. I didn't know how to answer. I fumbled my way through. "What was I supposed to tell them? That a werewolf killed a kid from my school?"

"Don't know. But now you're in here with me and a dead body you knew about. My guess is that you can't call them for some reason. Were you enemies?"

"Hey!" I snapped. "I'm the one asking the questions

here. What's your name?"

"Does it matter?"

I guess it didn't. I really didn't know what to do here, but I decided my first move was to find the key. If it was going to take me time to figure out my next move, I had to make sure this guy wasn't going anywhere.

Scanning back and forth over the cave, I couldn't find it. I covered the ground at least three times, but still nothing.

"Are you sure you had a key?"

"Yes. I'm sure." He nodded toward the body. "How about under him?"

You had to be fucking kidding me.

Still, it was the one place I hadn't looked. I trained the gun on him and tried to sound as intimidating as possible.

"Not one move."

The man flicked his hands off his knees in a *whatever you say* gesture.

I knelt down next to Trevor's corpse and reached under his ruined torso and around to his back. I carefully lifted him. The body was rigid and stuck to the rock below, the blood holding the corpse down like glue as I peeled it off the ground.

There was nothing on the ground below. I was perplexed. As I contemplated where it could be, a thought entered my mind. I pointed the light at Trevor's back as his body lay on its side.

Sure enough, there was a brass key stuck to his blood-soaked shirt. I grabbed it between my thumb and forefinger and pulled it off of him, repulsed by the whole scenario.

I turned my attention back to the man who, for the first time, looked hopeful.

"That's it!" he said, displaying a hint of excitement. "Please. Unlock me."

"Then what?" I asked.

"We clean up. I'll help you. I'll move on and find somewhere to lock myself up tonight. It's the last night of the moon cycle. After that, I can be on my way and let you get back to your life."

"The moon cycle?" I asked.

"Kid, didn't you take astronomy?"

"Sure, but we didn't cover the effects of the moon on werewolves in the syllabus."

"There's three nights every month that apparently affect a person in my... condition. It seems to be the night of the full moon and the nights immediately before and after."

"Seems to be?"

"I didn't exactly get an orientation."

"Were you born like this?"

"Do we really need twenty questions here? Listen, let me out and we'll clean this up and never have to see each other ever again."

I actually considered it. After all, his story tracked from what I could see and what he said. If he really wanted to hurt people, why had he gone through the trouble of chaining himself up inside a cave in the woods?

Still, I knew nothing about him other than the fact that he was apparently a werewolf. What if he was bullshitting me? And what if he wasn't the one who put himself in here? Maybe he'd been captured. Maybe someone was keeping him here so he wouldn't hurt anyone and he was trying to con me into letting him go. I needed to know more before I released him.

"On your way? Where are you headed?"

The man's face dropped and twisted in frustration. "Does it matter?"

"It might."

"I'm telling you, I don't want to hurt anyone. This was all just a freak accident. You and your fr— this kid... were in the wrong place at the wrong time."

"I can't unlock you."

"Damn it!" he yelled, the beast inside peeking out. "If we don't do something quick, you are going to be in just as much trouble as me. Maybe more. What's to stop me from telling the police that you were holding me captive and made me watch you kill your—what? Rival? Bully? When you think about it, this looks a lot worse for you than me. After all, your fingerprints are all over the body and the key to this collar."

I dropped the key as if it were on fire. The man lunged forward to grab it but the chain pulled tight, the steel digging into his throat. He reached up and grabbed, coughing and choking from the impact while I retrieved and tossed the key toward the entrance before he could make another attempt to reach it.

"Fuck!" he roared. "Let me out of here, you little bastard!"

I pointed the gun at him.

"Stop," I said, surprised at how steady my voice was. "I want to believe you, but I need to think about this."

The man didn't respond. He just stared me down, teeth clenched, face twisted with rage.

Kneeling back down to the corpse, I reached into Trevor's pockets. I was able to retrieve his phone. The display was cracked, but it lit up when I touched it, careful to avoid cutting myself on the broken screen. The battery was at three percent. I had to move quick.

I rolled Trevor onto his back and brought the phone to his face, hoping it was intact enough unlock it. A message popped up.

Face ID not recognized. Please try again.

I repeated my action.

Face ID not recognized. Please enter passcode.

Fuck! I had no clue what his passcode was. I looked at the screen.

Two percent. I was fucked.

About to give up, an idea hit me. In my desperation to get the phone unlocked, I hadn't even noticed that his wallpaper was a picture of him and Arianna. It actually turned my stomach for a moment seeing them together, but I put that out of my mind quickly since I had more pressing issues than being jealous of a corpse.

There was one last Hail Mary I could throw. I knew Arianna's birthday was November 30th. I typed in 1-1-3-0, hoping that, if it was his passcode, he hadn't changed it.

It worked, but the phone went black almost instantly. It didn't matter. Now that I knew the code, I could do what I needed to.

With the phone situated, I thought of something else. Holding my breath, I searched his pockets and found his wallet. I was only just formulating my plan, but I had an idea that would require his ID and bank cards.

Pocketing the phone and wallet, I turned and headed back to the cave entrance. I found where I had thrown the key and retrieved it, sliding it into my pocket as well. I regretted it right after, because now there was even more DNA on me, but I was in so deep it didn't really matter anymore.

Before I left, I turned back to the man who was once again calm and sitting with his arms resting on his knees.

"I'll be back," I told him.

Chapter 18

When I returned home, I hoped that no one would be there, but luck was not on my side. Dennis and my mother were sitting at the kitchen table, eating breakfast. Dennis had one of his fancy-ass omelets, with fruit and black coffee. Mom had her own cup, lightened with cream and probably an unhealthy amount of sugar. A slice of toast smeared with peanut butter rested half eaten on her plate. Dennis had his nose in the sports section of the paper while Mom scrolled her phone.

They both looked up when I came in. Mom actually looked concerned.

"Brady," she said. "Where were you?"

"Hunting," I said, turning my attention to Dennis to see if he'd bought it. "I saw a buck but couldn't get a shot on it."

"So, you're back already?" Dennis asked before turning his attention back to the paper.

"I had to use the bathroom," I said. It was the only thing I could think of.

"You couldn't pee in the woods?"

"I have to take a shit and I would rather wipe my ass with toilet paper then dry leaves."

Mom rolled her eyes. "Jesus Christ, always with the drama here."

Dennis didn't acknowledge her. She kept her focus on me.

"I'm heading back out," I explained, trying to stare a hole through the paper to Dennis. "After I'm done."

Dennis didn't respond and I walked toward the stairs.

"Brady?" Mom called after me.

I turned back to her. "Yeah?"

"What happened last night?"

"What do you mean?" I asked, knowing damn well what she meant.

"Brandi came home by herself. She looked upset."

"I'm not sure," I lied. "I'll check on her."

Mom narrowed her eyes. She didn't buy it.

"You know Brandi," I continued. "Someone probably said something that pissed her off. I'll check on her. I promise."

Mom nodded and went back to her phone. I was actually surprised that she cared enough to ask, the way she'd been lately. But regardless of me trying to pretend I didn't know what had happened to my sister, I still had every intention of checking on her.

I quickly made my way upstairs and directly into my room. Pulling out a charger, I plugged his phone in and tossed my jacket on top of it. I didn't think anyone would just go looking around in my room, but the way the last twenty-four hours had gone, I wasn't taking any chances.

Now I had to check on Brandi. Leaving my room, I crossed the hall to hers and again pressed my ear to the door. Not hearing anything, I knocked gently.

No answer.

I knocked again, a little harder this time.

"Go away!" Brandi's muffled voice ordered from the other side.

I tried the handle and, no surprise, the door was locked.

"I mean it!" she shouted.

"It's me," I said.

Just when I thought she wasn't going to let me in, the door opened.

Brandi stood there, looking a far cry from the girl in the scandalous clown costume from the night before. She was wearing flannel pajama bottoms and an oversized T-shirt with an array of Disney princesses on it. She wore no makeup and her hair was pulled back in a loose ponytail. For a minute, I saw the innocent little girl who'd once demanded I get out of the tree I climbed after my father's funeral. Her eyes were swollen and bloodshot. She'd clearly done more than her fair share of crying.

She stepped aside so I could enter. Once I was inside, she locked the door behind her, clearly not wanting Mom or Dennis to come in. With the room secure, she sat cross-legged on the bed, clutching a pillow tight to her chest.

"What happened after I left?" she asked, getting straight to the point.

"I went looking for Trevor," I said, knowing there was no way I could get away with lying about that part.

"And?"

"Didn't find him."

Brandi nodded, tears welling up again. "Probably better. Knowing you, you would have killed him."

I felt a lump in my throat. She didn't seriously believe I could kill anyone. But Trevor was very dead. And it was definitely because of me.

"I'm sorry, Brandi."

She attempted a smile. "Why? It's not like you sent nudes to Ryan. And, yeah, you *stole* Trevor's girlfriend, but I'm the one that broke them up."

"Yeah, but I should have done something."

"Brady, you can't save the world. I can take care of myself. This was my fuckup. I have to own it."

"What are you going to do?"

"I'm going to cry a whole fucking lot over the next two days. Then I'll ditch school for a few days until Mom forces me to go back. Then I'll put on my big-girl panties and face the music."

I chuckled a bit. Couldn't help myself. I felt bad, but I

saw a slight smile on Brandi too.

"That simple?"

She shrugged. "That simple."

"Well, I'll go in on Monday and scout it out for you."

I said it without thinking. Sure, I'll be in school Monday as long as this whole accessory to murder thing doesn't throw a wrench into those plans.

"Thanks, Brady."

I nodded. There wasn't much else to say. I turned to exit, but Brandi added, "Did you call Arianna? She was worried about you."

Yup. Another thing to add to my growing list of concerns. I had to square things up with her too if I were to maintain appearances while I figured this whole thing out.

"I will."

"She really likes you, Brady. Don't fuck up."

"I won't."

Unless I already had.

CHAPTER 19

I went back to my room and locked up my guns. My plan didn't involve going back to the woods yet. Changing out of my hunting gear, I threw on a pair of sweatpants, a T-shirt and a hoodie, adding a plain baseball cap for good measure. My goal was to not stand out.

Heading to my dresser, I checked Trevor's phone. It was up to thirty-eight percent. That would be good enough. I slid it into my pocket and left my room. I went back to Brandi's and knocked again.

"What?"

"I need the car keys."

***

I went back downstairs. Mom was nowhere to be found, but Dennis was in his recliner, watching TV. He looked at me strangely when he saw me come down. It puzzled me at first, but then I realized he was expecting me to go back into the woods after the buck. I had to think quick.

"Got hungry. Going to grab a quick breakfast with Arianna before heading back out."

It would do. I doubted Dennis would call Arianna to see if I was with her. Besides, he rarely cared where I was at, so why would he start now?

He went back to the TV and I exited the house, making a beeline for the Sentra. I pulled out of the parking lot and drove toward the highway. My excuse would give me two hours tops.

As soon as I pulled onto Interstate 295, I called Arianna.

She picked up on the second ring. "Brady? Are you okay? What happened?"

"Nothing."

She was silent for a moment. "You didn't go to Trevor's?"

"No... I mean, yes. He wasn't there. I guess that's a good thing."

"Yes," she answered sternly. "You could have gotten hurt. Or you could've hurt him."

Would have been better for him than what actually happened, I thought.

"Yeah," I said.

"Is Brandi okay?"

"She will be. Thank you for taking care of her while I ran off trying to be some kind of dumbass hero."

"You're welcome."

She paused.

"Brady..."

"Yeah."

"Before everything went down with Brandi...before we went back to the gym. I just want you to know, that really meant something to me."

Hearing her say that made me a little emotional. I wasn't expecting it. If I wasn't in the midst of the worst nightmare I could imagine, I'd be in a state of euphoria right now.

"Me too."

The silence hung on the line for a few moments. It wasn't awkward, but neither of us really knew what to say next. I finally broke the silence.

"Ari, I'm sorry last night ended like it did."

"It was out of our control," she said softly.

"I know, but I am going to make it up to you. I promise."

"What are you doing today?" Her voice had become upbeat for the first time since she'd picked up.

"Um, I have to take care of a few things. Kind of swamped actually."

"Oh." The disappointment returned.

"But, how about tomorrow?"

Another pause until she added wistfully, "I can do tomorrow."

"Great! I'll text you when I get home and we'll set it all

up!"

"Sounds good," she said sounding like she was about to hang up, but she added, "Brady. Please don't do anything that'll get you in trouble."

Way too late for that.

"I won't."

***

The hardware store I chose was about twenty miles from my house. I parked halfway down the lot and went inside, moving purposefully, but not too fast. I left my hood down. Wearing the cap was enough. The last thing I wanted was to look like I was deliberately trying to avoid attention.

Having been pretty handy from a young age, I knew my way around the store. I pushed the cart to one aisle to pick up a large tarp. Next, I went into the garden section and picked up two bags of topsoil and one of grass seed—Kentucky bluegrass: I always found it odd that it grew in Jersey.

After that I picked up a shovel and a rake. I grabbed cleaning supplies and contractor bags. Before leaving, I stopped and bought a bucket of exterior paint and some paintbrushes to pad out my purchases so as not to look like I was trying to hide a body. It probably helped that I was completely winging this and had no idea what I was actually doing.

I paid for the stuff without incident and loaded it up in my car. My next move was to drive to the train station about two miles away. I parked in the lot and took out Trevor's phone. I punched in the code and went to work. The first thing I did was send a group text to Brandi and Arianna.

Trevor: I know neither of u wants to hear from me, but I went 2 far. I know that. I'm so sorry for everything I put u through. I promise I won't bother u again.

Was it believable? Probably not, but they would never be able to prove otherwise. Neither replied. Next, I texted myself.

Trevor: Listen, man. This thing between us got out of hand and I'm sorry. I really have to figure out what's next for me, but I promise our issue is squashed.

A little over the top, but what else was I going to do? My phone buzzed upon the arrival of the message. I typed back.

Me: What u did was fucked up. I accept ur apology, but u and I r not gonna b cool. Let's stay out of each other's way.

I took Trevor's phone and responded with a thumbs-up emoji.

Apology texts out of the way, I went into his app store and downloaded the NJ Transit app. I used Trevor's credit card to purchase a train ticket to Philadelphia. It was arriving in ten minutes.

With those other tasks complete I had only one thing left to do. I opened his social media and typed out a post:

I know what I did to Brandi Bennett was wrong. I was angry and wanted to hurt someone, so I guess I succeeded. But she didn't deserve that. Stuff's been going on with me lately and I just need to get away for a bit. I'm going to figure out how to be a better person, but I can't do that here. I got kicked out of school anyway, so I might as well see what else is out there. I'm taking off for a while. Don't worry about me. I'll be OK.

One more text. I found a group chat with *Mom* and *Dad*. I felt a lump in my throat as I sent the text.

Trevor: I'm sorry for all the trouble I caused u. I need to get away for a bit, but I'm OK. I promise.

Trevor: I love u.

I felt gross doing this. I really did. But I didn't see any other way. I turned off his phone and took out a Lysol wipe, sanitizing the entire phone. Holding it with the wipe, I placed it on a dry paper towel and wrapped it up, sliding it back in my pocket.

Five minutes later, I was on the platform, waiting for the train. Now I had my hood up and sunglasses on because I knew there were cameras. Thankfully, Trevor and I had similar builds. Before stepping out to wait for the train, I bought a coffee and donut inside with Trevor's card, cementing the lie that he was here at the station if they tried to trace it.

The train arrived and I stepped inside. Luckily, on a late Saturday morning, it wasn't as crowded as it would have been during a workday. I quickly found an isolated section and sat just long enough to use the napkin to take Trevor's phone and wedge it under the seats. I already saw social media notifications popping up, no doubt in reply to my post. The phone was going to ride this train until someone found it or it died.

I got up from my seat and started patting my shirt and checking my pockets. As I passed an older couple seated near the exit, I muttered, "Forgot my damn phone."

They didn't even look my way, but I was pretty sure they heard me. Stepping off the train and onto the platform, I realized that the cameras may have caught me getting on then off the train, but there was nothing I could do about it now. I continued miming like I had forgotten something as I left the station and headed back to my car.

***

Making it home without drawing further attention, no one questioned me when I went back inside, dressed in my hunting gear again and went back into the woods, retrieving my fresh supplies from my trunk as I did.

When I made it back to the cave, the man was still sitting there, chained to the rock wall. Trevor's body was still there too. It looked bloated and what skin hadn't been ripped open was blistering and had an odd sheen to it. The stench was overpowering, but the man didn't seem fazed. He barely acknowledged me when I entered.

This needed to be done as quickly as possible so I dropped my gear and laid out the tarp. I rolled the corpse on top of it and wrapped it up, tying it tight with string. I dragged the husk that used to be Trevor Wright out of the cave while the man watched me expressionless.

Out of the cave, I had a quick look around, specifically to check if any other hunters were nearby. While most respected boundaries, it wasn't unusual for a fellow outdoorsman to wander onto someone's property by accident. I didn't see anyone so I picked up the body and slung it over my shoulder. It was heavy, but not as heavy as I expected. I couldn't help but wonder if his lack of internal organs had made him lighter.

I walked, not sure how far I was going to go, but I definitely needed to get him further away from my property. A lot of the homes out here had many acres, but there was a patch of county land in between. I had a fairly good idea where that was.

After about twenty minutes, I felt fatigue setting in. A glance at my surroundings told me I was likely as far away as I needed to be. There was a grassy patch between some trees that looked like a suitable spot. I set the body down carefully. Trevor had died so horribly, it felt disrespectful to manhandle his corpse before burying him. Weird fucking logic, I knew.

I started digging. As I shoveled the dirt from the newly forming grave, it hit me that I'd never actually dug anything this deep before. It was much harder than I thought. The ground was hard and it took a lot of effort to break through the dense soil, but I kept at it. Eventually, I had a pretty good-sized pit. I don't think it was the requisite six feet, but it would have to do. I rolled the body into the cavity, letting it fall in, too tired to be graceful about it.

Filling the hole back in was definitely easier, but still taxing, especially as tired as I was. I pushed through to get it done, though. I was losing light and I still had to do something about the blood in the cave. Once I had fully filled it in, I covered it with a layer of topsoil and sprinkled down the grass seed. I knew it would need water to grow, but there was rain in the forecast. I hoped it was enough to take care of it.

With the body buried, I made my way back to the cave. The sun was descending to the horizon. When I got inside, the man still didn't address me, but stared at me as I grabbed a large container of bleach, actually grateful that the chemical smell overpowered some of the rot stench as I twisted off the cap. I knew I couldn't possibly get all the blood out from the rocks, gravel and dirt, but I thought at least if I poured the mixture over the area, it would dilute it and maybe make it harder to test for DNA. I remembered that from the movie the *Boondock Saints*, where the protagonists sprayed bleach on blood splatter after they were wounded in a gunfight. They did that so the cops wouldn't be able to link them to the crime scene.

Great. I'm covering up a murder based on shit I saw on TV.

But what else could I do? I was completely winging it here.

Having covered as much as I could, I looked at the man. He was still staring at me, but something was different. His blue eyes seemed to take on a yellowish tint. There was something different in them. The man I met this morning was quiet and articulate, seeming genuinely remorseful. The man I was looking at now had an expression that I can only describe as sinister.

"Lose track of time?" he asked, his voice like gravel.

Oh, no.

The man smiled, displaying a row of sharpened fangs that were too big for his mouth, causing his lips to jut out at an odd angle. His beard looked longer and bushier than it had previously. His nose seemed to flatten.

I looked toward the entrance of the cave and, while

it was still light out, I could see the full moon in the distance. He was turning. I'd been so caught up with trying to get rid of the body, that it had somehow slipped my mind that I was sharing a cave with a goddamn werewolf.

"You should get out of here," the man growled.

I gathered my stuff and scrambled to the cave entrance. I knew I was further back than I had been the night before when the wolf couldn't reach me, but would I be so lucky again? Still, I had to see.

I had to capture this. If I could get it on video, I'd have some evidence to back it up. I could go to the cops.

Fuck!

I had thought about it when I first saw the wolf last night but didn't act on it. Now I had panicked and gotten rid of the body, so even if I could get video evidence, I had still disposed of a corpse. But it didn't matter in this moment. I had to get the footage, then figure out how to handle it afterward.

Turning on the video, I pointed my phone in the man's direction. He was standing now. He was tall, taller than he looked when I first observed him. Hair grew all over his body. His eyes appeared to be the same bright yellow as the previous night. His mouth and nose elongated and I heard flesh rip and bones crack as the snout jutted out of his face. My hands trembled as I tried to hold the phone steady.

It wasn't long before the man was gone and all that remained was the wolf. The beast rushed at me and roared. I fell back as the chains once again prevented him from reaching me.

Recovering and getting to my feet, I pointed my shotgun at the snarling beast as it salivated, no doubt thinking about devouring my insides like it had Trevor's. I wanted to pull the trigger. Blow this monster away. But I couldn't help but think of the man inside. The man who had locked himself in this cave to prevent the killing that was ultimately my fault.

I couldn't do it. I lowered my gun and exited the cave, taking the supplies with me. There was an outlet to the river about a quarter of a mile south. I made my way there and washed off the dirt. I filled the empty bleach container with water to weigh it down and tossed it in, watching it sink as the current carried it away. My work was done for the moment. It was time to head home.

The wolf was a problem for tomorrow.

CHAPTER 20

It was a little after 8 p.m. when I got home. Unsurprisingly, everyone was dispersed throughout the house, doing their own thing. Dennis was in the living room. Mom and Brandi were nowhere to be seen, likely in their respective bedrooms.

I didn't engage with Dennis as I made my way upstairs. I heard the TV coming from Mom's room, but the door was shut so I couldn't make out what she was watching. Not that it mattered. Brandi had music coming from her room, but lower than usual. She probably just wanted to zone out peacefully.

Immediately after entering my room, I shut the door and stripped off my jacket and shirt. No sooner did they hit the floor than I heard a knock at the door.

"I'm getting dressed," I called to the visitor, figuring it was Mom or Brandi.

"Ooooh, can I watch?" a different but familiar female voice called from the other side.

I opened the door, disregarding the lack of clothing on my upper body and saw that it was indeed Arianna, a mischievous grin on her face.

"Hey!" I said legitimately enthused to see her, forgetting for a moment about all the grim tasks I had undertaken today.

"Hey yourself," she said.

"I didn't expect to see you tonight."

"Well, I guess that's the downside of dating your sister's best friend. I may be around even when we don't have plans." The look on her face told me that didn't come out as intended. "I hope that didn't sound too stalkerish."

I laughed and kissed her. "No. Not at all. I'm happy to see you."

I legitimately was and her smile returned, but only for a second before it quickly faded as she looked me over. Mine followed suit.

"What?" I asked.

"What happened to you?" she asked pointing at my exposed torso. I looked down and saw the massive bruise covering my rib cage, the result of Trevor's attack the night before. In all the commotion of the past twenty-four hours, I hadn't even noticed. Thinking fast, I forced a grin.

"Oh, that. My dumb ass tripped trying to chase a buck in the woods, landed on a pile of rocks."

I don't think she bought it.

"You said you didn't actually find Trevor last night, right?"

"No. He wasn't home. I swear."

I hated lying to her but there was no way I could get her mixed up in all of this any more than she already was.

She didn't continue her line of questioning. Instead, she lightly ran her fingers over the purple area of my skin. I winced as she applied the slightest bit of pressure.

"It looks like it hurts."

I forced a smile through the pain. "It does."

Her seriousness melted into a smile of her own. "How can I make it better?"

"You can be here when I get out of the shower."

Her grin widened.

"Or I could join you."

***

We didn't stay in the shower too long, not wanting to arouse suspicion from my parents. Although, with their level of interest we could have probably made out on the kitchen table in the middle of dinner and neither of them would give a shit.

The shower was mainly just that. A shower. The events of the past few days were definitely catching up to me and my body ached all over. Arianna helped me wash my back and I returned the favor. We explored each other's bodies a bit, but outside of some kissing and light touching, it didn't go further than that.

Once we made sure the coast was clear and snuck back into my room, however, we discarded our towels and before I could really register what was happening, we were having sex on my bed. Since I'd just lost my virginity, it was still new to me, but it felt good. It felt right. It wasn't until we were done and Arianna was lying next to me, head resting on my chest, that I realized just how odd it was doing something as *normal* as making love to my girlfriend when there was a werewolf trapped in my backyard. Oh, and he just so happened to have torn apart her ex-boyfriend, whose body I had summarily disposed of earlier that day.

I felt a wave of guilt and anxiety wash over me. Arianna must have sensed it.

"What's wrong?"

I forced my smile again and kissed her forehead.

"Nothing as long as you're here."

***

Arianna left my house a little after midnight. I walked her downstairs, making sure that I'd be able to run interference if Dennis was drunk in his chair. Fortunately for the both of us, he wasn't.

I walked her to her car, even though she insisted she

could make it there on her own. I would have had no doubt under normal circumstances, but I couldn't shake my nightmare and all I saw was the wolf bursting out of the woods and clamping his jaws around my girlfriend's head. Ari didn't know that while she was using the bathroom before getting ready to go, I had slipped my pistol into the back waistband of my shorts. Just in case.

I kissed her goodbye and promised to call her tomorrow. I stood in the driveway, hand behind my back, fingers wrapped around the grip of the handgun as I watched her drive away.

***

With Arianna gone, I held my phone in my hands, hesitating to watch the footage I had captured earlier. Seeing that thing's metamorphosis in person was so much worse than I could have imagined—I could have gone my entire life without seeing that again.

But I forced myself to watch.

I pulled up the video and clicked play, stunned at what I saw.

There was a video clip but it was useless. The recording was blurred and obscured, the audio nothing more than a distorted crackle. I forwarded it all the way to the end and there was not even one second of usable footage of the wolf. I played it again. Still the same. I played it a third time. There was no evidence of the transformation.

I had nothing.

CHAPTER 21

I woke up early the next morning, sleep becoming a rare commodity in my world. Once again, I dressed for hunting but, before heading into the woods, I got in my car and drove to the local Wawa. It wasn't unusual for me to grab a sandwich to bring with me as I ventured on a hunt, so no one would question where I was going so early. I grabbed two Italian hoagies, a coffee and a sixty-four-ounce bottle of water.

Once I got home, I went back in the house and grabbed my shotgun and knife. But I also went into my drawer and pulled out an old pair of sweatpants and a zip-up hoodie. They were pretty worn and stained. They were my go-to clothes when I went out to clear the area I liked to hunt so I didn't care if they got dirty or torn. Adding a pair of heavy socks, I grabbed my oldest hiking boots. Shoving all the garments into my duffel bag, I headed out.

When I got to the cave, I was relieved to see the man was still there. He barely even looked up at me when I entered the cave. I didn't acknowledge him right away either. I simply reached into my bag and pulled out the clothes and tossed them in his direction. When they landed on him, he looked up for the first time.

"You must be cold," I told him.

He didn't answer, but he pulled the pants on. He eyed the hoodie, noticing that it was not a pullover.

"So, I guess you're not letting me go since you're providing me with collar-friendly clothing," he said.

I tossed the boots and socks toward him.

"I don't know what I'm doing yet," I said. "But I want to believe that you didn't want to hurt anyone, so I'm willing to listen."

"Listen?"

"To your story. How you ended up here."

He shook his head. "It doesn't matter."

"It kinda does."

He didn't retort and I didn't press any more. At least not yet. I reached into the Wawa bag and threw him the sandwich. He fumbled it but caught it before it hit the ground, even though the wrapping would preserve the food inside. He ripped apart the packaging unceremoniously and took a huge bite of the sandwich. I couldn't help but remember the wolf pulling Trevor's innards out as I watched him. I shook the image off as best I could and tossed him the water. He opened it and quickly downed about a third of the large bottle.

His appetite momentarily sated, he leaned back, droplets of water clinging to his beard.

"Where are you from?" I asked, resuming my line of questioning.

"Nowhere," he answered.

"What's your name?"

"Don't have one."

"Look, man, I'm trying to work with you here. I need to know if I can trust you enough to let you go."

"Trust me?" he scoffed. "You saw me turn into a fucking werewolf. If you trusted me, I'd question your sanity."

"So, I guess I'll just leave you here to die," I said only half bluffing.

"Go ahead. I really don't care at this point."

"How'd you turn?"

"Got bit by a werewolf."

"That's it?"

"Isn't that enough?"

I was getting frustrated. Whoever this guy was, he wasn't giving anything up. I was truly starting to think that he really didn't care if he lived or died, but I had to press forward.

"You said you remember what happens when you're... wolfed out. How much do you remember?"

"Everything."

"And you can't control it?"

"No."

At least I finally got some type of answer. Now I had to test a theory. I took out my phone and recorded a brief video.

"What are you doing?" he asked.

"Checking something." I looked at the video and saw the man clear as day. So my camera still worked. Was it a glitch last night or is there something that made it so the wolf couldn't be recorded on camera? After all, vampires didn't have a reflection according to those legends. Maybe there was something similar with werewolves.

"What are you checking?" the man asked, interrupting my contemplation.

"Can we film you when you're in wolf form?"

"What?"

"The video I took of you turning last night was blurred and distorted. Even the audio was fucked up."

"First I've heard of it, but it kind of makes sense."

"How so?"

"We can both agree at this point that werewolves exist, yes?"

"Kinda hard to deny."

"You ever seen actual video footage of one? On the news? YouTube?"

I guessed not. Sure, there was a bunch of fake shit out there, but I'd seen nothing resembling what I'd seen the past two nights. I guess this was a piece of lore that had never made it into any of the popular media. So much for getting video evidence.

"Can you die?" I asked, switching topics.

"Haven't yet."

"You know what I mean."

He splayed his hands in an *I don't know* gesture. "Nothing's killed me so far, kid. Not sure what would."

"Silver?"

"You got any on you?"

I froze. I definitely did not have silver on me. Bullets or anything else. What if it was the only thing that could kill him? If he were to break loose and a run-of-the-mill bullet wouldn't do the trick, I was screwed.

"Sure do."

He laughed. "You're a terrible liar, kid."

"Brady."

He looked at me confused.

"My name's Brady," I repeated.

"Now why would you tell me your name?"

"Call it a show of good faith."

"Well, Brady, you don't need to know my name."

This was getting frustrating. I thought about getting hostile and pulling my gun, but I doubted that would get me anywhere either.

"Fine," I told him. "If you're not going to tell me your name, I'll just give you one."

"And what name are you going to give me?"

"Gunther," I said, the most random name I could think of.

"Gunther?"

"Unless you want to tell me your real name?"

He didn't answer. Just took another bite of his sandwich followed by a swig of water.

"Look," I continued, "if I'm going to let you go, I need to know I'm doing the right thing. You have to give me something." The man ignored me and continued to eat his sandwich. I felt my blood boil at his obstinance. "Fine. If that's how you want it to play it, feel free to enjoy your accommodations for another evening."

***

It was still early so I decided to actually try to do some proper hunting, but my distraction prevented it from being a successful outing. I returned home just after five. Mom was standing over a pot of water on the stove, staring daggers into it as she waited for it to boil. Another pan with sauce was heating on the adjacent burner. It smelled tart and burned, like she hadn't stirred it the whole time it was on the heat.

She looked odd. Her eyes were glazed-over and sunken, like she hadn't slept in a month. Her lips were dry and cracked and she was hunched over as she observed the pot. I was pretty sure she was drunk.

"Pasta tonight?" I asked in a half-hearted attempt at conversation.

"What's it look like?" she snapped.

"Jesus, Mom."

She ignored me and I stood there watching her, feeling sad, unable to remember the last time my mother had had a truly warm word for either of us. I figured her attitude resulted from whatever was going on between her and Dennis. Even before the incident with Brandi's laundry, there seemed to have been a negative shift in their relationship. It didn't take long for my reflection to turn to anger. In my mind, no one could ever replace my father, but if there had to be someone, Dennis was nowhere near the top of the list. My mom was the one who had married him. If she wanted to be miserable, then the hell with her.

"Sauce smells burned," I remarked.

"How about you cook, Gordon Ramsay?"

Now it was my turn not to answer as I went back upstairs and stashed my gear.

While I was waiting for dinner, I called Arianna. We kept it light, not talking about the incident at the dance or my "hunting" injury. Just normal high school couple stuff. Although I wondered what would happen when people realized Trevor was missing. I kept trying to push it away but the sick feeling in my stomach came back.

I had just hung up when Dennis called us to come down for dinner. Brandi and I met in the hallway and made our way downstairs to the table. Mom and Dennis were already seated and had served themselves. They both had wine, with Mom's glass filled practically to the brim.

We ate in silence yet again, the tension the thickest it had ever been. I mean, awkward family dinners had clearly become the norm, but there was something tonight that felt even worse. An underlying sense that there was a powder keg ready to explode.

I took particular note of how Dennis watched Mom. He barely touched his food as he stared her down while she neglected her own plate in favor of her wine. He looked downright disgusted at her. Dennis and I being on the same page was a rarity, but I couldn't help but feel my own sense of revulsion watching my mother guzzle alcohol while the four of us sat around the table.

Brandi and I stole glances in each other's direction when we could, using our eyes and whatever twin telepathy existed to ask *What the fuck?*

Dennis abruptly rose from the table, depositing his plate in the sink, not even bothering to scrape the uneaten contents into the trash, before heading toward his den.

Mom didn't even acknowledge her husband's departure, opting instead to sit back in silence as she took generous sips of her wine. I was stunned when, after draining it, she reached for the bottle and poured the remaining contents into the glass, filling it almost to the top again. Brandi and I exchanged another *WTF* look.

"Mom, what's going on?" Brandi asked.

Mom took another sip, unconcerned with my sister's inquiry.

"This is so fucked up," Brandi added.

"I made you dinner. What else do you want?" Liz slurred, almost startling us by actually speaking. "You're free to go to McDonald's next time if you don't like my cooking."

Brandi shook her head. "It's the company that's the problem." She got up and took her dish over to the garbage can, looking it over before stepping on the pedal to open the lid. "But now that I think about it, your cooking has been shit lately. Maybe you should try using that wine in an actual recipe instead of pouring it down your throat."

Mom took another gulp, not giving Brandi the satisfaction of an answer. Nor did she spare a glance in Brandi's direction as she dumped both the food and the plate in the trash before storming out of the room.

Fuck this. I wasn't about to sit here either so I stood up and emptied the contents of my plate. Don't ask me why, but I also took a few moments to grab Dennis's out of the sink and Brandi's out of the trash and loaded them all in the dishwasher.

Honestly, whatever this bullshit was about, it was clearly a situation between my mother and Dennis that

Brandi and I were caught in the middle of. Sure, we were eighteen, but we shouldn't have to be the adults in the situation. I thought about saying something to my mother but thought better of it, leaving the kitchen and returning upstairs, making my way to Brandi's room.

"Well, that was fucking awkward," Brandi noted.

"No kidding," I said. "Something's up. More than the usual bullshit."

My heart sank for a minute. Could they know what was going on out in the woods? I quickly put it out of my head. There was no way. This family dynamic had been deteriorating for a while now. This was just an evolution.

I looked back at my sister. I saw tears forming in the corners of her eyes. With everything that had happened since Friday night, I almost forgot this had all started with her public humiliation. Throw in some increasingly fucked-up family drama and it was no wonder she was cracking.

I pulled her in for a hug, holding her tight as she cried.

"Hey," I said. "It's going to be okay. No matter what happens, you'll always have me."

She squeezed me tight. I felt her nod against my shoulder, nonverbally acknowledging that she believed me.

Like she had done for me on the day of my father's funeral all those years ago, I held her until her tears stopped.

***

After Brandi had settled and retired to her room, I waited until everyone else had fallen asleep. I had one more thing I needed to do. For what seemed like the umpteenth time this weekend, I gathered some gear and returned to the woods. I needed to make sure Gunther wouldn't change now that the moon cycle he had described was over. Assuming he was telling the truth, that is.

Before I left, I went into the kitchen and grabbed a Tupperware full of pasta and stuffed it into my bag along with another bottle of water.

When I entered the cave, I found Gunther was still there and still human. It was later than it had been the previous evening, when he had turned, so it appeared for the moment that he was telling the truth. Still, I knew I shouldn't let my guard down. After all, who was to say he wasn't fucking with me and he could turn at will? Or maybe the moon cycle thing was correct, but when whatever energy the phase gave off faded, it took longer. There were so many unknowns. I had to stay sharp.

"Here," I said handing him the Tupperware and a plastic fork.

He quietly accepted my offer, popping the lid off and

taking a bite, making a face as he did.

"Don't take this as me being unappreciative, but this sauce tastes burned."

No shit.

I didn't acknowledge the observation. Instead, I reached into my bag and tossed him a couple of old towels I had absconded with from the laundry room. They weren't much, but they would provide him with some extra cover. He held them in his hands and looked back up at me.

"You can't keep me here forever."

He was right. I absolutely could not. Beside the sheer logistics of having a pet werewolf in my backyard, I legitimately felt bad about keeping him here. It was no lie. I really believed him. Maybe I was completely off, but he didn't seem like a killer. Not in his human form, anyway. But what the hell did I know? I was just a teenager who would rather spend time with his girlfriend than engaging in hostage negotiations with a mythical creature.

"Maybe not," I admitted as I turned to exit the cave. "Goodnight, Gunther."

CHAPTER 22

As I approached my house in the dead of night, I recapped the past few days in my head. Since Friday night I had lost my virginity, gotten into a fight at a school dance, threatened a bully, then watched said bully get torn apart by a fucking werewolf—a werewolf I was now holding prisoner even though I couldn't actually prove he was a werewolf because I couldn't actually capture it on video.

I considered waiting until the next full moon and then calling the cops when he would have already transformed. The problem with that idea though was that I had covered up a murder. Plus, I still didn't know if the man himself was actually evil. What would the cops do? Kill it? Turn it over to the military for experiments? Did the man deserve that fate? Did *deserving* even play into this at all?

I honestly didn't know if I could write something more absurd.

Being careful not to make noise, I was wary as I ascended the stairs to the second floor. About midway up the landing, I stopped as I heard something coming from Mom and Dennis's room.

They were arguing.

It sounded pretty intense given the late hour. Mom was definitely louder. She would speak and I could hear her clear as day. Dennis sounded as if he was trying to keep the volume under control, but he wasn't doing a very good job.

I crept up to their door and put my ear up against it.

"You're repulsed by me!" Mom shouted.

"Oh my God, give it a rest, Liz," Dennis replied.

"Why won't you fuck me?" she yelled back.

I certainly could have done without hearing that. Mom's voice still sounded slurred. She must have continued hitting the bottle well into the evening.

"Maybe I don't want to have sex with a sloppy drunk. You ever consider that, sweetheart?"

The endearment was smattered with sarcasm. It was clearly a marital dispute. I should have just ignored it and continued on to my room, but something made me keep eavesdropping, even though I was unaware that the argument was about to exacerbate the gruesome nightmare I was living.

"Yeah, sure. That's the reason," Mom retorted. "You just want to fuck my daughter."

I felt like I was going to throw up.

"You're out of your goddamn mind, Liz."

"Don't talk down to me, you prick. I see the way you look at her! I used to have perky tits and a nice ass too, or have you forgotten? Ten years ago, you would have been sniffing my panties!"

Ten years??

"I'm not doing this."

His voice sounded closer. He was moving toward the door. I realized now was the time to make myself scarce. I started to back away when Mom said something that sent a chill up the length of my body.

"I guess you're done with me! Maybe I'll have an accident next? You'll have to come up with something original, though, seeing as I don't hunt."

Oh, my God. Was she saying what I thought she was?

"Shut the fuck up," Dennis whisper-yelled, sounding like he was mashing his teeth together.

"Yeah, something convenient. Maybe I'll fall down the stairs and then you'll make a move on my daughter before my body's even co—"

The last sentence abruptly ended with what sounded like a slap. Dennis had never hit my mother before, at least not to my knowledge. My normal instinct would have been to rush in and confront him for hurting her, but I had heard things that spun my head and froze me in place. It couldn't be what I thought. It just couldn't.

As I stood there paralyzed, I heard Dennis say, "Sober the fuck up and keep your damn mouth shut! I'm leaving."

Time to move. I willed my body to action and walked as quickly as I could to my room without alerting him, making it inside and quietly shutting the door a millisecond before I heard the master bedroom door open and shut. Dennis's footfalls faded as he made his way downstairs.

Now in the safety of my room, I collapsed on the bed. A wave of emotion flooded over me as I thought about the things I'd heard.

Mom said Dennis was more attracted to her ten years ago. My father died seven years ago. Did that mean they were having an affair? It might not be that scandalous. Maybe Dennis just had a thing for her. Brandi and I were so young that, if he had, it would probably have gone right over our heads.

But, then again, Mom had moved on pretty quick. They didn't tell us they were dating until a year after he died, but I did remember him being around a lot. The image of him descending the stairs the day of the funeral came back to me. I had wondered why it felt weird that he was up there now that my dad was gone. It made sense.

The revelation that my mom was probably fucking my dad's best friend for years before he passed was bad enough, but what did she mean by *Maybe I'll have an accident next? I don't hunt?*

Dennis knew my dad as well as anyone. They'd hunted together on plenty of occasions. He knew his strategies and routines. If he wanted my father out of the way so he could have my mother to himself, he could have easily sabotaged the tree stand. He could have caused the accident.

My whole body shook and tears flowed, a blend of rage and sadness. Sadness at what had been taken away from me and rage as I understood it was not some freak accident. It wasn't a cruel twist of fate.

Dennis killed my father.

CHAPTER 23

When I woke up the next morning, it surprised me that I had fallen asleep. I remembered lying there for a long time, the conversation playing over and over in my head.

Ten years.

Maybe I'll have an accident too?

My life was a lie. Mom and Dad's relationship. Dad's death. Dennis. All of it predicated on bullshit. The man who had been living under my father's roof for the past six years was responsible for his death. He had been his best friend, but he coveted his wife so badly, he resorted to murder. It wasn't enough that Liz—I couldn't even think of her as my mother right now; maybe never again—had willingly engaged in an affair with him. He had to have everything my dad had.

I wanted to go downstairs and stick my father's Glock in Dennis's mouth at the kitchen table and let him know I knew everything, right before I blew his fucking brains all over the backsplash. But I couldn't. There was the small matter of being an accessory to a classmate's murder by a hairy monster. Like every other move I'd made this weekend, I had to play this carefully.

It was still very early, a little before 5 a.m. Dennis usually got up around six thirty, so I had a little time. I quietly crept down the stairs and turned the corner into the basement. It was only partially finished, but there was a large open area where Dennis kept a treadmill, elliptical and some weights, a storage room off to one corner, and a small workshop in the other. Dennis kept it locked most of the time. He fancied himself a handyman in his own right and had all kinds of tools, that I rarely saw him actually use.

Just outside the workshop was a large filing cabinet where we kept all our important documents. Dennis was more than a little OCD, so I was sure that everything would be neatly labeled. I was glad to see I was right. Not only were the files labeled, but they were also alphabetized. I immediately found the file labeled *Life Insurance*.

Pulling the folder out, I opened it and saw that Mom and Dennis each had a policy, but I paid little attention to either of them. Behind those documents was what I was looking for—a sealed manila envelope marked *Blake Bennett Life Insurance Claim*.

Why the hell was it sealed? To deter us from exploring further if we found it?

I took a deep breath before ripping into the envelope. I really did not care in the least if Dennis or my mother found it like this. Let them wonder which one of us had found out the truth.

The first, and most striking, thing I saw was the amount that my mother had received because of my father's accident. The total policy was for two million dollars and they paid it out about two months after he died. I knew Mom hadn't really stressed about money, but I had no idea she'd gotten that much. I felt rage boiling inside. No amount of money was worth my dad's life. He'd made damn sure my cheating bitch mother was taken care of.

There was a police report behind the claim forms. I got emotional as I read it, recounting that my father's cause of death was a broken neck likely from a fall out of the tree stand. The details in the report stated that the stand had been assembled incorrectly, using the wrong type of pins to secure it to the trunk. They couldn't hold the operator's weight, causing the stand to collapse.

That cemented it. My father had hunted for over thirty years. He'd built more than a dozen tree stands. There was no fucking way he would use the wrong materials. No fucking way.

I gripped the documents hard, wanting to crumple them in my hands and just leave them on the floor, but that wouldn't get me anywhere. That wouldn't be justice for my father. I inhaled deeply again, followed by another long exhalation. Smoothing out the papers, I placed them back in the torn envelope before returning it to the filing cabinet.

I composed myself and returned to my bedroom.

***

After I got ready for school, I delayed going downstairs as long as possible, until just before I had to leave. As I walked down the hall, I heard music coming from Brandi's room.

"Brandi?" I called through the wooden barrier.

"Come in."

I opened the door and saw that she was lying in bed, covers bunched around her waist. She didn't have any makeup on and was wearing a black *Motionless in White* hoodie, the one she typically wore when she was sick. Her hair was disheveled and hung down over her eyes. When she brushed it away and tucked it behind her ear, I saw how bloodshot they were.

"I guess I can't convince you to come to school."

She laughed humorlessly. "Good guess. I changed my mind. Forget a few days off. I'm never setting foot in that building again."

"C'mon, Brandi. You know that isn't realistic."

"Try me. The entire school saw me naked on Friday. That can be the last image they have of me."

I didn't know how to convince her to go. Wasn't even

sure if I should. I was angry, but she was humiliated. People had already been saying nasty things about her before this incident. I couldn't fathom how she felt having those pictures put out there for all to see.

"I'm sorry for all this."

She nodded. "I know. But it's not your fault. It's that piece of shit Trevor. Don't get me wrong, I'm glad you didn't get into a fight or in trouble, but if you had found him and fucked him up, I wouldn't be shedding any tears for him."

I wondered if she would shed those tears if she knew what actually happened, but there was no way I was telling her that. Instead, I simply nodded and leaned over to kiss her on the forehead.

"I'll get the lay of the land. Maybe it's not as bad as you think."

"Doubt it. But thank you. Close the door on your way out, please."

I did as she asked.

When I went downstairs, I silently thanked God that neither my mother nor Dennis was around. I didn't know where they were and I didn't care. If I had seen either of them, I had serious doubts I would have been able to restrain myself. I grabbed a Pop-Tart and took it with me, not bothering to toast it, as I headed to my car.

***

When I arrived at school, I noticed the looks immediately. Glances and murmurs followed me from the time I walked through the doors, to my locker and into homeroom. I did my best to ignore them. No one dared come at me directly after they saw the way I went at Ryan at the dance. But the gossipy atmosphere justified Brandi's decision to play hooky. I meant it when I said she couldn't stay away forever, but a few days would probably be a good thing.

As I did my best to keep to myself, it surprised me to feel someone tap my left shoulder. I turned to see Kevin Blanton was the one trying to get my attention. I wouldn't call us friends, but I was cordial to him. Pudgy and afflicted with a slight lisp and a severe case of acne, Kevin didn't run in the more popular circles, but, for some reason, the bullies actually let him be. Probably because he was the most non-threatening person I'd ever met.

"Hey, Brady," Kevin said, "I heard you beat up Ryan."

"I didn't actually beat him up."

"You rattled him pretty bad."

"Where did you hear that?" I asked, genuinely curious, seeing as Kevin hadn't been at the dance to my knowledge and it was unlikely that anyone had just come up and filled him in.

"Hey, just because I don't go to things, doesn't mean my ears aren't open." He paused. "What did you do to Trevor Wright?"

I gulped involuntarily.

"I didn't do anything."

Kevin took a gulp of his own. His to clear the saliva pooled up in his oversized jowls rather than out of guilt like me.

"I heard them say you went looking for him. Now he's missing."

"Missing?" I asked, trying to sound surprised. "He's missing?"

"You don't know?"

"No. I haven't seen him since he got kicked out."

The words were such a blatant lie that they felt like they were coming from someone else's mouth. Kevin looked surprised in his own right.

"You haven't?"

"That's what I said, Kevin," I told him before turning around.

"Well, now no one can find him," he said before going back to whatever it was he was doing before.

***

For the rest of the morning, no one else had the guts

to question me about the dance or what may or may not have happened with Trevor. I tried my best to act normal, but my thoughts were all over the place as I moved from class to class. I had a werewolf problem, a missing classmate problem and a murdering stepdad problem. All having popped up over the past three days.

It wasn't until chemistry class that my thoughts came together. While Mr. Liptak was going on about chemical compounds and such, one of them stood out.

Silver nitrate.

The teacher held up a small bottle of the substance and talked about its practical applications, noting it was primarily used to cauterize infected tissue around a skin wound and to help it create a scab to prevent bleeding. He cited the example of a pediatrician dabbing an infant's belly button to remove the last remnants of the umbilical cord.

It didn't really matter what it was used for normally. Discreetly pulling up my phone, I checked to see if I could get a bottle online, half surprised to learn that I could. And with overnight shipping too. I quickly placed the order and stuffed the phone back in my bag. I'd need some other materials, but I knew where to get those quickly and easily.

***

At lunchtime, I met Arianna and we found a table to ourselves despite her friends' insistence that we sit with them. I was glad she blew them off. Outside of my sister, I didn't really know any of her friend group and today was certainly not the day that I'd make my best first impression.

"How's Brandi?" she asked once we got settled.

"Mortified," I replied.

"I can't even imagine."

A thought hit me. I was ashamed to even ask, but my stupid teenage male ego compelled me to. "There're no photos of you that might pop up are there?"

She looked irritated. *Nice one.*

"No, Brady. There are no photos of me."

I felt stupidly relieved. Murder, mayhem and deception all around me and here I am, grateful that my girlfriend wasn't sending nudes to anyone before me.

"I'm sorry, I don't know where that came from."

She smirked. "Well, I was going to send you some, but now I'll have to think about it."

"Don't think too hard."

We shared a laugh. There was so much tension in my world right now that any excuse to break it was a welcome one. Too bad it didn't last too long.

"Are you okay?" she asked. "You look tired."

"I am. This whole thing has been a lot and listening to the whispers in the hallway aren't helping."

"Tell me about it. It's like living in TMZ or something," she said, reaching out and grasping my hand. "But we'll help her get through this."

I put my other hand on top of hers. "She can't just drop out. I need your help to show her it'll be okay to come back."

"Of course. We'll get her through this."

She smiled. Her eyes sparkled and I completely believed her. Brandi and I were both incredibly lucky to have her in our lives.

"How about we pick her up after school and take her to the movies?"

"And see what?"

"That new movie with Jennifer Aniston?"

"Raunchy Comedy Jennifer Aniston or Rom-Com Jennifer Aniston?"

"Rom-Com?" she answered sheepishly.

"Brandi watches Rom-Coms?"

"Don't you dare tell her I told you, but she's seen *When Harry Met Sally* like a hundred times."

I chuckled. "How about you take her to the movies and I'll meet up with you after and we can grab something to eat?"

"Okay," she said, feigning disappointment. "I'll spare you."

I squeezed her hand. We said nothing else for a few moments, just held each other's gaze. If my plan worked, by this time next month, I wouldn't have to worry about anything other than spending time with this amazing girl.

But I had things to worry about. Most immediately was the announcement that came over the intercom.

"Brady Bennett, please report to the principal's office."

Shit.

CHAPTER 24

As I entered the principal's office, I immediately noticed a large black man in a dark-gray suit. He was probably pushing six foot five. His head was bald, but he had a thick, neatly trimmed dark beard speckled with gray. He looked like he should play linebacker for the Giants, not be standing here in the principal's office of Hillcrest High.

I was so distracted by the sheer size of the man, I barely noticed the police badge clipped to his belt. I don't know why I was surprised—I should have expected it.

Principal Koehler sat behind the desk, a beady-eyed little twerp with horn-rimmed spectacles and a Napoleon complex. Feared by some, disliked by most and respected by none, he was a typical pencil-pushing administrator who did only the bare minimum to keep the school running. He looked as if he were sweating.

"Mr. Bennett," the principal said, "this is—"

"Detective Dante Wallace. Hillcrest PD," the large cop finished for him, extending his hand as he did.

I accepted the handshake, not wanting to appear

hesitant or nervous. Even though I felt like I was about to shit my pants. He gripped my hand firmly, but politely. Not trying to squeeze extra hard to send a message. I guessed that could be a good sign.

"Nice to meet you, sir."

"Have a seat, Brady," Detective Wallace said, gesturing to one of the two chairs in front of the desk.

I did as I was instructed, compliance foremost on my mind.

The detective turned to my principal. "Mr. Koehler, may we have the room?"

Koehler was flabbergasted. "Detective, I don't know if questioning a student without an adult present is appropriate."

"How old are you, Brady?" Wallace asked, turning his attention back to me.

"Eighteen, sir."

He turned back to Koehler. "Mr. Bennett is a legal adult. It's not inappropriate for us to have a one-on-one chat."

"Am I in some kind of trouble?" I asked, hoping it sounded convincing.

"Just a few questions, Brady." Back to Koehler. "So, may we have the room?"

Principal Koehler clearly wanted to protest further, but he was also smart enough to know that he wasn't equipped to win this pissing contest.

He let out an exasperated sigh and locked his computer before heading out, offering as he left, "I'll be right out here if you need me."

"I think we'll be fine," Detective Wallace said as the principal shut the door behind him.

With the room to ourselves, the policeman gave me a once-over.

"You know why I'm here, Brady?"

No point in lying. There were too many witnesses.

"Because of what happened at the dance?"

"What happened at the dance?"

I was sure he knew, but I had no choice but to play along.

"Someone leaked private photos of my sister and put them up on the big screen during the dance."

"And who leaked them?"

"Ryan Marshall told me he sent them to Trevor Wright and he was the one who put them up there for all to see."

"And that made you angry, I take it?"

"Well, yes. She's my sister."

"Did you have an altercation with Ryan Marshall in the gymnasium?"

You know I did.

"Yes."

"What happened after that?"

"I went looking for Trevor."

"Did you have an altercation with Trevor Wright?"

You could say that.

"No," I answered, feeling sick as I've now added lying to the police to my list of indiscretions over the past seventy-two hours.

"Did you threaten him?"

"I didn't find him."

"How about over text message?"

Goddamn it.

"I did send him a text. I was really mad for my sister. Didn't really think about what I was doing."

Wallace cocked an eyebrow. "What would you have done if you had found him?"

Try to vandalize his car, then get into a fight before running off into the woods where he would be murdered by a seven-foot-tall werewolf.

"I honestly don't know. I guess we would have fought."

"That wasn't your first altercation with Trevor Wright, was it?"

I thought back to getting my head slammed into the locker along with the subsequent concussion. It seemed so long ago.

"No. He jumped me at my girlfriend's locker."

"Why?"

I didn't like where this was going.

"Because my girlfriend used to be his girlfriend."

Wallace nodded as if the puzzle pieces were coming together for him. I hoped my candor would keep him on my side.

"So he was pissed that she dumped him for you?"

"Not exactly."

"Why'd they break up?"

"Because he tried to cheat on her with my sister."

The detective shook his head. "Jesus Christ, you high school kids and your drama."

I couldn't disagree.

"We didn't start dating until after they broke up."

"Well, I guess he still held a torch for her if he's going to such lengths to go after you and your sister?"

"I guess."

He flipped a page in the notepad. "So, Trevor Wright wasn't home when you got to his house?"

"When I got to his house?" I asked, wondering how he knew. He answered by opening up a file folder I hadn't noticed on Principal Koehler's desk. I guess I assumed it was school paperwork and not police stuff. Inside was a fairly decent photo of me standing on Trevor's porch, pounding on the door with a manic look on my face.

His family must have a video doorbell. I hoped it hadn't caught anything else.

"He wasn't there. Guess I'm glad it didn't go any further than it already had."

"What did you do after?"

"I went home."

"Straight home?"

Not exactly.

"Yes."

"And you haven't heard from Trevor since?"

I knew it was coming, but it felt like my intestines were being tied in knots inside my stomach. Here was the point where I'd find out how well my deception would hold up.

"He texted me the next day. Apologized."

"Apologized?"

"Yes."

"Did he text anyone else?"

"My sister and girlfriend both said they got texts from him apologizing to them too. Plus, he put something on social media."

He eyed me for several long moments before continuing the interrogation. And make no mistake, this was an interrogation.

"You don't find that odd?"

If I didn't know it was all staged? I absolutely would find it odd. Guys like Trevor didn't typically have rapid onset crises of conscience.

"It surprised me to get it."

The cop nodded. He looked like he was choosing his next line of inquiry very carefully.

"Are you aware that Trevor Wright is missing?"

Now, I wanted to say no. But the social media post I had written as him implied he was going away. Plus, I recalled

215

my conversation this morning with Kevin Blanton. Even though I didn't think it was likely that they'd question him in all this, I couldn't leave that to chance.

"I heard something about that this morning."

"What did you hear?"

"That he was missing."

"Mm hm." The cop muttered as he jotted notes. When he finished, he flipped the notebook closed and slipped it into his inside jacket pocket. "So, here's the deal, Brady. Trevor's parents don't think he ran away. We have some evidence that says he did, but it's inconclusive."

I didn't know how to respond so I simply said, "I don't know, sir."

"Trevor, or someone pretending to be him, purchased a train ticket to Philadelphia. He didn't go home. Didn't get any clothes or belongings. Just went right to the train station. Which is odd considering he had a new car that he could have driven anywhere he wanted."

I felt sick. No matter how many bases I thought I had covered, there were more that I'd missed. I just hoped it wasn't enough to sink me.

"Security footage from the station shows a young man of similar build getting on the train, but he was wearing a hooded sweatshirt and sunglasses. How tall are you, Brady?"

Fuck.

"About five ten."

"I'd say closer to five eleven, but we'll call it five ten." He flipped through some papers in the file folder. "Trevor's five eleven too. That's a heck of a coincidence, don't you think?"

Fear paralyzed my body. It took everything I had to muster, "I guess so."

"Yup. Heck of a coincidence," he said as he shut the folder. "See, it seems his phone stopped tracking around Trenton, right before he would have had to switch to the River Line. We had the folks there pull the security footage. They're still going through it, but, as of now, it's like he just vanished somewhere between here and there."

His eyes felt like they were burning through me. It felt like I was on fire, hoping I wasn't visibly sweating. I tried my best to play it cool. I told myself I didn't kill him nor did I want to kill him, despite my empty text threats. It was a stupid feud that went too far, but the werewolf committed the actual murder. Although I could only imagine what the detective would say if I admitted everything that actually happened.

What was I going to do? Lead him into the woods where I had a man chained up in a cave? The moon cycle was over. He wouldn't turn for another month. With his back against the wall, he'd almost certainly say I kidnapped him and killed Trevor. By the time he wolfed out again, he'd be long gone and I'd either be in jail or some type of mental hospital. As messed up as this whole thing was, I had to stay the course.

"I'm sorry, sir. I wish I could be of more help."

"Of course, Brady. I looked through your file. You're a bright kid. Decent grades. Never in any kind of trouble before that fight last month. Even then, it's clear that Trevor was the aggressor. I have no doubt that if you knew something, you would come clean with me."

Come clean with him. Interesting choice of words. Implying that he knew I was hiding something. He was trying to use some kind of psychology on me.

"Yes, sir."

He stood up and retrieved the file folder from the desk. He stood in front of me for a few more moments, assessing me one last time before extending his hand again. Once again, I accepted.

"Thank you, Brady. I'll be in touch."

Chapter 25

The interrogation from Detective Wallace had seriously rattled me. As soon as I was out of view of the principal's office, I felt like my body was going to collapse in on itself and I had a hard time keeping my hands from shaking.

It took a while, but I finally composed myself enough to meet Arianna outside. She was understandably curious about why I had been summoned to the principal's office. As with the detective, I felt it best to be as honest as I could without telling her any more than she needed to know. I told her that apparently Trevor's parents don't think he ran away and that they filed a missing persons report. The police knew about the incident at the dance so they asked me a few questions. Arianna was obviously concerned, but I assuaged her fears and told her everything was okay, once again skirting the fine line between withholding certain facts and outright deception.

Fifteen minutes later, we were at my house and went straight to see Brandi. She was happy to see Arianna. We made small talk for a few moments, but then excused myself, saying I had some homework to do and that they should enjoy the movie. It surprised me how little resistance Brandi put up. I guess any excuse to get out of the house was a good one.

Back in my room, I put the next phase of my plan into action. I went online to the site where I normally buy ammo. I knew it was a long shot, but I did a quick check to see if there were silver nine-millimeter bullets available for purchase. There were not. Silver shotgun shells weren't a thing either, so I had to improvise.

I ordered an all-in-one shotgun slug mold. Without getting too technical, it's a device hunters use to make their own shotgun ammo. A little touch of silver nitrate in each slug and I would have my werewolf killers loaded and ready to go. The package would arrive in the next two to three days. Which would be fine since I still had some prep work to do.

After Brandi and Arianna left, I brought Gunther another sandwich and a bottle of water. I also brought a bucket of water with a sponge and some bath soap so he could clean himself up a bit.

Sitting down across from him, well out of his reach, my back against the opposite wall of the cave, I watched as he ate the sandwich. I'd fed him a few times now, so he wasn't devouring it like he had previous meals. He didn't seem to care that I was there. Finally, I broke the silence.

"Does it hurt?"

He looked up, a mouthful of sandwich straining against his left cheek. He didn't respond, but resumed chewing until he could swallow.

"Does what hurt?"

"When you... change."

He laughed. "Does it hurt?" he repeated in a mocking tone.

"Is that funny?"

"You remember having growing pains when you were younger? You know when your legs would hurt at night and your mom told you it was because you were getting to be a big boy?"

"Yeah, so?"

"The funny thing is—growing pains are actually a myth. There's no actual evidence that your body hurts as you grow. Most of the time, they can chalk those aches up to simple overuse during the day."

I didn't follow. He continued.

"But imagine your body growing and changing within minutes. I'm six one, but you saw me when I changed. The wolf is about seven feet tall. So, think about all your bones growing inside of your body while your flesh expands to accommodate it."

He pinched the skin on the back of his left hand and pulled at it, wincing once it got as far as it could.

"Try that," he said.

I did. It hurt.

"Now picture that feeling all over your body. You can't control it. You can't relieve it."

"I understand," I said.

"No, you don't!" Gunther snapped. "You have no fucking idea! My body sprouts hair, violently. Every follicle feels like it's on fire. My teeth expand and sharpen, like having a root canal without Novocain in every tooth at once. Every muscle in my body tears and reforms, every nerve gets mashed together."

"I'm sorry," I said.

Gunther took a second and composed himself. "Yes," he said, "it hurts. Worse than you can imagine."

We sat in silence after that. He took a drink of water and then went back to his sandwich. I kept quiet until he was finished, crumpling up the wrapper and tossing it aside before chugging half of what was left in the water bottle. That was when I spoke up again.

"I'm going to let you go."

That got his attention. For the first time, his eyes looked hopeful.

"You are?"

"I am," I said, prepping myself to toss in the kicker. "But not yet."

He rolled his eyes and leaned his head back against the wall, looking up at the roof of the cave.

"Fine, I'll play along," he said. "When?"

"I need you to help me with something."

Another laugh. "What could I possibly help you with?"

"I'll tell you when the time comes."

"Jesus, kid, you certainly know how to be vague. Let me ask you this, then. How am I supposed to help you while I'm chained up in here?"

I hesitated, wondering if I should even answer. But I did.

"I don't need you, exactly. I need the wolf."

He lowered his head and cupped his hands around his face, rubbing from his eyes down to the bottom of his beard.

"You're fucking nuts. You know that, right?"

"Starting to feel that way," I admitted. "But I wouldn't be doing this if I had any other choice."

"What do you need the wolf for?"

"I believe you," I said ducking the question.

"Believe me?"

"Yes, I believe you don't want any of this. I believe you were chaining yourself in here to prevent something like what happened. I believe that all of this was because Trevor and I were in the wrong place at the wrong time."

"So that was his name?"

"Yes. He hated me. He practically ruined my sister's life and wanted to hurt me. But, despite all of that, I did not want him to die. Do you believe me?"

Gunther surveyed me, assessing my sincerity or lack thereof. After a moment, he answered, "I do."

Getting that validation from him was almost a relief. I really cared that he believed me.

"But there's someone else. Someone truly evil. Someone that deserves to be punished."

"What makes you the one to pass judgment on this person?"

"Because he did ruin my life. My sister's too. And if he isn't taken care of, he's going to hurt us."

"So go to the police."

"The police won't be able to give me the justice I need."

"The justice you want."

"Want. Need. It's all the same. You do this for me and I let you go. No questions asked."

"So I kill someone for you, you let me go? You turn me into a murderer again and that gets me my freedom?"

I nodded. He stared daggers into me.

"I'll be back tomorrow with some more food," I said as I got up and moved toward the cave's exit.

"I'm not turning again for a month. You planning on keeping me down here all this time?"

I stopped and turned back to him.

"Why not? I'm guessing no one's coming looking for you at this point. At least not anyone you'd want to find you."

He hung his head, confirming my theory.

"But," I continued, "I have something in mind. I just need a couple days."

With that, I left the cave.

There was no dinner that night, nor was there any explanation given by Mom or Dennis as to why there wasn't. In fact, they didn't even interact with me at all. Guess it's hard to expect great parenting from a pair of adulterous murderers.

Whatever. They would get theirs. Dennis especially. I wasn't sure how I was going to handle my mother yet, but Dennis? My stepfather had a special surprise coming to him.

As I sat on the front porch, Arianna and Brandi pulled into the driveway. Before they could come to a complete stop, I approached them and put up my hand, signaling that they shouldn't even bother getting out of the car. I hopped in the back seat and told them we should head for the diner.

Brandi drove us there and we took our seats in a booth toward the back. As we waited for our food, the topic of Trevor's disappearance came up. Of course, I played dumb, but I filled my sister in on my encounter with Detective Wallace.

"Holy shit, Brady!" she said, trying—and failing—to keep her voice down. "Does he actually think you had something to do with it?"

"I don't think so," I lied. "But you know Trevor and I had gotten into it more than once. And I was out for blood for a minute there."

"Well, thank God you didn't fight him," Arianna chimed in.

"Yeah," I agreed as an ache ran through my bruised ribs almost as if they were calling out my perjury.

"I mean, if he didn't run away, who would go through all the trouble of texting everyone and posting to his social media? How would they get his phone unlocked?"

Not easily.

I shrugged and changed the subject. "How was the movie?"

CHAPTER 26

The next couple of days at school were uneventful. No cops. No classmates questioning me about Trevor. Sure, there was the odd look here or there, but no one approached me with anything.

After much coaxing from Arianna and me, Brandi agreed to go back to school on Thursday. She promised all she needed was a couple more days to get her head right. We made it clear that we would give her space but would not take no for an answer once Thursday rolled around.

Each day, I ate lunch with just Arianna again, keeping it light. As far as she was concerned, we were all trying to put the events of the previous week behind us. I wished that was actually the case, but it wasn't yet for me. My peace would come in just under a month from now, assuming everything went to plan.

At the end of the day on Wednesday, Arianna was apologetic. She wanted to hang out, but she had gotten a little backed up on a history project that was due at the end of the week. That was actually perfect as it would give me enough time to finish my preparations. I told her not to sweat it and that I had plenty to do myself (which was accurate—just not schoolwork). I promised that, once we got through this week, I would plan an amazing weekend for the two of us. She was excited by the prospect and we shared an extra-long kiss as we said our goodbyes for now.

Arriving home, I was happy to see my package from the online ammo shop sitting on the porch, having arrived a day early. I was also thankful that my snake of a stepfather wasn't home, sparing me the irritation of having to explain the contents of the parcel.

I rushed up to my room and locked the door behind me. I completely cleared off my desk and unpacked the box, laying each piece out individually. Before I started, I opened both of my windows to make sure the room was well ventilated because, even though I'd never done this before, I understood the process could produce some gnarly fumes.

I cleaned the mold with soap and water and made sure it was completely dry before I moved on. Next, I took a match and held it up to the cavities, smoking them so the soot left behind would fill any grooves, preventing the shells from sticking.

I poured the lead alloy that came with the kit into the melting pot and started heating it. It needed to get to about seven hundred degrees. While it was warming,

I rested the mold on top of the pot to heat that as well. After about five minutes, the mold was up to temperature, so I removed it, placing it carefully on the old pan I had stolen from the kitchen.

Typically, you would place the shell mold under the downspout of the melting pot but before I did, I filled it about a quarter of the way with the silver nitrate. After that, I followed the normal process and released the smelted lead into the mold and pressed it shut. I plunged it into the water to cool it and released the newly cased shell onto the pan.

I repeated the process until I had eight silver nitrate-laced shotgun shells. If it would actually kill a werewolf, I didn't know. But my hope was I wouldn't need to find out. I had every intention of honoring my promise to Gunther. I just hoped it wouldn't come back to bite me.

Literally or figuratively.

***

As she promised, Brandi returned to school on Thursday. It was mostly uneventful. Of course there were looks and a few whispers in the hallway, but no one directly accosted or harassed my sister. She was definitely uncomfortable, but soldiered through, doing her best to ignore the occasional sidelong glance.

After school, I completed the rest of my preparations after obtaining a few other items from various stores around town. It took a while, but I was able to get what I needed done before heading back for dinner.

There actually was a dinner tonight. It consisted of the four of us eating Chinese takeout in silence. I couldn't even look at Dennis or my mother. I wanted nothing more than to flip the table and call them out on everything I had learned, but I knew I had to be patient. Once we finished up and dispersed, I found the opportunity to sneak back out.

It was time to move Gunther.

***

As I once again entered the cave, Gunther shook his head.

"I guess you haven't changed your mind?" he asked.

"The deal is the deal. You do what I need you to do and I let you go."

I pulled a zip tie out of my bag and tossed it to him.

"Put this around your wrists," I instructed.

He did as he was told. Once he was secured, I retrieved another tie and bound his legs at the ankles.

"What the hell are you doing?" the confused man

asked.

"Just relax," I told him as I pulled out the key I had pocketed when I first found him. I tossed it to him and he immediately reached his bound hands up, slid the key into the lock and turned it. The shackle clicked open and fell from around his neck.

"Son of a bitch," he uttered as he rubbed his neck, taking a deep sigh having been relieved of his confines.

"Sorry," I said, actually meaning it. "Toss it back."

He did as he was told. I caught the key and slipped it back into my pocket. Next, I took out a small pair of wire cutters. I used them to clip the tie around his feet. As he got up, I raised my shotgun in his direction.

"Don't think about running," I told him. "These shells are loaded with silver."

"Why should I believe you?"

"Try me," I said.

He didn't. He simply held his hands up like he was a train conductor and I was a bandit robbing him.

"Let's go."

***

For the next forty minutes, we marched silently through the woods. The boots were a little tight on Gunther, but it was better than walking barefoot over the rough terrain.

He walked ahead of me, his hands tied in front of him.

I kept a few feet back at all times, holding my gun on him. The whole thing felt wrong to me, but I had to stay the course until this ordeal was over.

"Where are we going?" he asked, finally breaking the silence.

"We're almost there."

The silence returned and we walked for another ten minutes before we finally reached a clearing. Through the trees, a large, decrepit three-story building came into view. The brick exterior was still in pretty good shape, but there were a myriad of broken windows with rotted wood frames. A pretty sizable red oak had fallen against one corner of the structure. The entire building was covered with patches of moss, giving away the fact that it hadn't been occupied in years.

"What is this place?" Gunther asked.

"My dad and I came across this building on one of our hunting trips years back. He told me it used to be a mental hospital," I answered. "Closed down about twenty years ago. Administration was cutting corners or something. There were also rumors of patient abuse. Most of us grew up thinking it was haunted."

"Is it?" he asked.

"You believe in ghosts?"

"Don't you?"

"Not really."

"You realize you're talking to a werewolf, right?"

He had me there.

"C'mon," I said. "Around here."

I led Gunther around the side of the building to a rusted pair of bulkhead doors. The lock on them was busted which wasn't a surprise since I was the one who had busted it. I pulled the heavy metal door open with a loud creaking noise, not overly concerned with anyone hearing. People steered clear of this place because of its overall creepy atmosphere. Even if there were some fellow teens drinking or getting high in the vicinity, they'd hear the doors groaning and would more than likely take off running.

"This way," I said, gesturing to the basement that was now open.

"Can't see a thing."

I handed him a flashlight. He flicked it on and made his way down the stairs. I followed behind him, holding a second flashlight against the barrel of my shotgun.

Using my beam, I illuminated the path around the corner and down the hall. The corridor was lined with doors, some open, others shut tight. Each had a small, reinforced window at about the eye level of an average-sized man. About four inches under each was a small slot, enough to slide a cafeteria tray through.

"Looks like jail cells," Gunther noted.

"Kind of," I replied. "I think this is where they kept

their more problematic patients. The ones they needed to keep from hurting themselves. Or others."

"So, if they had a werewolf, this is where they would keep him?" Gunther said, catching my drift.

I ignored the question. "It's the one on the end."

I shined my beam at the open door at the very end of the corridor. Gunther made his way down and into the room. It wasn't exactly a five-star hotel suite. The walls were padded, likely to keep the occupant from injuring themselves. But there was a bed that I had made up, with clean sheets and a pillow. There was a small metal chair and table bolted to the wall over in the corner. On the table, I had laid out a pack of cookies, a bag of potato chips, a box of Captain Crunch, and a 24-pack of bottled water. Next to them, I had stacked some magazines and old paperbacks I had grabbed at the used bookstore.

On the chair, I had piled several T-shirts, sweatpants and socks, along with a cozy-looking sweatshirt. I'd gotten them all for twenty dollars at the local thrift store.

Gunther surveyed his surroundings.

"So, I'm guessing this is my new home for the time being?"

"Perceptive," I quipped, unable to help myself.

He went over and thumbed through the magazines, holding up the copies of *Gallery* and *Juggs* that I had slid in between the more mainstream offerings like *Men's Health* and *Sports Illustrated*.

"Really?" he asked.

I shrugged. "I figured you have needs. There's a box of tissues over there too."

He shook his head and made his way over to the bed, sitting down. He tried not show it, but I could tell he was relieved to actually sit on a mattress with soft sheets as opposed to his week on the cold, hard ground of the cave.

"So, let's get this straight," he said. "You're going to lure some bad dude here that you want me to kill for you. What are you going to do when I turn? Are you sure that door is going to stop the wolf if it wants out?"

"I thought of that," I replied. "It's reinforced. I'm going to lock it with three heavy-duty padlocks when I leave. It'll hold a grizzly bear if need be."

"If not, it's your funeral."

No kidding. But this had to happen. Dennis had to pay.

"I'm sorry about all this," I told Gunther. "That's the truth. I wish our paths had never crossed. And when we're done here, I hope you find what you're looking for."

"It may be too late," the man solemnly replied.

"Maybe for the both of us," I agreed as I tossed him the wire cutters. He turned them in his hand and used them to clip the zip tie off his wrist. He shook his hands back awake now that they were free.

I held out my hand and curled my fingers toward me in a *give it here* gesture. Gunther didn't argue and tossed the small tool back to me. I stepped out of the room and shut the door, taking my time to make sure each padlock was secure. Once I was confident it wasn't opening, I gave it one last tug. It didn't budge.

Peering back into the room, I noticed Gunther was standing right on the other side, looking at me through the window. I felt like I should say something else, but I had no clue what that would be.

I took one last look before making my way back home.

CHAPTER 27

The next full moon was due three nights after Thanksgiving. Based on what I'd learned, Gunther would turn the first time in the new cycle on that Saturday night. Sleep became harder to come by as the days passed and the time to enact my plan drew near.

While tensions had eased somewhat in my house over the past few weeks, we were still nowhere near where we used to be, even in the early days of Mom and Dennis's relationship. They were talking again, but not much. As the holiday approached, it was clear no one in the Bennett–McGill household had much interest in a big festive dinner, so, a week before the holiday, when Arianna invited Brandi and me to Thanksgiving dinner at her family's house, we jumped at the opportunity and neither Mom nor Dennis protested.

The whole day was such an amazing experience that, at times, I wanted to cry. First, and most importantly, I learned that Arianna's dad was a Giants fan. We instantly bonded over our contention that Eli Manning should be a first ballot hall of famer and debated who was the worse first-round draft pick—Kadarius Toney or Eli Apple. We talked about how excited we were about the new coaching staff and had a great time watching the Cowboys get their asses kicked during the late-afternoon game.

Arianna was the oldest of three children. She had two younger brothers, Darren, eleven, and Victor, eight. They were two of the coolest little kids I'd ever met. It was especially funny to watch Darren try to flirt with Brandi. I have to admit the kid had some game. Brandi smiled and laughed at his silly little comments in a way that I hadn't seen in years. It felt like what life could truly be like if we hadn't all been dealt the shitty hand I was trying to play.

After dinner, while Mr. Kenton was fast asleep in a food coma in his easy chair during the eight o'clock game between the Cardinals and the Commanders, and Brandi was helping Mrs. Kenton in the kitchen, Ari and I snuck upstairs to her room. Our clothing came off quick and we did our best to not alert the rest of the house to our lovemaking. When we finished, I lay on top of her and, for a moment, got lost in her eyes.

"What are you thinking about?" she asked as she caught her breath.

"I'm thinking that I love you," I told her, a sudden wave of panic washing over me. It wasn't a premeditated thought. I just blurted it out without thinking. I hoped it wasn't too much.

She smiled. "I love you too."

***

Brandi and I left Arianna's house that night with full bellies, full hearts and full containers of leftovers. As we drove, I felt my good feelings wash away the closer we got to our house. The whole day had been so amazing that I'd almost forgotten what I had to do.

Almost.

One fortunate twist of fate was that Arianna was going to be away with her parents visiting family out of state for the weekend, so I didn't have to worry about explaining where I was or what I was doing over the next few days.

"I'm really happy for you and Arianna, Brady."

She offered me a smile. It was so genuine and pure that it made me rage inside. It was another reminder of what Dennis had stolen from us.

"Thanks, sis. I'm really happy."

"So is she."

I nodded. I was so anxious for all of this to be over so we could just move on with our lives.

"How are you?" I asked.

She leaned back in her seat, focusing on the road again for a moment before turning back to me.

"I'm... okay. I really am. Today was a good day."

"Yeah."

"I want to figure out who I am again," she said.

"What do you mean?"

"I mean, since Dad died, I have been looking to figure out how to fill that emptiness. I tried it with dating, but most guys are assholes. No offense."

"None taken."

"And you're great. I really couldn't ask for a better brother, but sometimes, I resent the fact that you feel you need to take care of me."

"Brandi—" I started.

She cut me off. "It's not like that. I understand why you think I need to be taken care of. I haven't been the most responsible, that's for damn sure. But I really want to take control of my life. I want to figure this shit out and be the best person I can be."

"You're a great person."

"Thank you, but I see you and Arianna and there's a difference in you. A confidence. It's like you found that piece you needed to level up. Now I need to find mine."

"Like, find a boyfriend?"

She chuckled. "No. I need to figure out how to be okay with myself. College is coming up. I haven't even thought about applying. But I think I want to. I don't know what I want to do yet, but I want to figure out what the rest of my life is going to look like."

"I'll tell you this much," I said, nodding. "Once you

decide what you want to do, you're going to be great at it."

She bit her lip, trying not to get too emotional. So, I figured I'd make it even harder on her.

"I love you, sis."

That did it. The tear dropped from her eye and she laughed, knowing that I got her.

"I love you too, bro."

We didn't grow up in a house where that was said too often, even when our dad was alive. But tonight, knowing what was ahead of me, it was important to tell the two most important people in my life how much I loved them.

***

We got back to the house and found it empty. Dennis's car was gone. Mom mentioned that one of Dennis's co-workers had invited them for dinner since they weren't doing anything big either.

Maybe Dennis would drive home drunk and run them both into a tree, solving all our problems.

I shook the thought out of my head. I certainly had conflicted feelings about my mother right now, but I didn't want to hurt her. Not physically.

Dennis, on the other hand...

Brandi went straight to her room. I told her I felt like

going for a drive.

"Too wound up from your little romp with Arianna after dinner?"

"How'd you...?"

She smirked. I shrugged and wished her good night before getting back into the car.

I could have made the forty-five-minute trek through the woods, but it was easier to drive to the scenic overlook and park there. From that location, it was only a fifteen-minute walk to the old mental hospital.

I'd gone to visit Gunther every couple of days to bring him a sandwich or some other non-processed food. On the weekends, I'd bring him a Dunkin' coffee and a donut. We didn't talk much. It was a little awkward, being that he was my prisoner and all.

When I entered the abandoned building and made my way to his cell, I could see him pacing through the window. He looked agitated.

I opened the slot and slid the container of leftovers and a plastic fork and knife through the opening. He stopped when he saw them.

"Did you have a nice Thanksgiving, Brady?"

I did but I wasn't about to rub it in his face. I noticed his voice sounded different. It reminded me of how Batman used that deep gravelly voice while in costume.

"I bought you some food," I said.

Gunther slapped the container away, its contents

splattering the floor and the wall.

"Fuck you."

"This is almost over."

"It's never over!" he growled at me. "You think you're going to use me to kill your enemies and then we're all just going to go on our merry fucking way? You think there's such a thing as normal for you and me after this?"

"We... we can try."

He put his face right up against the glass, his hot breath steaming it up.

"Try? You're a fool. The wolf. He gets into your very being. He changes you, twists you. The harder I try to keep him at bay, the more he infests my soul."

"We'll find you help."

"That's what I was trying to do!" he bellowed. "But I got stuck in a fucking cave where some pissant little twerp is using me to do his dirty work!"

"Fuck you, man!" I shouted back at him. "That son of a bitch was chasing me! He was trying to hurt me! I was just trying to get away. I didn't tell him to go into your fucking cave!"

Gunther stepped away from the window and started pacing again. He lowered his voice.

"I thought I could run from this. I thought I could stop this."

"You can," I said, not really believing it myself.

He came back to the window, keeping a little more

distance this time.

"Every cycle since I first turned, it gets worse. Every base instinct I have is amplified. As the full moon gets closer, I get more aggressive. Angrier. Hungrier. But last month, when the wolf killed and ate that boy, I woke up feeling better. God help me, for the first time since that initial cycle, I felt like myself again. It was like the wolf needed to be fed. When it was satisfied, it was easier to hold back."

I gulped. "You mean, if you kill... if you feed, you can control it."

"I thought so at first, but now, with the full moon coming, I feel those urges stronger than ever. The more the wolf feeds, the more it needs to."

I didn't know how to respond to that.

He continued. "Before this cycle ends, you're going to make me kill somebody. Maybe they even deserve it. But do you know the worst part of all of this?"

I didn't answer. My silence beckoning him to continue.

"I'm looking forward to it."

CHAPTER 28

I barely slept that night. Gunther's deteriorating mental state haunted me. Maybe I'd made it worse by keeping him locked up. Even in human form, I had caged an animal. And there was nothing more dangerous than that. Maybe if I had let him go, he would have been able to suppress those animal urges better.

Still, it was too late to turn back now. Thankfully, there was no school the Friday after Thanksgiving. I thought about maybe going on a hunt, but to be honest, I'd had more than enough of the woods for a while. I had things I needed to do out there, but I wasn't going to spend a second longer out there than I needed to.

Dennis was actually in a good mood that morning. His knee had finally healed up, on schedule. This was good because my entire plan revolved around him getting back out there to hunt again. He went out early to prep his tree stand, clear off the brush around it and to fill his feeders. The next morning, Dennis McGill would be back in the great outdoors.

I killed time as best I could until he got back. I watched

TV, called Arianna for a bit and tried to catch up on some sleep, an endeavor in which I was only mildly successful.

Dennis got back around three o'clock and, at five, we all convened for dinner. I don't know why we put ourselves through this ordeal night after night, but I guess pantomiming a happy family made everyone feel a little better.

But tonight would be different. I made conversation.

"So, you're all set to get back out there tomorrow, Dennis?"

He was so startled that I addressed him he nearly choked on his roast beef.

"Uh, yeah, Brady. I'm all set."

"I never did get that eight-pointer. He might still be out there."

Brandi eyed me suspiciously, wondering what I was up to. Mom remained disinterested.

"Well," Dennis said, his initial surprise giving way to arrogance, "if I see him first, I'm shooting him, pal."

"May the best hunter win," I told him, before adding with a slight smirk, "Hell, if my dad were still around, he'd get him before either of us. He was the best hunter I ever knew."

Dennis squirmed. Mom put her fork down and took a large gulp of her wine, draining the glass to about a third before refilling it near to the brim.

"Yup," Dennis said without looking up at me. "Your dad

was an excellent hunter."

"Better than you?" I goaded.

"I don't know about that."

"You ever get a twelve-pointer like the one mounted over the fireplace?"

He didn't answer right away. He shoveled food into his mouth and pretended he was chewing to avoid the question.

I kept it up. "You probably wouldn't have to think so long if you did."

Brandi went wide-eyed, fascinated and a little anxious as to where I was going with this.

"I guess not, Brady," he finally answered. "But one big deer doesn't make you the best hunter out there."

"Guess not," I said, taking a bite of my food. "If you think about it, how good could he really be if he couldn't even properly install his tree stand?"

"Brady!" Mom snapped, finally out of her stupor.

I held my hands up in an *I surrender* motion.

"Sorry, Mom," I said putting on my best remorseful tone. "I just get so angry sometimes, thinking about it."

Everyone had their forks down now. They were all staring at me.

"Brady..." Brandi started but stopped not sure how to respond to what I said.

"I guess I'm mad that he wasn't more careful. It just seems so irresponsible to not take the proper precautions when setting up your tree stand. You know what I'm talking about. Right, Dennis?"

Sure you do, you smarmy cocksucker.

"Not sure I follow," he said with trepidation.

"Well," I explained. "You're an expert hunter. I'm sure you confirm your stands are one hundred percent safe before you get up there, don't you?"

"Of course."

You arrogant son of a bitch.

"Of course," I parroted. "He left us all because he couldn't take a few minutes to make sure his tree stand was secure. No offense to you, Dennis. You've been so great taking care of us all these years, but I'm really pissed at my dad sometimes for leaving us. It all feels so... unnecessary."

"I miss your dad too, Brady. He was my best friend. And I'm sure it's a little strange sometimes that your mom and I found each other through all of this, but grief looks different on everyone."

I'm going to dance on your grave mother fucker.

"You're right. I'm sorry I haven't always given you a fair shake."

Mom and Brandi were flabbergasted. Brandi mouthed "What the fuck?"

"It's okay, Brady."

It will be when Gunther shits you out.

I couldn't prevent these vile thoughts from entering my

mind. It was like the wolf was getting into my own soul. I was angry and bloodthirsty. But I was also ashamed at how badly I wanted this vengeance.

Getting up from the table, I loaded my plate in it in, before turning back to my bewildered family.

"I'm going to go chill in my room."

At least until everyone's asleep so I can make my final preparations.

I walked out of the kitchen, but right before I stepped onto the stairs, I turned back.

"Hey Dennis?"

He looked up at me.

"Good luck tomorrow."

CHAPTER 29

Today was the day. Once again, I barely slept after I had done what I needed to in the woods. Once all this nasty business was finished, I'd need to sleep for at least a week to catch up. But right now, I couldn't worry about little things like being tired.

Dennis had always been an early riser on hunting days and I knew he'd be really amped up today to get back out there. The good thing about not sleeping is you don't have to worry about not being where you need to be on time.

I dressed quickly, as if going on my own hunt—which I suppose I was—and went downstairs just in time to see Dennis checking his gear in the kitchen.

"Feeling good about today?" I asked, keeping up my cheery facade from the night before.

"Uh, yeah. Gonna nab that buck," he said, trying to sound more confident than he actually was.

"Not if I nab him first," I said, presenting my fist for a bump. "May the best hunter win."

Dennis hesitated. I don't think I'd ever offered him a

fist bump in my life. But he accepted, even if he didn't know what to make of it.

"See you later," I said as I cheerily exited the house.

My area was a good distance away from where Dennis had set up his stand. I started in that direction, but only went far enough to make sure I was out of sight. Once I was, I watched as Dennis made his way into the woods.

I followed as far back as I could without losing him. Even if I did, I knew exactly where he was going, but I needed to be there to see it when it happened.

When I finally saw him ascend his tree, I hung back and crouched in the bushes. It was unlikely he'd have been able to see me, but I didn't want to take any chances. I watched with anticipation as he climbed each rung of the ladder to get to the stand, holding my breath at one point when I thought I saw it shake. But it held firm and he made it to the top.

No sooner did he rest on the seat, however, than the entire structure came tumbling forward out of the tree. I watched my stepfather flail as if he were trying to fly away from the collapsing stand, feeling a great deal of satisfaction as he hit the ground with a thud.

I ran over and saw him dragging himself out of the seat. He was writhing in pain as he did.

"Dennis!" I called. "Are you okay?"

He turned on his side and saw me approach.

"Brady?" he asked, confused about why I was in his

area, but grateful that I was. "My leg. I think it's broken."

"Oh, no!" I exclaimed with mock concern. "Don't move. Let me see."

I crouched over his lower body and saw that right leg was twisted at an unnatural angle.

"It definitely looks broken," I said.

I pulled up his pant leg and had some trouble getting it just over his shin. He yelped as I did and it was there that I saw a jagged piece of bone sticking through his flesh, blood seeping out around it.

"Oh, shit," I said.

"Is it bad?" He asked.

"Yeah," I confirmed. "What happened?"

"I don't know. Damn stand collapsed as soon as I got up there."

"Let me see," I said. "Don't move."

I took my time inspecting the ruined apparatus, knowing damn well what had happened but not about to let Dennis in on that little tidbit. So, I just took a few minutes pretending to investigate when, in actuality, I was enjoying watching him writhe in pain.

Finally, I held up one of the straps.

"Here's your problem. Looks like the straps broke."

"How?" he asked through gritted teeth. "I checked them yesterday. They're brand new!"

I turned the torn strap around in my hand and held it out toward them.

"They didn't break," I confirmed. "They were cut."

Dennis flailed back as a wave of pain shot through him. "How do you know?"

I stood up and walked back over to where he was lying and stood over him again, this time by his upper body.

"Because I'm the one who cut them."

Before he could respond, I kicked him as hard as I could in his face, knocking him out cold.

***

I could only imagine what Dennis was thinking when he woke up with me pushing him through the woods in a wheelbarrow. Fortunately, I'd had to field dress and drag bucks weighing over 200 pounds out of the woods. Loading Dennis into the wheelbarrow wasn't much different.

As soon as he regained awareness, he tried to yell what I imagine was, "What the—?" But I couldn't be sure since I had stuffed an old rag in his mouth before duct-taping it in place.

He tried to thrash about, but he had no mobility. Before loading him up, I zip-tied his hands and ankles, so he couldn't yell and he couldn't get away.

"Don't bother, Dennis," I told him. "You aren't going anywhere."

He settled a bit, but still thrashed about occasionally, just on principle, I suppose. He yelled something indistinguishable but no doubt profane.

"I'm pretty sure you have a good idea what this is all about. And, in just a bit, it's going to be crystal fucking clear to you."

Even with the wheelbarrow, it was still physically taxing getting my stepfather to his destination, but no matter how much fatigue I was feeling, I still pushed forward. Finally, the abandoned mental hospital came into view.

Dennis started getting agitated again as we got close. I slapped him in the head.

"Calm down. I'm just showing you to your room."

He didn't put up much of a fight the rest of the way. Not that he could if he wanted to. I wheeled him around to the bulkhead doors and opened them up, pushing the wheelbarrow right up to the threshold and tilting it forward, dumping Dennis down the stairs. He tumbled down, smacking into the hard concrete floor below, screaming in pain through his gag.

I rolled the wheelbarrow behind some bushes and entered the building, closing the doors behind me.

It wasn't too far to where I needed to bring him, so I just reached under his armpits and dragged him. As I turned into the main corridor, I saw Gunther looking through the window, watching with an blank face as I dragged the half-conscious man. I stopped halfway down the hall and pulled Dennis into an empty room. There was no bed or any other furniture here so I leaned him up against the wall.

Once he was set, I searched his pockets and came up with his car keys and cell phone. I held his phone up to his face and it unlocked. Unlike Trevor, his face wasn't mangled when I attempted it, hence the success.

I sent a text to my mother.

Dennis: Had to go get some supplies. Saw a big buck. Won't be home for dinner.

With the message delivered, I put the phone and keys in my pocket and left the room. Dennis was moving, but not alert. I locked the door, not needing to reinforce it like I had with Gunther: he turned into a seven-foot-tall monster. My murdering stepdad was a zip-tied 180-pound man with a head injury and compound fracture in his leg. He wasn't going anywhere.

I left the basement, stealing a quick glance toward Gunther's cell, but I didn't see him through the window anymore. I felt it best not to engage with him until tonight's task.

Exiting the building, I retrieved the wheelbarrow and pushed it back through the woods to my house, an easier undertaking than it had been while Dennis was in it. I checked his phone occasionally, but Mom didn't respond to the text. It didn't even come up as read.

I made a pit stop at the tree stand where Dennis had fallen. Removing the sabotaged straps, I replaced them with new ones I had bought a few days ago. I hastily put the stand back up. It wasn't the best job and probably wouldn't hold, but I just needed it to look intact. It didn't need to be functional. After that was done, I gathered Dennis's rifle and tossed it in the wheelbarrow.

When I got home, I deposited the wheelbarrow by the shed and hosed it down. There was no blood inside that I could see, but it was best to err on the side of caution.

I went inside and made myself a sandwich. Truthfully, I was too wound up to eat, but I needed an excuse to make sure no one was around.

Upstairs, I saw both Mom and Brandi's doors shut. I heard the TV coming from Mom's room, so I knew she was distracted. Similarly, Brandi was blasting music. I was in the clear.

Quickly, I went outside and got into Dennis's SUV. He had a large Chevy Suburban which worked great for my purposes. My mother and sister's rooms were on the other side of the house, so even if they were looking out their windows, they wouldn't see that I was the one driving it.

Ten minutes later, I parked at the scenic overlook. Exiting the car, I went back into the woods and navigated to the spot where I had stashed some materials. I put on gloves and retrieved the shovel, axe and garbage bags I had purchased over the past few weeks. After inventorying the items, I tossed everything inside the wheelbarrow . I'd disposed of the stuff I originally used to bury Trevor, but I didn't have to worry about someone finding this new batch of tools. That was the point.

I took a deep breath. This next part was going to be very distasteful.

***

Digging up my dead classmate was not something I had planned on doing, but I needed something of his to plant on Dennis. If this worked, he would not be a problem anymore and, if anyone ever suspected foul play on Trevor, all signs would point to him.

When I had dug deep enough to find the body, I hesitated before unwrapping the tarp from around his face. The first thing I noticed before I even uncovered him was the smell. It was a vilely repugnant odor that nearly made me vomit. It took everything I had to hold it in, not wanting any of my DNA in this hole with him.

Exposing his corpse was even worse. He had been in the ground, un-embalmed and rotting, for a month. What was left of his face was withered, and dried green crust surrounded every orifice, I'm guessing from the fluids leaking out as he decomposed. The remainder of his skin was a mess of red-and-black sludge. His gums appeared to have receded but only a scant few yellowed teeth jutted out of his mouth. I assumed the rest had fallen out somewhere but I wasn't about to look. I couldn't believe that this had once been a human being.

I stood up and grabbed Dennis's rifle. I aimed it at the decaying husk in the hole and fired a single bullet in the space between his now empty eye sockets.

Would that hold up as evidence that he was the one who killed him? I didn't know. I'm sure advanced forensics would show that the bullet wound was inflicted postmortem, but at least it was a bullet from a gun registered to Dennis McGill.

And he wouldn't be around to proclaim his innocence anyway.

As if all this wasn't bad enough, the worst part was yet to come. I picked up the axe and swung it immediately, knowing that if I hesitated for even a second, I might not go through with it. The blade came down on the corpse's neck, detaching the head easily, like cutting the tip off a rotten banana.

Holding back tears, I continued to chop the body into small pieces, depositing them into the garbage bags and wrapping them up as quickly as I could. Once he was in pieces, I pushed the bags back into the hole and covered them up again.

It would have been simple if I could just have stashed

the body in Dennis's trunk, leaving a nice little setup for the cops to get an anonymous tip, but I knew it would raise too many additional questions. Primarily, why was Dennis driving around with a rotting corpse in his trunk for a month? And how did no one notice the smell?

No. I had to dispose of the body somewhere else. After pouring two whole bottles of bleach in the hole and covering it with dirt once again, I piled the bags in the wheelbarrow and rolled it through the woods to the river, taking great care to survey my surroundings at all times to make sure I didn't run into a hiker or fellow hunter just making their way through the woods.

When I got to the river, I pushed the wheelbarrow over and let the current take the garbage bags downstream. I had weighed each one down with weights I had taken from Dennis's home gym. That, combined with the weight of the body, was enough to make them sink before they made it too far down the river.

I returned to the car an hour later, tired and dirty. I opened Dennis's trunk and deposited the shovel and axe inside. After that, I unwrapped the small rag and let Trevor's severed pinky finger fall inside. Before I put his left arm in the bag, I had chopped and wrapped the finger so I could stash it, driving the point home that Dennis was the one behind his death. Using the rag, I pushed it behind the wheel well, hidden at first glance, but not so camouflaged that it wouldn't be found in a thorough search.

My watch showed it was just after 3 p.m. I still had a couple hours before the main event.

***

That evening, Brandi told me that mom said Dennis would not be home and she didn't feel much like eating so she gave Brandi and me money to order takeout. I told my sister I wasn't hungry either so she should just get whatever she wanted.

She shrugged and didn't ask questions, which was good because I didn't want to have to lie to her about what I was up to.

A little after five o'clock, the sun fell over the horizon. It was time.

CHAPTER 30

The sun was almost down by the time I entered the building where my captives were held, my shotgun loaded with silver slugs slung over my shoulder. I headed first to Dennis's room and unlocked it. He was half asleep when I walked in, but his head popped up as soon as he saw me. He started shouting through the gag again. I slapped him hard.

"Shut. The fuck. Up," I told him.

I grabbed his collar and dragged him out of the room, down the hall toward his fate. I let him fall to the floor when I reached the reinforced cell and quickly unlocked each of the padlocks before opening the door and shoving him inside.

Gunther was sitting on the bed, watching quietly as I delivered his next meal.

Dennis looked at the man, confused, then back at me, his eyes pleading for an explanation.

"Dennis, meet Gunther," I said, nodding in the bearded man's direction.

I dragged my stepfather over to the chair by the

window and hoisted him up. I pulled out my hunting knife and his eyes went wide.

"Calm down, I'm not going to stab you," I told him.

That was true. I had no intention of using the knife for anything other than cutting the zip tie around his ankles, which I did in one swift motion. His legs instinctively drifted apart and he cried in pain as his broken one moved.

Next, I reached behind and ripped the tape that held the gag off, a nice chunk of hair coming with it, eliciting another yelp of pain from the man who had killed my father. I almost laughed as I did, inappropriately recalling the body waxing scene from *The 40-Year-Old Virgin*.

"What the fuck?" Dennis exclaimed. "What are you doing, Brady? Who the fuck is this?"

I punched him in the face. His head flung back and blood gushed out of his nose immediately.

"I'm not going to tell you again. Shut up. I'm doing the talking here."

"You better talk fast, kid," Gunther interjected. I looked at him and he added, "Time's running out."

I focused back on Dennis.

"You killed my father," I said bluntly.

"Are you crazy?" he asked. "I didn't—"

I slapped him.

"Don't deny it," I told him. "You sabotaged his tree stand and he died. All because you were fucking my mother behind his back."

"Brady," he said, trying to act calmly. "Where did you get this idea? Your dad was my best friend. I loved him."

I yanked the gun off my shoulder and pressed the barrel against his forehead.

"Don't you ever say that, you piece of shit. I know the truth. There was no way my father would have used the wrong pins in his tree stand. It was you."

"That's all you're going on? The wrong pins? You're going to kill me based on that? You're so sure, you're going to make your mother a widow for a second time?"

Dennis was trying to get into my head, but it wasn't working. He'd always been a con artist and he was just trying to throw me off.

My stepfather knew he wasn't going to get through to me so he turned his attention to Gunther.

"How are you involved in this?"

Gunther didn't respond.

"Listen, friend, I don't know what my stepson has told you, but he's emotionally unstable. Help me get out of this and I'll make sure you don't get in any trouble. I'll forget you were even here."

Gunther shook his head and stood up. He looked taller to me. "Sorry, mister. This is out of my hands. It's just like I said to Brady when he brought you in here."

He faced me and Dennis and I saw that his eyes had turned yellow.

"Time's up."

I had to act fast so I backed out of the room as quick as I could and slammed the door shut, hurriedly working to secure each padlock.

With the locks secured, I looked in just in time to see Dennis lunging forward. His broken leg couldn't support his weight so he fell to the floor, but he immediately started dragging himself onward, trying desperately to get to the door.

Gunther was standing behind him. He now had hair all over his face and he was smiling with a mouthful of razor-sharp teeth, saliva dripping into his ever-expanding beard.

Dennis stole a glance behind him and screamed. It was a high-pitched wail that gave me great satisfaction.

There was no doubt Gunther had grown at this point. His head was almost touching the ceiling. The hoodie and sweatpants he wore were ripping at the seams as his muscles bulged and stretched. A steady groan of pain gave way to an animal growl as his nose and mouth widened into a snout.

Dennis had reached the door at this point and used the knob to pull himself upward. He gripped the bottom frame of the window and was able to hold on just enough to support himself in a standing position.

He pounded on the glass, a look of fear in his face unlike anything I'd ever seen.

I met his eyes. I had nothing left to say. It was Dennis's time to pay for his sins.

The last thing I heard was him say the word "please" before the monstrous wolf head appeared behind him and sank its teeth into his shoulder, my stepfather's pleas turning to a screech of agony.

I turned away as he continued to scream. When I decided to carry through with this plan, I expected I would relish watching the man who killed my father get torn apart by a werewolf, but now I couldn't help but look away. Maybe I would feel some satisfaction in the coming days and weeks, but right now I was watching the ugly outcome of my quest for vengeance.

The screaming stopped and I willed myself to turn back to look. Only, this time, I came face to face with the werewolf on the other side of the glass. Its eyes were narrowed and its mouth curled into a snarl, blood and saliva flowing from its mouth. It was as if the creature was staring into my very soul.

I stood transfixed, unsure whether I should run but, as I tried to decide, the beast thrust all its weight against the door. I jumped back. Before I could register what was happening, it slammed into the barricade again, and this time the hinges groaned and bent.

The door wasn't going to hold.

I raised my shotgun and aimed it at the window, hoping it could see. Hoping that would deter it from continuing.

"Gunther!" I shouted. "Stop!"

The beast backed up and barreled into the door once more. I heard the door frame crack as the whole thing came loose.

The werewolf was free.

CHAPTER 31

The creature stared me down as it stepped out into the hall. I trained my gun on it.

"Gunther. Don't," I pleaded.

It leaped toward me, going low. I pulled the trigger, but the blast went over its head as it dove into my midsection, knocking me halfway across the room, the shotgun sliding from my grip. Until this point, I had only seen this thing in captivity. I was not prepared for how fast it actually was. One second, I had a clear shot. The next I didn't.

The werewolf started approaching me more slowly this time, stalking me. My weapon was gone so it must have perceived that I was no longer a threat. As it drew closer, I reached behind me and pulled the Glock out of the holster affixed to the back of my belt. I didn't hesitate, firing six times center mass.

I hit on all six shots, but all it did was knock the wolf back maybe half a step. As I theorized, regular bullets had no effect. I had to get out of there.

I ran down the hall, firing wildly behind me as I did.

The clip held ten bullets so I could only get off four more shots and I don't know if any of them actually hit the creature. All I knew was that it was still moving toward me. I pressed the release on the grip of my gun and let the clip fall to the floor.

With the wolf hot on my trail, I ran around the corner and toppled an old filing cabinet next to the entrance, I turned back just in time to see the monster bound over it, not slowing for even a second. I was running as fast as I could, but Gunther was gaining ground on me. The bulkhead doors were only a few feet away and my only hope for escape.

As soon as I hopped up the small stairway, I pushed as hard as I could against the metal door. Over the past few weeks, it had been an effort to open and close them every time I came here to prepare. This time was no different. The door groaned as I tried to shove it open, but it moved only slowly.

Just as I became aware I wasn't going to make it out in time, I felt a vice grip around my ankle. I looked down to see the yellow eyes and white, blood-slicked teeth emerging from the darkness of the basement as the wolf pulled me in close. I tried to break free, but it was too strong. It started dragging me down the stairs.

I did the only thing I could think of at that point: I pulled the spare clip for the Glock from my pocket and quickly popped it in and chambered the round before firing three more shots directly into the werewolf's face.

It reeled back but didn't release me. Its free hand went to the fresh wounds in its face and wiped the blood away. While it tried to clear its vision, it let out the most vicious roar I'd heard yet, its mouth opened wide.

I aimed the gun at its open mouth, but before I could pull the trigger, I felt my body yanked abruptly, like the freefall ride at Six Flags. The wolf tossed me clean across the room, and my body skidded across the concrete. I thanked God I had several layers of clothing to cushion me. It still hurt like hell. Why he threw me instead of just biting me, I'll never know, but even though the bullets didn't seem like they were doing significant damage, they still must have hurt like hell. He must have been trying to put some distance between us before I could shoot again.

When I made my way up to a sitting position, the wolf was already bounding toward me, I rolled to the left, narrowly avoiding the hulking beast landing on me. I got to my feet and fired twice more, the second shot clipping it in the shoulder. It grabbed the wound with its hand, but, again, the regular bullets did nothing.

I ran toward a door in the distance, not sure where it led. The wolf was blocking my way back to my shotgun and I didn't have time to get through the bulkhead doors, so I only had one option. Hopefully, the door wasn't locked.

Thankfully, it wasn't. I was also lucky it was a *push* and

not a *pull* because, losing even a step right now could mean certain death.

Shutting the door behind me I saw that I was in a stairwell. I didn't think; I just ran up the stairs, barely making it to the first landing when I heard Gunther burst through the door. I turned the corner and headed up to the second flight. There was a door at the end, but I could see debris through the window. Not wanting to chance it, I pivoted and ran up to the next landing, I could hear the wolf behind me. It was not moving as fast, but I still wasn't putting enough distance between us.

The staircase ended on the next level and, from what I could see through the window, it wasn't blocked, so I ran and grabbed the handle, this side being a *pull*. Only, this time, the door didn't open. It was locked. This decrepit fucking piece of shit building still had locked doors. No matter how hard I pulled, it didn't budge.

I turned and aimed my gun down the stairs. I didn't see the werewolf, but I heard it, a small, low growl accompanying its slow ascent. It was stalking me now, savoring the anticipated kill.

Looking around in panic, I was unsure of what to do. I braced my foot against the wall and tried to pull again. Still nothing. I turned back and saw it.

The wolf was at the landing right below me. It stood there, chest heaving as it breathed heavily, salivating in anticipation of what it would do to me. I saw half a dozen bullet wounds in its chest, face and shoulder, not a single one appearing to impede it.

It looked like it was almost smiling.

I turned back and frantically pulled the handle, to no avail. The wolf took the first step toward me. It knew it didn't have to rush. One step followed another, slow and deliberate.

The wolf was halfway up the stairs now, almost to where it could swipe me with his claw if it really wanted to.

With one last desperate move, I took aim at the door handle and fired three shots. The last one did the trick, as I saw the door pull away from the frame. I slid to the right and yanked it open, pushing my way in, just as the wolf lunged. I tried to shut the door, but its massive arm prevented me from closing it all the way. I shot twice more, one lodging in its elbow joint, the other in its bicep as the beast pulled its arm back in pain. That was the good news. The bad news was that the gun was now empty. I pulled the door all the way shut, even though I knew it wouldn't stop it.

As I ran as fast as I could down the hall as I heard a mighty crash which I could only assume was the door being completely ripped off. Once I made it to the end, I moved around the corner. On my right, I immediately saw a pair of elevators. One set of doors was completely open. I looked inside and saw the car was down below me. Looking back down the hall to my left, I tried to see if there was another viable exit, but there wasn't. The wolf would be back on me in only a few seconds, so I did the only thing I could.

I jumped.

When I hit the elevator car, it shuddered under my weight. I thought it was going to collapse, but it held. There was a maintenance hatch with a handle in the corner. I guess they weren't just convenient plot devices in movies. Even so, I wasn't going to question this stroke of luck. I pulled it open and dropped inside the elevator.

The doors inside were shut. I wedged my fingers in the gap and tried to pull them apart. They moved, but slowly, likely rusted from being abandoned all these years. I put all my strength into it, trying to get them to open just enough for me to squeeze through.

It took effort, but they did move. Finally, it looked like it was enough for me to get through. Unfortunately, that was also the moment I felt a huge weight land on the top of the car. The whole thing shook and then fell.

For the second time in the past ten minutes, I was reminded of the freefall ride. My stomach took a vacation to my throat as we fell. It was only one story, but the impact when we landed knocked me off my feet and back against the wall.

The shock disoriented me and, for a minute, I couldn't move. It wasn't until I felt something wet drip on my forehead that I regained enough of my faculties to rouse myself and assess my surroundings.

I saw the wolf through the maintenance hatch. The beast growled and reached its clawed hand through, swiping at me. If it was toying with me before, the game was now over. I had well and truly pissed this thing off and it wanted nothing more than to tear my head from my shoulders.

Rolling to the front of the elevator, I stood up. As the wolf continued to flail its arm through the opening, I realized it couldn't get through the hatch. This was my chance.

I pushed my way through the opening and out into another hallway. I was back in the basement after the fall, so I ran in the opposite direction from which I'd come on the top floor. Sure enough, I found the door to the wing with the cells. My luck held: this one was unlocked, which was good considering the lack of ammo in my pistol.

The shotgun was where I had dropped it. I ran toward it and scooped it up off the floor, heading to the cell that had been Gunther's home for the past few weeks. I stepped over the busted door and went inside, a small gasp escaping when I saw Dennis on the ground. In all the commotion and effort to stop myself from becoming werewolf food, I'd forgotten he was even here.

He was propped up against the wall. His shirt was

completely ripped open and a huge chunk of flesh was missing from his shoulder, right below his neck. I couldn't help but think how similar it was to what had happened to Trevor. There were claw marks, blood and chunks of flesh everywhere. It did not disembowel him like my classmate, but he looked very dead. I guess Gunther was focused on getting his revenge on me before he was going to stop and eat.

"Fuck you, you piece of shit," I said in a farewell to my stepfather, before focusing my attention back on the corridor.

The wolf would be here soon. There was no doubt. Time to find out if these homemade shells worked.

Before long, I heard the heavy footsteps of the seven-foot-tall lycanthrope. It appeared in the doorway at the end of the hall and crouched to get through. The wolf stood across from me, ready to end this. But so was I.

The creature didn't hesitate. It ran toward me. I pulled the trigger.

The blast hit it directly in the chest and flung it backward. The wolf landed hard on its back, incapacitated for the first time that I'd seen. Slowly, it reached to its chest to feel the wound, but its arms fell back to its sides. It was motionless.

I pumped the shotgun and expelled the casing while simultaneously loading the next one. I led with the gun as I cautiously approached the felled monster.

When I got close enough, I could see the large cavity created by the blast. It was oozing blood as the edges smoked. I thought that was a little odd seeing as I'd never seen that effect on any deer I'd ever shot.

Whether or not it was dead, I really didn't know. It sure looked dead, though.

It wasn't.

The werewolf lunged forward, arms outstretched, but it didn't go for me; it just started flailing around. I jumped back, putting some distance between us.

More smoke started pouring from the wound as the beast screamed in unholy pain. It opened its mouth for what I thought would be another roar, but instead it vomited up a copious amount of dark-red blood. It kept spewing long after I thought it would stop.

The wolf writhed in pain as its body convulsed so hard that I wouldn't have been surprised if bones snapped. I watched as it changed, this time in reverse. The creature shrunk back down to human size as its hair receded. Its snout and mouth sank in on itself and soon resembled a person once again.

I was now looking at the man I'd first found in the cave, his massive chest wound leaving no doubt that he would not survive. He let out one last gasp as the rest of his breath left his body and he fell back to the ground, eyes wide and blood seeping from his mouth and chest.

The silver had worked.

Gunther was dead.

I lowered my shotgun, the barrel still smoking, I saw blood everywhere. And the bodies, ravaged and mangled. It wasn't supposed to go like this. I had just tried to help and now there was nothing but carnage and death surrounding me.

I had fucked up big time.

CHAPTER 32

My plan had totally gone off the rails. I hadn't thought that the wolf would be able to break free, but he had and now I was fucked, with no clue what to do next. The only thing I could think of was to run. I'd get in the car and drive as far as I could. Find somewhere to lie low.

I could have taken the shorter route and run back to where I parked Dennis's car. With all the evidence I had planted inside, the idea of driving it made me more than a little uneasy, so I opted to run instead. My lungs burned and every bone in my body ached, but I made it home, not slowing until my house emerged from the tree line.

Once I arrived, I didn't bother trying to be quiet as I rushed inside, despite the fact that it was well after midnight. No one was on the first floor, so I made my way to my room. I immediately pulled out a large duffel bag and started tossing clothes inside. I also grabbed my phone charger and my wallet before retrieving a box of nine-millimeter ammo and reloading both clips for the Glock which I also tossed in the bag.

As I packed, I caught a glimpse of myself in the mirror. I

was a total mess, covered in dirt, dust and blood. Quickly shedding what I was wearing, I tossed it in another bag. I'd get rid of these articles on the way to wherever the hell I was going.

I wrapped myself in a towel and hurried to the bathroom, turning on the shower and stepping in without even letting it warm up. The cold water was shocking and it felt like every nerve ending in my battered body fired at once. But I couldn't worry about that now. I had to clean myself up and get out of here as soon as I could.

Once I had scrubbed all the grime off, I got out and dried myself quickly. As I stepped into the hallway, I saw Brandi's door open. She peeked her head out and looked surprised at the sight of me.

"Brady?" she asked. "What's going on?"

"Be quiet," I whispered. "Come here."

She followed me into my room and I shut the door behind us. I asked her to turn around as I got dressed, my clothes sticking to my still wet skin.

"Okay," I said when I was done.

Brandi turned and looked confused as ever. "What the hell are you doing?" she asked.

I stopped and approached her, putting my hands on her shoulders.

"Listen, I can't explain everything right now. I have to go away for a bit."

"What the hell are you talking about?"

"I'll explain when I can but listen to me very carefully. Dennis is gone."

She looked both confused and frightened. "What do you mean, gone?"

"He's gone. He's not going to hurt us anymore."

"*Hurt us?* What..."

"I'd say you should come with me, but I don't want you mixed up in this any more than you already are."

"Mixed up in what?"

"You can't trust Mom."

"Holy shit, Brady. What the fuck are you talking about?"

"Mom and Dennis..."

Before I could finish my sentence, there was a pounding knock at my door.

"Brady! Open up!"

It was my mother.

"What?" I yelled through the door.

"Open up."

I went into my bag and grabbed the Glock. Brandi was stunned.

"What the fuck are you doing?" she whispered.

I held my finger up to my lips, shushing her as I went to the door and cracked it open, the gun behind my back. Mom stood there, her robe sloppily tied over her nightgown, still looking like she was half-asleep.

"Brady, what the hell is going on? Why are you running

around up here like a crazy person?" she asked before she noticed Brandi over my shoulder. "What are you two up to?"

"You really want to know?" I asked, ready to drop the hammer on her.

Before she could respond, we heard a loud crash downstairs in the direction of the kitchen. Mom jumped with a start and looked back at us. I shut the door for a second and then reopened it, trying to make it look like I had to go get my gun and not that I had it ready to use on her if necessary.

I pulled the slide back to ready it as I took the lead, Mom and Brandi following close behind me. We slowly made our way downstairs, not hearing anything after the initial commotion. Cautiously, gun drawn, I entered the kitchen and my blood ran cold at what I saw.

Dennis was sprawled out on the kitchen floor in a growing pool of blood. My mother and sister screamed at the sight of him. I thought for sure he'd been dead when I left him, but somehow, he'd made his way all the way back here. I looked out the window and saw his car parked in the driveway, the door open. He must have had the wherewithal to crawl to it and drive back here. I never should have left it so close to the building.

I was in complete shock, a million scenarios running through my head. He wasn't moving. He wasn't speaking, but when he did, he would surely pin this on me. I should put a bullet in his head right here, right now, but then Brandi would be a part of this too.

The choice was taken from me because while I was standing in a state of complete stunned paralysis, I hadn't noticed that my mom had grabbed her cell phone. Not until I heard her say: "I need an ambulance, now!"

CHAPTER 33

Mom, Brandi and I sat in the emergency room waiting area while the doctors worked on Dennis. I couldn't believe he'd survived all of this. He hadn't regained consciousness between the time we found him and when we got here, but I had no clue what was going on behind those doors.

I thought about leaving. Following through with my plan to run, but I didn't want to rouse my mother's suspicion. She had grilled me in the car on the way over. Had I seen him while we were hunting? Were there bears loose in the area? Did I know what could have done this to him?

I played dumb even though I knew damn well what had done this to him.

A werewolf mauled your murdering garbage pile of a husband, you unfaithful bitch.

Brandi kept looking over at me, that twin telepathy in play again. She knew I had more information than I was letting on, but she also was going to keep it to herself until she knew exactly what was happening. She wasn't going to betray me. I was sure of that much.

My mother alternated between a zombie-like trance and fits of crying. Her tears pissed me off. I didn't know if they were legitimate or not, but I couldn't care less. If there was genuine pain behind them, I was glad. I had no more love for this woman. Our relationship was strained the second she inserted Dennis into our lives. Now knowing the origins of their coupling, the only thing I felt toward her was hatred.

But I had to play along for now. If I was lucky, Dennis would die back there and just maybe I would have a chance at salvaging my plan. I would have to let Brandi in on more than I was comfortable with, but I was sure that once she knew what they had done to our father that she would be on board. I just hated that she would end up being an accessory to this mess I created.

While I was lost in thought, a voice broke my concentration.

"Mr. Bennett."

I looked up and instantly felt the lump in my throat. Detective Wallace was standing over us. This had just gone from bad to worse.

"Detective," I said. "Uh, what are you doing here?"

He sat down in the row of chairs across from us.

"Well, Brady," he said, pulling out his notepad. "When I heard the call come in about an... animal attack... at your address, I told my colleagues I would handle this call, since we've met before."

Mom and Brandi looked confused.

"When did you meet this man?" Mom asked.

Wallace didn't give me a chance to answer. "Brady and I crossed paths while I was investigating the disappearance of one of his classmates. Trevor Wright."

Brandi shot me a look. I didn't look at her; I just willed her to be cool.

"Why didn't you tell me about this, Brady?" Mom asked.

Again, Wallace answered for me. "It was just a few questions at school. Nothing formal."

I nodded to corroborate. The detective turned his attention to my mother.

"Mrs. McGill, I'm sorry about your husband."

Mom started crying again. I tried hard not to look too disdainful.

"Thank you, Detective."

"Can you tell me what happened?"

Mom recounted what little she knew. Dennis went out hunting in the morning. He texted her later in the day to let her know he wouldn't be home for dinner in the late afternoon. That was the last she heard from him before finding him mauled and bloody on the kitchen floor. Wallace took notes the whole time she spoke.

"What about you, Brady?" he asked.

"What about me?"

"Did you see or hear anything?"

"No. Just like my mom said. We woke up and went hunting, but I didn't see or hear from him until we found him tonight."

"So, you're a hunter as well?"

Fuck.

"Yes, but we cover separate areas."

"Mm hm," Wallace said, scribbling more notes. "Did you see anything in the woods? A bear perhaps? From what the officers on the scene said, it looked like he had been attacked by a rather large animal. One of the guys thought it may have been a wolf, but it would have to be one hell of a giant-sized breed. But, as far as I know, there aren't any wolves in the wild in New Jersey, but I'm not an outdoorsman like you. Is that your understanding? No wolves around here?"

"I don't believe so."

"I suppose one could have escaped from a zoo or something, but we would have gotten a report if that was the case."

"I guess."

The policeman wrote a few more notes and then stuffed the pad back in his jacket pocket. He leaned toward us.

"We won't know until Mr. McGill regains consciousness, but we'll send a team out to the woods tomorrow to see if we can find whatever did this."

My blood froze. If they made their way into the old mental hospital, they'd find a very dead man with a very large hole in his chest. Courtesy of my shotgun.

I tried to play it cool, though. I just nodded.

Detective Wallace stood and walked over to us, shaking Brandi's hand, then my mother's.

"I'm very sorry for what you're going through, Mrs. McGill. I'll say a prayer for your husband."

Save it for someone who deserves it.

Mom continued her poor, grieving wife act and thanked him through her crocodile tears. The detective then walked over to me and reached out his hand. I stood and shook it.

"Stay out of trouble, Brady. You seem to have a knack for being in the wrong place at the wrong time."

"Yes, sir," I said.

Unlike that day at school, he held the handshake a little longer than I was comfortable with, but he eventually let go and left the waiting room.

As soon as he was gone, I felt an overwhelming need to get out of there. Fortunately, the doctor came out a few minutes later as I was contemplating how I could sneak away. He told us that Dennis lost a lot of blood and was suffering from a host of other injuries including the compound fracture in his leg, a collapsed lung and a separated shoulder. Despite all that, the doctor said he was stable, which the staff concurred was nothing short of a miracle.

"Can I see him?" Mom asked.

"Once we get him set up in the ICU, we'll bring you back."

That was my chance. I stood up and tossed my keys to Brandi.

"Sis," I said, "stay with Mom, okay? I need to go back and check the perimeter around our house to make sure it's safe."

Brandi was shocked. Two hours ago, I told her she couldn't trust our mother and now I was asking her to stay with her. It didn't matter how untrustworthy my mother was, I needed both of them away from the house while I cleaned up.

"Brady, I don't want you going looking for some dangerous animal," Mom said.

Like you actually fucking care.

"I'll be safe. I promise."

"Brady," my sister added. "Maybe she's right."

"Brandi. Trust me. Please."

She saw the conviction in my eyes and gave me a slight nod. I made myself a promise that I would make this up to her.

"I'll be fine."

***

I drove home as fast as I could without attracting attention. The last thing I needed was to get pulled over. As soon as I parked in the driveway, I hopped out and ran inside the house and straight to the kitchen. I almost slipped on the blood that was still pooled on the tile floor but avoided it just in time. I retrieved a pair of latex gloves from under the sink and pulled them on. With my fingerprints shielded, I headed for the front door, grabbing Dennis's spare keys off the hook by the entryway. I exited the house and hurried to Dennis's car. I couldn't do what I needed to using my own.

When I opened the door, I immediately saw bloodstains all over the interior so I grabbed a blanket out of my trunk and laid it across the seat before I sat, repulsed at the squelching sound the combination of fabric and blood made as my body weight sank down.

I drove to the abandoned mental hospital.

When I arrived, I looked around. It appeared the coast was clear. I went back in through the bulkhead doors and headed right to the corridor with the cells.

An overwhelming feeling of guilt washed over me when I saw Gunther's dead body lying there. I didn't know why. We weren't friends. He was just a strange man who turned into a monster. Maybe he was a raging psycho even as a human. On the other hand maybe he was just a man who'd ended up getting dealt a bad hand. Maybe he was trying his hardest not to hurt anyone when

I came into his life and fucked that all up. Now he was dead and it was my fault.

"I'm sorry, Gunther."

It felt wrong using the made-up name I'd given him as a joke, but that was the only way I knew him, so it would have to do.

Once again, I went about the business of wrapping up a dead body. I brought him up and out and put him in the trunk of Dennis's car. There was far too much blood to clean up, even more than when I had left, the result of Dennis dragging himself up and out of the building.

I drove twenty minutes to the next town. There was a small marina about five minutes off of the exit. Since it was almost December, it was likely there wouldn't be anyone there.

When I arrived, I parked as far back as I could. As I thought, there was no one around, so I opened the trunk and dragged Gunther's body to the nearest pier and rolled him off into the water. I watched as the current took him away.

I mouthed one more silent apology and then drove home.

Brandi and my mom still weren't home when I got there, so I went about making sure the trunk was clean of Gunther's blood, even though I'd seen enough crime shows to know there was always some manner of evidence left behind. But it was Dennis's car, so my hope was any blame would fall on him and hopefully he'd be dead by then, so he couldn't deny it.

But what if Dennis didn't die? Sure, he was in bad shape, but the way he looked back at the asylum, there was no way he should have even made it this far.

I wondered if my plan was a bust. It had certainly gone far off the rails. I thought about getting rid of the evidence I'd planted in the trunk, but I held off. This had gone too far to turn back.

I had to see how it all would play out.

CHAPTER 34

The next week was tense. Dennis remained in the hospital in a coma, but the fucker just wouldn't die. I wondered if he had been infected by whatever had made Gunther become a werewolf. After all, wasn't that what Gunther had said happened? That he got bitten by a werewolf?

So now, not only did I have to worry about the fact that my stepfather might wake up at any moment and tell the police that I tried to have him killed, but I also had to worry that he would turn into a fucking supernatural monster.

Mom went up there every day. She gave us some updates, but there wasn't much to tell. Brandi pushed me to tell her what was going on. I promised her I would, but we needed to see what happened with Dennis first. She was scared, but I assured her I wouldn't let anything happen to her.

Arianna was supportive. She knew there were issues between me and Dennis, but I hadn't shared my newfound knowledge about my father's death. I spun my stressed-out state into concern for my family. She had also learned since we'd started dating that my relationship with my mother was strained, but she was still my mom and my concern for her right now was easily believable.

By Friday, it was getting clear to me that there was a very good chance that Dennis might not die. The fact that he'd survived his injuries only lent credence to my theory that he was going to end up like Gunther. In our limited interactions, the stranger had at least tried to come off as a decent person and I wanted to believe that was true. Dennis, on the other hand, had been a killer from the start. If he became a werewolf, he may not go to the lengths Gunther said he did to keep himself from harming others.

I had to end it.

My mother had spent most of her time at the hospital that day, but she came home late in the afternoon, looking exhausted. She told us she was going to rest and go back up tomorrow. This was my chance.

Just after 6 p.m., I knocked on Brandi's door. She let me in and I sat on her bed. She sat down next to me.

"I'm going to tell you what I can."

She didn't answer, she just nodded for me to continue.

"Dennis killed Dad."

My sister shook her head like she didn't comprehend what I was saying. "What?"

"I overhead him and Mom arguing a few weeks ago. They'd been having an affair for years before Dad died."

"No," she said sounding irritated. "She wouldn't."

"Wouldn't she?"

She opened her mouth to protest, but I think she realized it was a very plausible scenario.

"Why would she do that?"

"I don't know and I don't fucking care. She betrayed Dad. And he died because of it."

"You don't think... that Mom..."

"Yeah. Not directly. But the way she was yelling at Dennis, saying that he was going to make her have an accident too. She knew damn well what Dennis did."

Brandi sat silent for the next few minutes. Her eyes were welling up and she bit her lip, looking like she was trying to keep from a full-on breakdown. Finally, she asked, "So what changed between her and Dennis?"

"I don't know, but she said Dennis wasn't attracted to her anymore. That he was lusting over you or something."

Brandi looked disgusted.

"I think I'm going to be sick," she said as I continued.

"When Mom made that comment about having an accident of her own, it prompted me to do some digging. I looked at the life insurance forms. The accident report said Dad's tree stand wasn't put together right. There was no way he would have done it wrong. Dennis sabotaged it."

"Jesus Christ, Brady. How do you know that?"

"I just know."

"I'm not a lawyer, but I think you need more than that."

"Brandi. It was him. It was."

I could tell she wanted to believe me, but she didn't have the same conviction. Something must have popped into her head because her face screwed up and she asked me another question.

"Did you have something to do with what happened to Dennis?"

I didn't answer, but she saw it in my face.

"Oh, my God, Brady. What did you do?"

I dodged the question. "I'm going to finish this. Please, stay here and steer clear of Mom. Once I do this last thing, it'll be over. I promise."

"Brady, what are you saying?"

I got up and kissed her on the cheek.

"I love you, sis."

She didn't respond and I couldn't bear to glance back in her direction.

I left the house.

***

On my drive to the hospital, I called Arianna. She picked up on the second ring.

"Hey!" she said, her exuberant voice full of cheer.

"Hi," I said.

"What's wrong?" she asked, immediately recognizing the stress in my tone. "Did something happen with your stepfather?"

"No. Nothing like that. Just wanted to hear your voice."

"Brady, Come on. I know you a little better than that by now."

"I... I just... I love you."

"I love you too but you're freaking me out."

"I'm sorry. I've just got myself in a jam. I'm not sure how I'm going to handle it, but I just wanted you to know how I feel about you."

"Of course I know. What's this really about?"

"I have to go. I love you."

"Brady, don't do anything stupid. Please."

I hung up.

I was about to do something stupid.

CHAPTER 35

When I had to sign in at the hospital, I figured that would seal my fate. By the time I left, Dennis would be dead and the police would see that I had been the last person to visit him. The autopsy would no doubt show the silver nitrate pumped into his veins via the IV and a quick search of my online shopping history would show I was the one who bought it.

I'd have to run, but I knew I wouldn't get far before the cops caught up to me and I'd end up in jail. Despite all that, however, I felt a sense of peace. I had been living a nightmare for over two months and, to be honest, any ending would be a welcome one as long as no one else got hurt. I couldn't risk Dennis turning into a werewolf. If that meant my life, so be it.

The elevator dinged as I arrived in the ICU. I went to the front desk and asked what room Dennis McGill was in, identifying myself as his stepson. A kindly older nurse pointed me toward his room. It was back at the end of the corridor, which suited my purposes.

I reached into my pocket and felt the syringe and the

small chemical bottle that would finally rid the world of the monster that had killed my dad and corrupted my mom. It was time to end this once and for all.

Except that it wasn't going to end tonight. I felt like I was going to faint when I entered the room and saw Dennis sitting upright in bed. He was covered in bandages and his leg was in a cast, but otherwise looked okay. He didn't seem the least bit surprised to see me. In fact, he looked... happy.

"Brady!" he exclaimed. "I'm so glad to see you!"

I couldn't figure out what to make of this. If it wasn't for the bandages, it wouldn't have even looked like he was injured at all.

"Uh, hi, Dennis," I said not knowing what else to say. "How are you feeling?"

"You know, I actually feel great. Like I just caught up on some badly needed sleep. But now I'm finally awake."

His cheeriness made me very uncomfortable.

"In fact, I just woke up not that long ago. The nurse told me I was attacked by some kind of animal."

"You don't remember?"

"Nope," he replied. "It's the damnedest thing. I remember leaving the house that morning, but after that, it's all blank. Crazy, right?"

Bullshit.

"Yeah," I agreed. "Crazy."

"Come on over," he said gesturing to the chair next to

the bed. "Have a seat."

I thought it best to play along. I couldn't exactly inject the chemicals into the IV now. Not without him alerting the staff. I took a seat next to him, inching the chair back a little to keep some distance.

"Any luck finding that buck?" he asked.

"No. Didn't see him."

"Too bad," Dennis replied with a nod before adding, "I'll tell you one thing, though: I'd love to have seen whatever animal had a go at me. They thought it was a bear or a wolf or something."

"That's what they told us."

"You didn't see anything like that out there?"

"No."

"Hmm. Oh well."

We sat in awkward silence. Well, awkward for me anyway. I still wasn't buying the amnesia act. After a few minutes, he broke the silence.

"You were with Brandi before you came here?" he asked.

I was confused.

"Yeah. Why?"

"No reason. I can just... smell her on you."

Fuck. He knew. He knew everything that happened and everything that was happening. He was fucking with me.

"I guess she was wearing perfume or something."

"No. It's not her perfume. I can smell *her*. It's very distinct. You can't smell it?"

"No, why would I? That's a weird thing to say."

"Oh. I'm sorry. Didn't mean to offend."

He absolutely meant to offend.

"How is your sister? The nurses said Mom's been up here, but Brandi hasn't come to see me."

"She came with us to the emergency room when they brought you in. But you know Brandi. She's not great with these kinds of things."

"Yeah. I guess you're right."

I stood up, needing to get out of there. "Well, Dennis, I'm glad you're healing up. I should get home."

He grabbed my hand and held it in one of his, covering it with the other. "Thank you, son."

That sent me into orbit. More so than usual. I wanted nothing more than to jam the syringe in his eye. But I didn't. I'd been ready to go to jail when I walked in here, but Dennis being awake and alert threw me off.

"You're welcome," was all I could think to say before I walked to the door.

"Oh, Brady?" Dennis called after me. I stopped but didn't turn around. "I'm looking forward to getting out of here. See you soon."

Chapter 36

I dialed Brandi as soon as I got out of the elevator on the first floor. It went straight to voice mail. Goddamn it. Was she out? It was a Friday night, but given that she hadn't been very sociable since the incident at the Halloween dance, that seemed unlikely. Was it not charged? As I pondered what was going on, her voice recording came over the line.

"This is Brandi. Don't know why you're not texting me but leave a message if you must." Beep.

"Brandi, call me back ASAP!"

I clicked the phone off and ran to the car. When I got in, I dialed again. Again, right to voicemail. We hadn't had a house phone in years, so I couldn't try there. Even if I could, I wouldn't want to risk my mother answering.

This time, I drove as fast as I could, completely disregarding pretty much every traffic regulation. I had no choice but to run now and I would have to convince Brandi to come with me. All that business about being able to smell her on me. That was a direct threat. She would be in danger as long as she stayed in that house.

When I got home, I left the car running and ran inside. "Brandi!" I shouted as I took the stairs two at a time.

I got to the second floor and went right to her room. I opened the door without knocking, only to find it empty. Where the hell was she? Had she gone out? Maybe she was with Arianna.

I could call Ari from the road to see if Brandi was in fact with her. If she wasn't, I had no clue where she'd be. I ran into my room and got my duffel bag, which I had kept packed since I realized I may need to make a quick getaway. I slung it over my shoulder and went back downstairs.

My mother was sitting at the kitchen table clasping a steaming cup of tea in her hands. I hadn't seen her when I rushed in. Had she been there this whole time? I would have thought she'd have commented on the way I burst in, but she was eerily quiet.

"Where are you going?" she asked.

"Out," I said, not having the patience to play games.

"Have fun," she said in an odd tone, taking a sip. She had been a drunken, miserable asshole for months and now she was casually telling me to *have fun*? Something felt very wrong about all of this.

"Have you seen Brandi?" I asked.

"She's in the basement."

"The basement? Why is she down there?"

"She said she was looking for something."

She must have been looking for the files I found when I was trying to find the evidence against Dennis.

I didn't say anything else to my mom and went straight for the basement. I flipped on the light and immediately realized something was wrong. Why was she down here in the dark? I dropped my bag and ran the rest of the way down the stairs.

"Brandi!" I shouted in a panic. "Where are you?"

I didn't get a response. Was she actually down here?

I surveyed the area and saw the door to Dennis's workshop open. I ran over and went inside, shocked to find Brandi tied to a chair with a thick length of rope. She saw me and her eyes went wide. She tried to say something but I couldn't hear her since her mouth was covered in duct tape.

As I went to free her, she shouted something I couldn't make out through the gag.

"Stop, Brady," a voice said from behind me.

I whirled around to see my mother. She was pointing a revolver at me. No doubt one of the guns from Dennis's collection.

"We need to talk."

CHAPTER 37

"You fucking bitch."

Uttering those words to my mother would have been unthinkable a few months ago. Now I wanted to grab that gun and blow her fucking brains out. Dad was dead because of her. Brandi was hurt because of her. My life was ruined because of her.

"I know you're upset, honey, and I know this looks bad, but I just needed you to stay here and calm down. Just give me a chance to explain."

"Slide that gun in your mouth and pull the fucking trigger," I said defiantly.

"Brady, please stop talking. You're only going to make this worse. We can still figure out a way out of this."

I laughed in her face. "Sure, Liz," I said, never intending to address here as *Mom* ever again. "You think there's a way we come back from this?"

"There is," she said, desperation creeping in. "Dennis and I talked about it. We can smooth all of this out. As soon as he comes home, we'll all talk this out and we can be a family again."

"We stopped being a family the day Dennis killed Dad."

"Stop saying that, Brady. It's not as simple as you think."

A familiar male voice joined the conversation from behind her. "Actually, it is."

I looked over my mother's shoulder to see Dennis standing in the doorway. He was dressed and looked one hundred percent healthy. Like nothing had ever happened.

Liz lit up when she saw him, somehow glossing over his confession to my father's murder.

"Dennis! Honey! Thank God you're okay!"

She ran up and hugged him. He wrapped his arms around her. I took a step forward hoping to use the distraction to get the drop on them, but Dennis was too fast, He grabbed the gun from Liz and pressed it against my forehead.

"Don't do something foolish, Brady."

I'd been hearing that a lot lately. I guess I was getting a reputation.

"Liz, please tie our son to the chair until he calms down?"

"I'm not your son, you fucking piece of shit!" I bellowed.

"That's exactly the kind of thing I'm talking about," he said. "Sit the fuck down, Brady."

I complied. What other choice did I have? Liz went to work wrapping thick layers of duct tape around my chest, my hands and my legs. Once it was clear I wasn't going to be able to move, she taped my mouth just as she had Brandi's.

Once we were secure, Dennis walked into the room, only the slightest hint of a limp on a leg that had suffered a compound fracture less than a week ago. He grabbed a folding chair and set it up, beckoning for Liz to sit in front of us.

"They let you out?" she asked.

"I let myself out. The doctors tried to stop me, but I told them I was leaving. What could they do? It's a hospital, not a prison. But that's not important now. Time for a family meeting!"

Dennis walked behind the woman I used to call my mother and put his hands on her shoulders, rubbing them slightly as he stood there. It made me sick to watch.

"Kids," he started. "Sometimes, you reach a crossroads in life. And that's where we're at as a family. Clearly, we've all made mistakes along the way, but those mistakes don't have to define us. We can be happy again."

"Fuck you!" I tried to yell through my gag. Not the most original comeback, but it was all I had.

"Brady, I know you're upset. I know you blame me for your father's death, but you shouldn't."

"See, Brady?" Liz said, almost manic. "Dennis didn't kill your father."

"Don't lie to the children, Liz. You know damn well that

I killed him." He turned to us, his eyes burning a hole into mine. "And they know it too, so let's not insult anyone's intelligence here."

Dennis said the words as nonchalantly as one would order a coffee. Liz was stunned that he would confess in such a casual manner.

"Dennis, they weren't supposed to find out," she said, focusing on us as her house of cards came tumbling down. "It's not what you think. I swear it's not!"

"Shut the fuck up, Liz."

Liz acquiesced but she looked like she was on the verge of spontaneous combustion. How could she not be? I had caught her in a decade-long lie and a full-on murder cover-up. Despite my rage toward her, given my own recent escapades, I understood her panic.

"Now, as I was saying before I was so rudely interrupted—yes, I killed your father. I swapped the pins in his stand and it fell. But you know the funny thing? The fall didn't actually kill him. I kind of knew it wouldn't. I mean, it certainly would have been easier on me if it did, but you gotta do what you gotta do, right, Brady?"

Dennis gave me a great big shit-eating grin. He remembered everything.

"Your dad was actually relieved to see me coming out of the woods toward him," Dennis continued. "I mean, he was hurt pretty badly, but he would have been just fine."

He paused, looking off into the distance as if trying to

draw the memory from the recesses of his mind to the forefront.

"Well, he would have been fine if hadn't snapped his neck like a fucking twig."

I jumped against my restraints, trying in vain to get to him.

He laughed and kept going. "It was so much easier than I thought. And a lot more satisfying that shooting a deer. Almost gave me a chubby if we're being completely honest."

Liz had tears streaming down her cheeks now. She wasn't moving, but she was breaking before our eyes. I would have loved to have known what she was thinking when she held a gun on us and tied us up. How in her right mind could she think we would just talk it out and go back to normal life again? But that was just it: looking at her, I could see that she had lost it. Whether it was guilt, fear or some combination of both, the woman who used to be my mother had gone insane.

I looked over at Brandi, who was crying as well, the tears rolling down the duct tape as they fell.

"Dennis," Liz said. "Please stop."

He slapped her hard. She let out one gasping sob before she covered her mouth to stop herself. If I didn't despise her, I'd almost pity her.

"I will not tell you again, sweetheart. Shut the fuck up."

She put her head down and whimpered softly.

Dennis kept his diatribe going. "Your dad was a good guy, but he was a pussy. Too much of a pussy to satisfy a woman like your mom here. She needed a real man to fuck her and who was I to say no?"

Everything was red. I struggled against the restraints, frustration exacerbating my rage.

"But, you see, your dad wasn't just unable to satisfy her needs sexually, he also couldn't give her the life she deserved. I mean, he tried. He bent to her every whim, but he just didn't have the cash to support it. Your family was in so much debt when he died that you never would have made your way out of it. The creditors would have taken the house, the cars and everything he had. You would have lost everything if he'd lived."

Liz let out another sob. I thought Dennis was going to hit her again. I kind of wished he would.

But he didn't.

Instead, he turned and walked over to his workbench, bracing himself on either side of it. He took a deep breath.

"I saved this family. I made your mother happy. I put your father out of his misery. He would have just kept fucking up, but I took care of it. And, by doing so, I secured all of our futures. With the money from the life insurance, along with my income, we don't have to worry about money ever again. But none of you appreciate it."

"We do!" Liz blurted. "I... I love you. I appreciate

everything you've done!"

Dennis scoffed. "Sure, that's why you dried up on me, right?"

"What?" she choked out in shock.

He didn't turn away from the bench.

"You used to get so hot for me. Now you just lie there like a dead fucking fish. A man has needs, you know."

"Dennis, how could you..."

"The things I did for you. I killed for you. I saved your fucking life and you can't even meet my basic needs."

She put her head in her hands and started to full out sob. "I don't know what you want... tell me what you want and I'll do it."

"What do I want?" Dennis asked, almost as if he were contemplating it himself. He reached over to the side of the bench, but I didn't see what he'd grabbed.

"I want to end this marriage."

Liz raised her head just in time for Dennis to bring the hammer down on top of it. The tool landed with an audible thunk as it left a dent in the center of her head. Surprisingly it didn't drop. She somehow lifted her body from the chair and staggered to her feet as blood poured down her forehead.

"I... I... I'm... I'm sorry," she said to us, having a lot of trouble actually forming the words.

Brandi and I both screamed through our gags. Despite all my hatred for what she had done, a lifetime of happy memories prior to my dad's death flooded my mind.

Mom pushing us on the swing at the park.

Family vacations.

Getting pizza after a little league game or dance competition.

Snuggling and watching movies on the couch.

In my mind, she became my mother again, if only for a moment. I meant what I said earlier. She died with my dad, but it didn't mean it wasn't completely horrifying to watch her die so violently in real life.

Dennis took a single finger and poked her between her shoulder blades, sending the wobbly woman crashing to the floor, hitting her face on the concrete, not even raising her hands to brace herself. I heard a sickening crunch followed by a splat as the hard surface obliterated her nose. Dennis moved around her. He rolled her head on its side so she was facing us, her mangled nose caved into her face. Her eyes were wide and blood-streaked tears trickled down from them. Subtle movements indicated that she may not be technically dead, but there was no life in those eyes either.

Dennis raised the hammer again and brought it down right on her zygomatic bone. It crushed her eye socket and the orb popped out, rolling as far as the optic nerve would let it. He hit her again, this time on the cheek right in front of her ear, shattering teeth that tumbled out of her drooling mouth.

The next series of blows were all directly on the cranium. On the fourth shot, it cracked like an egg. Each subsequent strike sent pieces of pinkish-gray brain matter out of her ruined skull like cookie dough seeping from its package.

He kept hitting her and hitting her and hitting her while Brandi and I thrashed and cried. When he was finally done, he tossed the hammer aside and stood up, covered in blood and chunks of flesh.

The thing that used to be our mother lay sprawled out on the floor, her face a hollow cavity that had been demolished by the hammer.

Dennis wiped some blood from his face and took off his gore-soaked shirt, tossing it aside. I was shocked at the sight of him. There were still traces of Gunther's attack, but the wounds had healed much more than they should have at this point.

He noticed me looking at him. He checked the injuries himself and laughed.

"Yeah, I healed from this little incident very quickly. It's why I decided to check myself out of the hospital. The doctors would ask way too many questions once they saw how far along I was."

He set the chair back up and sat in front of us, but he focused his attention on Brandi.

"Your brother has been keeping a few things from you, sweetheart."

She looked at me then back to Dennis.

"You see," he continued. "He captured an honest-to-goodness werewolf."

Her eyes went wide.

"Yup. My thoughts exactly." He turned to me now. "Especially when he locked me in a room, hoping the werewolf would make a meal out of me."

Back to Brandi.

"He nearly did too. I mean he certainly fucked me up pretty good, but the thing about a caged animal is that they'll turn on their captor before focusing on anything else."

Back to me.

"I guess your dad never taught you that one."

I was too tired, both emotionally and physically, to react.

"Now, I'm no expert, but based on how quickly my wounds have healed, not to mention how fucking great I feel right now, I'd say at the next full moon, I'm going to... well, let's just say I'll be a whole new man."

He stood up.

"I'm just glad we can experience this as a family."

CHAPTER 38

The next full moon was three weeks away. Just in time for Christmas. Dennis kept us tied up in the basement, but he came downstairs often.

At first, he said little. He moved his workbenches and tools out of the room, leaving it empty except for Brandi and me. He also moved our mother's corpse, wrapping it up and carrying it out, a process I, unfortunately, was all too familiar with. What he did with the body, I don't know. He was gone for quite a while.

When he returned, he went to work soundproofing the room, adding foam and acoustic panels on all the walls, the floor and the ceilings. He worked almost around the clock that first day, but he took occasional breaks doing God knows what upstairs. First thing Sunday morning, he brought down two tray tables and plates with scrambled eggs. He set up the tables and placed the food in front of us, but before he maneuvered them so we could eat, he looked me dead in the eyes.

"I know that when I take the gag off, you're going to have the urge to scream and yell and make a fuss and tell me to go fuck myself. But I'm telling you right now that's a bad idea. Because if you do, I'm not going to hurt you. I'm going to hurt Brandi. Badly. Do you understand?"

I believed him. I nodded.

"Good," he said with a cheery smile.

He adjusted our restraints so we could use our hands and removed the duct tape from our mouths so we could feed ourselves. I didn't really have an appetite and I'm guessing Brandi didn't either, but we ate to try to keep our strength up. When we were done, Dennis removed the tray tables, restrained our hands again and covered our mouths with fresh tape.

Dennis continued working through the morning and into the afternoon. Once he finally finished the soundproofing, he took off our gags and kept them off since we couldn't be heard outside the room.

His next task was to change out the door. The new one looked very heavy. He told us it was steel. He installed it shockingly easy for one guy doing the work himself. There was no doubt he was getting stronger. He added a heavy-duty padlock on the outside. When he was finished, we ended up in a room not all that different from the one I had kept Gunther in, other than the door which I could see was much more secure than the one in the asylum.

There was a single window visible in the main section of the basement whenever the door was open. It was dark outside. But once Dennis closed the door behind him, there was no window and no clock, giving us no way to track the time.

***

The next time the door opened, Dennis came in dressed for work. I could see the sun shining from the window on the other side. I guessed it was Monday morning but I was already losing track of time.

Dennis brought us pop tarts. After he freed our hands, he placed them on the tables in front of us and sat down for another chat.

"I called your school. I told them that, unfortunately, your mother and I are separating and that you guys went with her to visit her aunt out of state. You'll be staying there and enrolling in school in the next few weeks. So you can forget about anyone from the administration trying to find you."

That had crossed my mind. I figured once we didn't show up for school, they'd come looking for us and maybe we'd have a way out of this, but the bastard was smart. Our mother didn't even have any out-of-state relatives, but they probably wouldn't bother to check that.

"Anyway, I have to get to work. You kids have a good

day."

He left and locked us in.

CHAPTER 39

After Dennis left the room and locked us in, ungagged for the first time, I turned to Brandi. She looked at me and as soon as we made eye contact, I began to cry.

"I'm so sorry. I'm so very sorry."

She looked at me, her own tears wetting her cheeks. "It's not your fault," she said.

"Yes, it is. This is all my fault."

I told her everything. How I went to Trevor's house. How he was killed. How I got rid of the body. I told her how I set Dennis up and tried to have him killed even though it backfired.

She listened to me but didn't seem surprised by any of it. It had been clear to her for a while that something had been going on.

I broke down again at the end. "Please forgive me."

"I do," she said. "You were only doing what you thought you had to do to help us. I just wish you hadn't tried to take this all on yourself. That you had let me in."

"I was trying to—"

"Protect me. I know. But you didn't have to. We could

317

have faced this together."

"Better late than never," I said in disbelief that I'd actually cracked a joke.

Brandi let out the slightest hint of a smirk, but it looked pained. My heart broke seeing her like that.

"We're not getting out of this, are we?" she asked.

"I'm out of ideas."

I wish I could have reassured her, but I couldn't. Barring some kind of miracle, Dennis was going to kill us. It was just a matter of when and how.

The room we were in didn't have windows so it was tough to track the passage of time other than scant glimpses when Dennis came in and out to check on us and to occasionally provide us with meals. When he brought breakfast, he'd set up an LED lantern in the corner of the room. It was unexpectedly bright for such a small device. It was no substitute for sunlight, but at least we could see. He'd lock us in while he did whatever it was he did during the day. We couldn't hear anything outside the room, so if anyone came looking for us, we'd have no idea.

At night, Dennis would come back one last time and remove the lantern, causing our makeshift prison cell to descend into darkness. With no light and no windows, it was pitch black. I tried to scoot my chair close to Brandi. Even though we were tied, I wanted to be close so she could at least hear me breathing, and she would know I was close.

"I'm still here, Brandi," I said. "I will be with you as long as we're here. You're not alone."

"Neither are you."

I tried to spread my fingers, see if I could even brush hers with my pinky to give her some reassurance beyond my words.

I couldn't reach.

The first few nights we talked long after the world went dark. I don't think anyone knows what the protocol for conversation during captivity is, but we figured we may as well try to come up with something to prevent us from going insane. Plus, we needed to stay sharp in case an opportunity to escape presented itself. The room was devoid of tools and we were bound tightly to the chairs. If there was a way out, I just couldn't see it.

We reminisced a lot, talking about the good times with our family while our dad was alive. Brandi said she couldn't believe they were having financial problems. We always had food and went on vacations, and Christmas was always loaded with presents. But maybe that was it. Maybe they just binged on credit cards and home loans and got underwater.

It didn't matter. Dad had done his best for us. The man simply tried to be there for his family and he got killed for it. It was so fucking unfair.

***

We did our best to track the time, but it was an almost impossible task. Dennis would come in once in the morning with a small breakfast and again in the evening with dinner. He rarely stuck around too long.

After a few days, Brandi and I came up with the idea of quizzing ourselves on what meals we had each day. There certainly wasn't a lot of variety, but listing each meal allowed us to count how many days had passed.

With some effort, we figured we had been down there six days at that point.

My extremities were numb. I tried my best to shift in the seat to somewhat manage my blood flow, but my effort was futile. I wondered if Brandi was experiencing the same thing, but didn't ask, not wanting to draw attention to it if she was.

On day eight, we started playing trivia games. We both considered ourselves movie buffs, so one of our favorites was always *Six Degrees of Kevin Bacon*. The concept of the game was that Kevin Bacon had been in so many movies that any other actor could be linked to him in six movies or fewer.

"Bruce Campbell," challenged Brandi.

I scoffed. "Please. Bruce Campbell was in *Spider-Man* with Kirsten Dunst who was in *Interview with the*

Vampire with Brad Pitt who was in *Sleepers* with Kevin Bacon."

"You and that fucking *Sleepers* loophole."

"It isn't my fault that everyone and their mother was in *Sleepers*," I said.

She wasn't lying, though. To be successful at the game, *Sleepers* was a great one to go back to because of the all-star cast that was with Kevin Bacon. Robert DeNiro, Jason Patric, Brad Pitt, Minnie Driver and Dustin Hoffman. If you couldn't get a six-degree link with those actors, you probably shouldn't even bother playing.

"Jim Carrey," I challenged back.

"You're kidding, right? He was in *The Truman Show* with Laura Linney, who was in *Mystic River* with Kevin Bacon."

"Oh, so you'll give me shit about using *Sleepers* but then you pull out *Mystic River?* Sean Penn, Laurence Fishburne, Tim Robbins, Emmy Rossum. It's way easier to use that one than *Sleepers*!"

"Whatever you say, dude."

We both laughed. It felt weird, but I was glad we were keeping each other occupied, otherwise our minds would have cracked like Mom's. The figurative way, not the literal one.

We were so distracted with our banter that the sound of the door opening startled us.

Dennis came in with our dinner as usual. Tonight's

offering was a plate of buttered noodles for each of us. He set us up and then went back upstairs, returning a few minutes later with a steak, a baked potato and a bottle of wine for himself. For the first time since our captivity began, he sat and ate with us, asking us stupid questions like how our day went.

We didn't respond, but it didn't seem to bother him. He kept refilling his wine as he ate, pounding it down in a way that I'd never even seen my mother do even when she was at her worst. He finished his meal and let out a contented belch.

"Mm. That was a hell of a meal," he said, leaning back in the chair. "Don't know if you guys have been keeping track of things, but Christmas is coming up! I feel bad that we haven't really decorated yet but you guys are in no position to help and your mother is certainly useless right now, so it's just me and I've been terribly busy with work. I'm sure you understand."

"Well, why don't you untie us so we can help?" I asked.

Dennis laughed. "Nice try, Brady. Listen, I know we haven't had many family dinners recently, but I figured since you guys won't be here for Christmas, we could kind of do our holiday dinner tonight."

"Where are we going to be for Christmas?" Brandi asked, afraid of the answer.

"Oh, sweetie, the full moon is going to happen before the 25th. I mean, that's how this works, right, Brady?

Once the moon is full, you're going to meet the new me."

"I don't know how it works," I lied.

"Oh, I think you do," he replied. "But it doesn't matter. I can feel it inside. It's coming."

I swallowed hard, my dry throat burning with the effort. Dennis didn't say much else. We ate in silence. Truth be told, I wasn't hungry, but only ate in an effort to keep my strength up as much as possible.

When he was finished, he grabbed the plates, bound our hands as usual and left the room, taking the lantern with him.

Brandi and I didn't talk too much more after dinner. Despite my unsettled state, I eventually dozed off. Sleep over the past week or so we'd been down here had come in fits and starts, but the fatigue was really washing over me. I didn't know how long I was actually out when I heard the door open again.

Dennis walked in, holding the lantern out in front of him. The light showed that he was wearing nothing but a pair of tight boxer briefs, a not-so-subtle bulge protruding from the front. There were no longer any visible signs of wounds anywhere on his body. Even though I wasn't looking at her, I could feel Brandi tense up next to me.

"Evening," he said. "So, I was lying in bed when I got a sudden craving for some dessert."

Where was he going with this? Was he about to

change? No, it was still too soon. He was after something else.

"Would you like some dessert, Brandi?"

"Stay away from her!" I shouted.

He ignored me. Brandi shook her head vehemently. Dennis walked over and crouched next to her, running his hands over her knees to her upper thighs. She was wearing leggings, but the material was thin and she closed her eyes tight, recoiling at his touch.

Dennis lowered his head and sighed.

"See, I framed that as a request, to be nice. But you really don't have a choice here."

She shook her head again, more violently this time, tears beginning to fall.

Dennis stood up and turned to me. Without warning, he punched me in the face, knocking me and the chair back to the floor.

He grabbed the back of the chair and pulled me back upright. I looked over and saw my sister watching the scene, her face red and streaked with tears.

"So, let's get this straight. You're coming with me one way or another. But, if you don't do it willingly, I'm going to hurt your brother. We still have about ten days until the big event—I can torture him every single day until he dies slowly and painfully."

I shook my head as hard as I could, blood flying from my nose, which I was pretty sure was broken.

"So, what do you say?" he asked Brandi. "Dessert?"

She looked over at me again. I tried to will her not to do it, but she apologized to me with her eyes before turning to Dennis and nodding. He smiled like the fucking Grinch.

"Good girl."

CHAPTER 40

I woke up the next morning and Brandi was still gone.

I'm not sure when I actually fell asleep. Passed out was probably more like it. After Dennis had taken my sister away, I broke down and sobbed for a long time, the weight of everything that had happened crushing my soul. A few times I thought I might even choke to death due to the mixture of blood, saliva and snot running into my mouth. I would have actually welcomed it at that point, but I needed to know what had happened to my sister so I spit it out every time it felt like it was getting full.

After what seemed like an eternity, the door opened up and Brandi walked in, Dennis right behind her.

I felt sick looking at her. She wasn't wearing the same clothes as she was when she left. She was only clad in an oversized Philadelphia Eagles sweatshirt. Obviously one of Dennis's. I couldn't tell if she was wearing pants, but the shirt covered her to mid-thigh. Her hair was disheveled. She had makeup on, but it was smeared and streaked with lines of mascara running down from her eyes.

The worst part was the myriad of scratches and fresh bruises that covered her body. It looked like she had lost a fight with a stray cat. She looked practically comatose as she sat back down and Dennis tied her back up to the chair.

"Thanks for dessert, sweetie," he said, kissing her on the cheek before turning to me.

I seethed. I opened my mouth to curse him, but he cut me off.

"Save the empty threats, kid. You should know by now that you're not in control here."

I stayed silent. He was right. I couldn't insult him to death.

"Why don't you just kill us?"

"Oh, I'm going to," he said with a smirk. "I just want you to see what you made me before I do. What fun would it be to just shoot you in the head at this point? Don't you think we're beyond that?"

I had nothing else to say. It wouldn't do any good. All we could do is just sit and wait for the end.

"See? It's good to be nice and quiet. Your actual death is going to be excruciatingly painful, but if you and your sister play nice, I'm okay leaving you be until we get there."

He left the room and locked us in. I turned to Brandi. She didn't look at me.

"Are you okay?"

No response.

"What did he do?"

Still nothing.

I wanted to cry but nothing came out. My tears were exhausted and I felt hollow inside. Not only were we going to die, but Dennis had clearly done something unthinkable to my sister.

We sat in silence for a long time, so I did the only thing I could do. In my mind, I prayed for it to end quickly.

CHAPTER 41

Dennis made an unscheduled visit a couple hours after breakfast the next day. Besides the usual lantern, he also set up some extra lights in the room. I could see through the open door it was daytime out. A decent amount of snow was piled up at the bottom of the window. Not long after Dennis moved in, he had hired a company to install an energy efficient HVAC system and heavy-duty insulation, so our house was always well controlled when it came to temperature, even in the basement. It could be a blizzard or a heat wave outside and we'd never know if we couldn't see it.

He left the door open and disappeared. I couldn't hear him outside, but I also couldn't be sure he wasn't there. I thought about hopping forward on my chair to get out. My mind raced as I desperately searched for any means of escape, but there was nothing feasible.

I considered yelling as loud as I could. It was highly unlikely that anyone was wandering around outside and would hear me. And when my plan almost certainly failed, how would Dennis react? I didn't care anymore what he did to me, but what if he took it out on Brandi? She'd already been through enough with inevitably more to come. I wasn't going to make it any worse.

A few minutes later, Dennis came back in, carrying a Christmas tree under one arm. It was an artificial one, but it still looked heavy enough that he should have had more trouble lifting it than he did. He set it up in the corner of the room.

"Yeah, I know," he said answering an unasked question. "Usually, we put the tree up the day after Thanksgiving, but things have been a little chaotic this year, wouldn't you say?"

I said nothing.

He continued. "We only have a few days left, but I figure we can make it festive."

He left again and returned with a box of ornaments. He started affixing them to the tree, whistling various Christmas carols as he worked. We continued to watch in silence as the maniac who had married our mother trimmed a holiday tree in our fucking prison.

Dennis pulled out a large, spherical object wrapped in tissue paper. He gently unwrapped it and held the crystal ornament in his hands. I recognized it immediately. It was a photo ornament with my dad and Liz holding Brandi and me as babies on Main Street in Disney World, in front of the castle. The fancy script read:

Babies' First Christmas – 2004

Dad had told me they had been invited on a trip to Disney World with his cousin and their two young kids. Dad and Liz had been married a few years but she hadn't gotten pregnant yet, despite them trying almost right away. While they were looking forward to the trip, lo-and-behold, Liz found out she was having us. She told Dad we should cancel the trip, because we would only be about three months old at the time. Dad refused. Liz argued we would be too young to enjoy it.

Dad simply told her that was true, but they would enjoy having us there.

Liz agreed and when we were old enough, they showed us all the pictures they took of us as babies on the rides, in the parks and with the characters. Dad said Liz had thanked him for talking her into it and they'd bought that ornament to commemorate the trip. The same ornament that the man who destroyed our lives was holding in his hand right now.

"What an absolutely precious memory," Dennis said as he carefully rolled the ornament in his hand.

Then he looked me right in the eye as he dropped it to the ground, shattering it.

I didn't react. I wanted to curse and spit in his face. Bite his fucking nose off if he got close enough. But I couldn't. I couldn't risk further harm to Brandi.

I stared stone-faced, trying, and failing, to fight back the emotion. Dennis grinned.

"Sorry. Guess I'm a little clumsy these days. Oh, well." He turned and looked the tree over, resting his hand under his chin, stroking it with his thumb as if he was contemplating something. "You know, it looks pretty good, but I think it's missing a final touch. Something that really emphasizes the spirit of the season." He snapped his fingers and exclaimed, "I've got it! Don't go anywhere!"

He laughed as he bounded out of the room. I looked down at the shattered ornament. Hearing a sniffle next to me, I turned to see Brandi was crying now too, breaking out of her catatonia. I thought about what to say to her but couldn't find the words. We just continued to sit there in our despair.

After a while, Dennis returned with a heavy black contractor bag. It didn't look like there was much in it. The bottom bulged as if there was something like a bowling ball, or maybe a watermelon, inside.

I didn't have to wonder too long as Dennis dropped the bag and reached inside, retrieving the head of the woman who used to be my mother.

He had fully severed it from her body, a jagged piece of bone dangling from the stump of the neck. There was really no face to speak of after what Dennis had done to her. Now we saw he had made some more modifications after the fact. He wrapped the head in Christmas lights with two large bulbs in the general vicinity of where the eyes should have been. A large candy cane was embedded in the mouth, sticking out through a hole in the bottom lip. It was obscene and horrifying.

Brandi came back to life, screaming, "You sick fuck! You piece of shit!"

Dennis shifted the severed head to his left hand and belted Brandi in the mouth with his right, cutting off her verbal assault.

"Now, Brandi. Don't talk to Daddy like that."

I raged when he said that, seething as I listened to her whimper next to me. I again threw away my agnostic leanings and prayed for God to strike him dead.

No such luck. He turned back to the tree and lifted the head up over the apex before slamming it back down, impaling it on top. He turned to us and stepped aside so we could get a full view of the severed head topping the tree where normally there would be a star.

"Shit!" he exclaimed. "I almost forgot!"

He plugged the cords into the sole electrical outlet in the small room and the tree lights coming to life from the base to the tip where the mangled head rested, glowing from the makeshift eyes.

"Perfect! Merry Christmas to all and to all a good night!"

***

Dennis didn't stick around much longer after setting up the tree. He told us we hadn't been spending enough time with our mother and would give us some privacy to do so.

I had lost any love I had for that woman over the past few months. Hell, I'd even wanted her dead. But seeing her annihilated head stuck on a Christmas tree was not something I was keen to see.

Brandi started crying harder once Dennis was gone. I focused my attention on her, avoiding the macabre decoration in the corner of the room.

"Brandi," I said. "Don't look. Just look at me."

She did, her eyes swollen and her lip quivering.

"I wish I could say something," I told her. "Tell you that things are going to be okay. I wish I could save you and I am so sorry that I can't."

She nodded, her face scrunching as tears pooled up in her eyes.

"I know, Brady."

"I love you, Brandi. Just know that. And know that I'm here with you until the end. I promise."

She nodded again, closing her eyes tight as she sobbed.

As we hung our heads in defeat, we were both startled to hear the door open again. What sick plan did Dennis have in store for us now?

You would think after the scene with the Christmas tree, I would have been ready for anything.

I wasn't.

Arianna stood in the doorway, a look of abject terror on her face as she saw us.

"Oh my God..." she muttered before being shoved into the room. Dennis was standing behind her, holding a gun to her back.

"Tsk tsk, Arianna," he said. "This is family time. You shouldn't have interrupted."

CHAPTER 42

Dennis set up another chair and tied Arianna to it.

"What's happening? I don't understand!" she said as she cried.

"Let her go," I pleaded. "She's not part of this. You don't need to do this."

"Brady," Dennis said in a condescending tone. "What do you think? She's just going to go home and forget that you two are tied up down here? Little Miss Kenton has been stubbornly persistent even though I told her I couldn't get a hold of you, but she came by again. And again. This last time she brought you a present and asked me to forward it to you. That really tugged at the ole heart strings, so I told her you had actually just gotten home and were down here. I said you'd be thrilled to see her."

He tossed a beautifully wrapped box onto my lap and said, "Go ahead. Open it. Oh, wait, you can't. Silly me."

He ripped the paper off and revealed a plain white gift box underneath, the kind you'd find clothing in from Macy's or JCPenney. He flipped the lid off and pulled out a T-shirt and a framed picture. It was a *Scene Kids* shirt, the band we'd seen on our first date. The picture was a framed selfie of the two of us she'd taken the same night.

"Well, isn't that sweet," Dennis remarked before tossing both items at the base of the tree, the picture frame shattering upon impact. I struggled against my restraints.

"She won't say anything! I swear!"

He looked at Arianna.

"He swears, Arianna," Dennis said to her. "But you and I both know that if I were to let you go, you'd walk right out of here and go straight to the police."

"She won't!" I screamed desperately.

"I... I won't," she agreed.

"Yeah. I don't believe you."

Once she was restrained, Dennis stood and looked her over and whistled. Then he looked at me.

"You know, Brady, I never really paid much attention, but your girlfriend here is one really nice piece of ass," he said before turning back to her. "I mean that as the highest compliment, Arianna. You are one beautiful girl."

She didn't answer, too scared to speak.

"So," he continued, "you two fucking?"

"You pig," Brandi said defiantly, earning another slap for her troubles.

"Don't be rude, Brandi," Dennis said.

He looked over to me, then back to Arianna.

"Yeah, you're fucking. You got a few more miles on you

than my stepson here. He leaves a little to be desired in the masculinity department. But I bet you'd let a real man do all kinds of nasty shit to you. You'd probably love every second."

He reached out to stroke her cheek. She withdrew in revulsion as far as her restraints would allow her.

"Looks like my stepdaughter isn't the only one with a rude streak running through her."

He took a few steps back and looked the three of us over.

"So, listen, Arianna," he said. "You've caught us at a bit of an awkward time. If you'd shown up a few days ago, I might have let you stay for dinner. Maybe even some *dessert* afterwards."

He looked at Brandi when he said the last part. She looked down. Dennis continued.

"But the thing is that we have something to do soon as a family. Something very important. I know you're *like family* to my kids here, but you really just don't belong. So, after thinking about it, you just can't stay here."

My heart sank. I knew that didn't mean he was letting her go.

"Dennis," I begged. "Please... please."

I couldn't get anything out except the word *please* over and over. It's like my brain stopped working and I couldn't form any other word.

"Brady, stop talking or I will re-gag you."

"Please..."

He rolled his eyes.

"Please..."

Dennis walked over to me and ruffled my hair.

"I get it, champ. There's nothing like your first love. I know you don't want anything to happen to her.

"Please..."

"But that's the thing about life. You can't always stop bad things from happening to good people."

With that, he pulled his gun and shot Arianna in the stomach.

CHAPTER 43

I tried to scream, but no sound came out. My vocal cords were paralyzed. I heard Brandi's scream. It was loud and anguished as we both watched the blood soak through the wool of Arianna's sweater.

Ari was silent, but she stared down at the wound in shock, the pain not registering yet.

Dennis said nothing else. He simply left the room and locked the door behind him.

Once it was shut, I found my voice.

"Arianna! Baby!" I shouted.

"Brady..." was all she said. "It... it hurts."

"I know, baby. I know."

"It's going to be okay," Brandi said, not sounding like she actually believed it.

The blood was running down Arianna's jeans now. Her clothes were fresh and her hair and makeup was done. I didn't know if it was a weekday or weekend. I wondered if Christmas break had officially started. What I knew was that she should have been anywhere but here. At school, with friends, with her family. Anywhere but shot and bleeding in the basement while we were all tied up.

I thought about how this was supposed to be our first Christmas together, picturing the two of us going shopping. I'd sneak away at some point to get her a gift. I would have gotten her as many as I could, doing my best to make her feel special.

We were supposed to drink hot chocolate and sit by the fire. All the corny family stuff that I'd been missing, that I now realized I'd been craving these last few years. Thanksgiving at her house was such a beautiful experience that I wished it was possible to spend every holiday like that.

But that would never happen because no matter how hard I tried; I had no way to get free. We needed to stop the bleeding if she was going to have a chance to get out of this. I knew from my hunting experience that a gut shot was a slow and painful way to die. Dad always taught me not to be cruel when we shot our prey, but Dennis picked that spot deliberately because it was cruel. Cruel like he was.

I struggled mightily, trying to somehow burst through the restraints that held me to my seat. It was a metal folding chair so I couldn't even try to break it to get myself free. There was nothing I could do.

We had no choice but to sit there while Arianna bled out. After a while, she stopped crying and moaning in pain. We tried to talk to her but she stopped answering, the only sound she made being her labored breath. I cursed myself for not being more religious. Maybe that's why my prayers down here had stayed unanswered. But still I tried. I prayed and prayed that someone would come in and save us. Even if I had to stay behind. Just let Arianna and Brandi get out of here.

While I searched for help from a higher power, I heard Arianna cough. It was a wet, choking sound, accompanied by a trickle of blood out of her mouth. A death rattle.

Brandi and I looked at each other, devastated.

I craned my head to see Arianna on the other side of my sister. Her head was hanging low. Her skin was turning a pallid shade as the life seeped out of her through the wound in her stomach.

"Arianna?" I called, the words barely above a whisper. I swallowed and tried again. "Ari!"

She looked up at me, her eyes a glazed red.

"Do you remember our first date at Jester's?"

She nodded ever so slightly.

"I was so scared driving to pick you up that night. I was in complete disbelief that you would even give me the time of day."

Brandi looked at me. She was crying but trying to hide her tears from Arianna.

"I... always thought you were... kinda hot," Arianna said, barely above a whisper.

I laughed despite myself, my own tears flowing now.

"Well, when we get out of here, I'll take you to get glasses," I said.

The words tasted foul in my throat. I knew we weren't getting out of here. She was in bad shape. I just hoped she somehow didn't realize it.

"When you kissed me that night... that was the best moment of my life."

"It...didn't...suck."

"I love you, Ari. I'm sorry. I'm so, so very sorry."

Arianna didn't respond. Her head hung low and her eyes registered nothing.

She was gone.

I didn't react at first. My entire body was numb. My girlfriend, my first love, was dead. But just when I thought the emotion wasn't there, that any feeling I had at all was gone, I felt something start in the pit of my stomach. Before I knew it, the flood of rage, guilt and sorrow rampaged through my insides and escaped in a primal scream.

I yelled until my voice finally gave out and then it gave way to heaving sobs, rattling my body against my restraints. My only thought was that I wanted to die in that moment. I wanted nothing more than to leave this earth and go be with Arianna.

Lost in my sorrow, I didn't even hear Brandi calling my name at first. It was only when I heard the desperation

343

in her voice as she shouted at the top of her lungs that I snapped out of my grief-induced stupor.

"Brady!"

When I turned to face my sister, terror washed over me.

Her eyes were yellow.

CHAPTER 44

"No! No! No!"

I shouted the words over and over as I stared into my sister's glowing yellow eyes. I thought I didn't have any tears left after Arianna died, but more found their way down my face.

"How?"

"When he brought me upstairs. He bit me."

I didn't want to ask where, but she answered me anyway, nodding her head toward her right shoulder. Seemed that was a werewolf's spot of choice when it came to biting people.

"Was he... turned?"

"No," she said. "I don't think it matters."

Panic was overtaking me. I didn't know what to do. Didn't know if there was anything I could do.

"Brady," she said. "I can smell everything. Arianna's blood. I can smell your blood inside of you."

"Brandi, please fight it."

She laughed. I saw the ends of her teeth growing jagged.

"Sorry, bro. I don't think it works."

All I could think was that I fucking deserved this. Everything I had done had led to this point and if I had to die at the hands of my twin werewolf, then I guess that was my fate. I closed my eyes, not wanting to see her actually change.

I had every intention of keeping them shut, but, before I knew it, the door opened and Dennis walked in. He was completely naked and his eyes were yellow too. His mouth was lined with sharp fangs. I didn't know what time it was, but I saw the dark of night through the window behind him.

"Daddy's home!" he exclaimed in a deeper, raspier voice than usual. "Can you imagine my surprise when this started to happen tonight? I thought it was going to be on the night of the actual full moon, but I guess we can start the party early!" He looked like he was going to say something else, but he stopped dead in his tracks when he saw Brandi. A look of delight came over him.

"Well! Looks like Daddy's little girl is growing up."

I looked to Brandi for her reaction but was horrified to see that she didn't look angry. In fact, she was smiling, fangs protruding from her own mouth.

"That's right, Daddy," she said licking her lips before turning to me with a smirk. "And I'm starving."

Dennis laughed, an inhuman cackle, as the transformation began. "Looks like you're the odd man out, son."

"Let me out, Daddy," Brandi said in a seductive tone that felt wrong for me to hear. "I need you."

Dennis ripped away her bonds, displaying inhuman strength. Brandi was free.

"Brandi," I said my voice barely above a whisper, "Don't..."

She ignored me as she walked up to Dennis. She ran her fingernails, now double their normal size, down his chest. He watched me the whole time as she leaned forward and kissed his neck. He put his arm around her waist to pull her close.

"That's right, baby," he said. "Come to Daddy."

"You're not my daddy, motherfucker!" Brandi bellowed as she sank her teeth into his neck, tearing out a large chunk of flesh, a geyser of blood squirting out from underneath.

Dennis roared in pain as he fell to the ground. Brandi spat the large piece of skin right back in his face as he clamped his clawed hands over his throat, trying to stifle the flow of blood.

I was in complete shock as my sister turned her attention to me. Her nose was reshaping itself and her ears were pointy like an elf's. Tufts of hair were popping out from underneath her sweatshirt.

"Hurry!" she said as she ripped off my restraints just as easily as Dennis did with hers. "Lock us in here!"

"No!"

"There's no time! Fucking do it!"

I knew she was right, but before we could get to the door, Dennis was back on his feet, now covered almost head to toe in hair. He looked about half a foot taller than when he'd walked into the room. He struck Brandi with a mighty backhand wallop and sent her flying across the room before flailing back and roaring with what sounded like pain. I remembered Gunther describing the agony of the transformation. Hopefully that would buy me some time.

Not enough, apparently, as Dennis recovered enough to lunge at me, but, in his pain, he was imprecise and I ducked as he slammed into the wall behind me. I ran for the door, but Dennis reached out and grabbed my foot, yanking me back much like Gunther had in the mental hospital that night.

Whirling around, I saw he was almost in full wolf form now. I pulled my foot back and kicked him as hard as I could, aiming for his still sputtering throat wound. The blow landed close enough that he whirled back in agony, releasing me in the process.

Back on my feet, I ran through the door. I tried to slam it shut, but Dennis was too fast, busting through before I could close it. I stumbled back and ran for the stairs, hoping that he hadn't locked the basement door.

It was unlocked.

I ran through and shut it behind me, knowing damn well that it would only buy me a few seconds, if that. I hurried to the kitchen intending to head out the back door, but it startled me to find Liz's decaying, headless corpse sitting at the kitchen table, a bottle of wine and a half-filled glass in front of her. Dennis no doubt having posed her for his own sick amusement, a sociopath even without the wolf's curse.

The delay was enough that Dennis was right behind me. I flipped the table toward him and ran in the only direction available—toward the stairs. It hurt to run, but I moved as fast as I could and went straight for my room, hoping he hadn't moved my shotgun.

Thankfully, the case was where I left it. I pulled it out and placed it on the bed, hurrying to enter the combination. In what was becoming a trend, I was too late. My bedroom door exploded and my werewolf stepfather burst through. He caught me around the neck and lifted me off the ground with one hand. My shotgun was completely out of reach. I was done for.

He pulled me closer to him until I was right up against his jaw. His breath was hot and rancid as he opened his mouth, ready to bite down.

I looked away, not wanting the last thing I saw to be the bottom of this monster's throat. That's when I saw it.

The bottle of silver nitrate was sitting there half full on my desk. On pure instinct alone I swooped it up and smashed it into Dennis's mouth.

As soon as the chemical hit his tongue, he released me. I dropped to the floor with a thud as the werewolf thrashed about in pain. There wasn't that much left in the bottle, but it was enough to hurt him. The question was, would it be enough to kill him?

He was no longer paying attention to me. He was scraping at his tongue, trying to get the burning liquid off, but couldn't manage it. But he was still blocking my shotgun. If I made a lunge for it, he could grab me with no problem.

After a few more seconds, the wolf recovered enough to focus back on me. He roared as he started toward me. I curled up into a ball and braced for him to tear me apart.

That's when I heard another roar.

This one came from behind Dennis. He whirled around, allowing me to see a second werewolf standing in the door. Its fur was the same color as my hair, save for a generous amount of platinum-blond streaks on its head.

Brandi.

She snarled as she leaped forward, but not at me. Instead, she lunged for Dennis, barreling into him with all her might, the momentum sending them both crashing through my window, smashing the glass and the frame in equal measure as they tumbled to the ground below.

I quickly ran and grabbed my shotgun and returned to

the window. A blast of frigid wind hit me in the face as I looked down to see Dennis running off into the woods with Brandi hot on his trail.

CHAPTER 45

By the time I made it downstairs, both wolves were gone. I'd seen the direction they initially went and a trail of blood in the snow confirmed it so I followed suit. Besides my shotgun, the only other thing I'd brought with me was my flashlight because, despite the full moon, it was very difficult to see once I was in the trees, even with the bright white snow lining the ground. It was freezing and I didn't have a coat, but I tried to put that out of my mind as I pushed forward.

I couldn't help but wonder why Brandi attacked Dennis instead of me (not that I wasn't grateful for it). I remembered Gunther saying that he remembered things while he was the wolf. Dennis also talked about Gunther going after me because he was a caged animal and I was his captor. Maybe because Brandi had only been bitten right before this moon cycle, she still had more awareness? Was her human hatred for Dennis carrying over to her as a werewolf?

I hoped I'd live to find out. My first order of business was to find Dennis and put him down. I prayed I didn't have to do the same to Brandi. Arianna was gone. I couldn't imagine losing my sister as well. Maybe once Dennis was dealt with, we could find a cure. I wasn't sure how, but I did not want to give up on her.

For the first few minutes, I heard nothing as I drew deeper into the woods, slowing my pace, not wanting the crunching snow below to give away my position. Like those times right before everything started, they were quiet. Not even the normal ambient sounds were audible. The silence chilled me along with the winter air.

After a few minutes, the blood trail disappeared. I continued in the direction that I was heading, constantly looking left, right and behind me, switching positions often while still moving forward, trying not to let either wolf get the drop on me. Just because Brandi had attacked Dennis didn't mean I thought she wouldn't go after me if it was just the two of us.

Since I didn't see where they went once they were out of sight, I figured it was as good an idea as any to head to where this all started. To the cave.

Now that the initial adrenaline burst from my escape from the basement had worn off, every muscle was clenched as I made my way toward that damned place. Fatigue wracked my body, my muscles atrophied from sitting bound to a chair for the past few weeks. Each step felt like my legs were going to give out. But they held and I kept pushing forward.

I didn't see or hear either werewolf as I made my way to the cave. When I got there, I froze, looking at the entrance and wondering if Dennis or Brandi was inside. I had guessed that the entrance was too small for Gunther to get in or out while in wolf form, but I'd never actually tested it. One of them could have been in there. I had to check.

One step at a time, I moved toward the hollow, gun and flashlight pointed right at the opening, finger on the trigger. If a wolf burst out of there, I don't think I would have enough time to identify which one it was before I pulled the trigger. I would have to shoot first.

Please don't let it be Brandi.

Closer and closer I moved, my heart pounding so hard, I thought it would burst out of my chest. I choked and realized I had been holding my breath. I expelled a gasp of air that burned as my chest tightened with the exhalation.

I crouched to see inside. As the light spanned the visible portion of the cave, I didn't see anything but rock. I knew there was still a portion that could not be seen from the outside. I needed to find out for sure if anything was hiding in there.

Only this time, if a werewolf was there, it wouldn't be chained to the rocks. If I didn't get a shot off, I was dead.

As I took my first step inside, I heard something behind me. The now-familiar growl of a giant wolf.

I turned quickly, ready to fire, but saw nothing. I surveyed the area quickly, but there was nothing there, neither seen nor heard. Maybe my mind was playing tricks on me. The stress, fatigue and lack of sleep or any real nutrition may have been fucking with my head.

It wasn't in my head.

The next growl was louder and came from above me. I looked up, shining my flashlight into the trees. That's when I saw the massive figure perched in the very same tree I had used to hide from Trevor. If I had time to think I may have wondered if my scent was on it. The wolf in the tree did not have the blond streaks on its head. It had blood in its fur around its neck and its mouth looked odd—odd for a werewolf, that is—in that it was twisted and drooping in spots. It almost looked like the monster had suffered a stroke or something.

The silver nitrate. It was Dennis.

I fired at him but missed, as he had already leapt out of the tree. I still couldn't get over how fast these giant monsters were. He landed on me, his gargantuan weight knocking me down and sending my weapon and flashlight flying. This must be what Wile E. Coyote felt like when he had an anvil dropped on him.

With the wolf on top of me, I couldn't move. I couldn't even raise my arms to defend myself. This was it.

Dennis roared, and, as he opened his mouth, I saw the damage inflicted by the chemical silver. A few teeth were missing and, from what I could see of its gums, they were marked with pockets of pus and appeared to melt down over the remaining teeth. There were lumps and craters all over the roof of its mouth as foul fluids and blood oozed from many of them. The left side of its jaw was indeed drooping and missing clumps of hair.

If only that had been enough to kill it. Maybe it still would. Maybe it was just going to be a slow death over weeks, months or years. I'll be real with you, though. That wasn't a comfort to me in this moment as I was about to be eaten by my evil stepfather.

I closed my eyes and braced myself for the end.

But the end didn't come. As my eyes stayed shut, I suddenly felt the weight lifted off my body. I opened my eyes and turned to see another werewolf rolling on the ground, snapping at Dennis. This wolf had the unmistakable blond streaks on top of its head.

For the third time tonight, Brandi had saved my life.

With the moon shining down on this part of the woods, I could get a good view of the battle even without my flashlight. The wolf that used to be my sister powered her opponent onto his back and swiped at his face with a mammoth claw, sending fur, flesh and blood splattering onto the neighboring oaks.

The Dennis-wolf howled in pain as Brandi brought her teeth down directly on its wounded neck, ripping another chunk out, resulting in an arterial spray. I was a little surprised that Brandi was manhandling it like this. Dennis was bigger and seemed stronger, but maybe the silver nitrate had weakened it. Plus, Brandi had gotten the drop on him and was not letting go. Or maybe she was just taking out all her rage, both human and supernatural, on the monster that had abused her.

But would it be enough to kill it? I'd seen these wolves soak up bullets like a sponge. Would a flesh wound be enough?

In all the confusion, I remembered my shotgun. I looked and saw the beam from my flashlight on the ground about thirty feet away. While the wolves were distracted with each other, I tried to get up to my feet, but I collapsed. I pushed up to my knees and bear-crawled to the light. I grabbed it and glanced around for my shotgun. As I did, the light illuminated the continuing werewolf brawl.

I saw Brandi raise her claws again, ready for another strike, but Dennis grabbed her by the throat. Brandi stopped mid-attack as Dennis pushed her entire weight off of him, never releasing the grip on her throat. On his feet now, he raised her off the ground with one hand and slammed her down hard with a chokeslam. My sister writhed in pain as a guttural howl escaped her mouth.

Dennis was over her now, still holding her throat. He thrust his own claw into her side, stabbing her just under her rib cage. He pulled his hand out, causing a generous spurt of blood to stain the ground below and then thrust it back in again, ripping at the newly formed wound.

"Stop!" I shouted, drawing my wolfen stepfather's attention.

He snarled at me, still clutching Brandi's throat, lifting her as he rose and slammed her into a tree, the thick trunk cracking from the impact of the giant wolf. Tossing her aside, he turned his focus back to me. She hit the ground hard and whimpered like a scalded dog.

I immediately regretted not finding my shotgun before I got the creature's attention, but it was too late now. The flashlight illuminated the multitude of injuries Dennis had suffered, with blood-matted fur, disfigured features and missing chunks of flesh.

The beast roared and lunged toward me. I scooted back as fast as I could. Just before it was back on top of me, I felt the barrel of the shotgun on the ground. I grabbed it and was able to aim just as Dennis was above me. Without even a thought, I pulled the trigger.

The blast hit Dennis on the left side of his chest and knocked him backward. An unearthly cry emanated from the werewolf as it convulsed, still standing on its feet. I pumped the shotgun and fired again, hitting him just to the left of the initial wound.

The second impact knocked him to the ground. He started shaking violently as the wound smoked, sizzled and bubbled. Like Gunther, he vomited a torrent of blackish red blood that erupted from his mouth before falling back down, choking him as he suffered.

Getting to my feet, my entire body screaming at me for doing so. I ignored the pain, needing to see this.

Making my way to my dying stepfather, I looked down at him as his face receded into its human form. I stood over him and cocked my head, making eye contact with him for one last time before he died.

I spat in his face.

"Fuck you, Dennis. Rot in hell."

As he died, I didn't feel any real satisfaction. The world needed to be rid of him, no doubt. He caused so much pain and suffering. My family had been destroyed. All that was left were Brandi and me—and Brandi was cursed. I thought about Arianna and the life we could have had. I thought of her parents and brothers and how they would have to deal with her loss. Same with the Wrights once they learned their son's true fate. Vengeance was necessary but it was no substitute for everybody who'd been lost.

I also had another problem that I had temporarily forgotten about.

A growl from behind me reminded me that there was another werewolf here. I turned and held my flashlight on Brandi, now back on her feet and staring directly at me. One of her hands was at her side, trying to stifle the flow of blood from Dennis's attack. She roared when she came into the light.

I reached into my pocket and grabbed the last silver shell I had. I loaded it and brought the flashlight back up, the gun barrel directly over it and pointed at the thing that used to be my twin sister.

She started toward me. Slowly. Stalking.

"Brandi!" I shouted. "It's me!"

The wolf kept coming, but it seemed like its pace had slowed slightly.

"Sis, please don't," I begged, tears flowing. "Please don't make me do this."

It slowed a little more but still moved, a snarl curling its mouth back as it salivated.

"Please," I said, knowing I only had time for one last plea. "I love you."

Brandi stopped. The snarl stopped and the wolf let out a whimper as it fell to one knee, gripping its side tighter. It looked down at its wound, then back up at me. Its eyes were different this time. They were still that terrifying bright yellow, but they looked almost sad. I could see a hint Brandi in them. She was in there. I knew it.

"Brandi..." I started, not knowing what else to say.

She got back to her feet, never breaking eye contact. I was still ready to shoot, but I hoped against hope that she wouldn't make me pull the trigger.

Thankfully, she didn't. She turned and ran off into the trees.

I lowered my gun and collapsed to the ground again. I looked over and saw Dennis was now back to human form. He was also very much dead. I was sure of it this time. His wounds from Gunther's attack had healed, but now there were fresh ones from Brandi. His eyes were wide and he looked like he'd died scared.

He deserved it, but I still felt hollow. My parents were dead. Arianna was dead. Brandi was infected and was God knows where. My actions had gotten Trevor and Gunther killed. It was a pyrrhic victory.

Pushing myself back against a tree, I rested my shotgun in my lap and waited to see if Brandi would come back.

She didn't.

CHAPTER 46

I woke up in the cave as the sun fought its way through the entrance. I had crawled in to rest after the battle, both to protect myself from the elements and to prevent Brandi from reaching me if she came back in wolf form. Not only that, but I didn't know if I'd even be able to make it back to my house in the exhausted state I was in. I didn't know how long I'd been out, but it must have been quite a while, my body needing to recover from the trauma it had suffered.

It took a bit of effort, but I braced myself against the rock wall and made my way back to my feet. I took my time to make sure I was steady as I exited the cave, the freezing air greeting me as I did.

I was relieved to see Dennis's body was still there and still human. His skin had lost all color and blisters were forming, some of which had burst already, giving certain areas a type of sheen. He also looked bloated, which, I remembered from biology class, was the result of gases being released.

I leaned my head back against the trees, wondering

how I was even going to clean up this mess, but I had something more important to deal with at the moment. I had to find Brandi.

And I had an idea where she was.

***

It took me twice as long to get to the abandoned building as it typically did, my injuries slowing me considerably. When I got there, I saw that the bulkhead doors were open and I was immediately thankful because it would be quite a task for me to move them in my current condition.

I dragged myself down the hallway to the end cell where I had kept Gunther. Relief washed over me when I saw Brandi sitting on the bed, human once again. She was against the wall, knees drawn in, the blanket I had given the room's last occupant wrapped around her.

"Brandi!" I exclaimed when I saw her.

She looked up at me with tear-streaked eyes. "Brady?" she asked in a daze.

I dropped my gun and ran over to hug her, pulling her in close and holding her like I never planned on letting go. I was the first to get emotional. She followed not long after. We held each other and cried for a long time.

***

Once we'd composed ourselves, we had to figure out a way out of this mess.

"Why did you come here?" I asked her.

"I— I don't know," she said. "I think I followed a scent. It was yours, but also something different. Something like me."

That made sense. I'd been here over a dozen times in the past few months and while I didn't know much about wolf packs, there had been a wolf from what I supposed was her bloodline staying here. There must have been something that attracted her to this spot.

"Brady," she asked breaking through my musings. "What are we going to do?"

I hadn't known at first, but seeing my sister back in human form made me realize I had lost a lot, but not everything.

"I have an idea," I told her. "Do you trust me?"

***

Brandi dressed in some of the spare clothes that I had left for Gunther. They were all too big, but they would protect her from the elements over the next few days. We made our way back through the woods to the cave. I had to lean on her at certain points to keep moving forward, but we did.

When we got to the cave, we went inside. Thankfully, I still had the key at home for the steel collar which was still affixed to the wall. I hated the idea of Brandi spending the next two days here after all she'd been through, but from what I'd learned from Gunther, she was likely to turn two more times and she needed to be missing until this cycle was over. I couldn't have her go to the cops right now. They may hold us. Probably send us to the hospital. What would happen at night when Brandi turned? It would be a massacre. Enough blood had been shed.

I wanted to keep her in the cells at the asylum but after the last werewolf had escaped, I had no confidence it would hold her and I didn't have the time or strength to prep anywhere else.

This would have to do.

Brandi didn't argue with me when I explained it. She agreed this was the best course of action. I stayed with her for a while and explained my plan. When I mentioned Arianna, her face screwed up and twisted as she remembered that her best friend had been murdered. Her best friend who I also loved.

"Oh, Brady," she said. "Arianna..."

I fought back my tears. There would be time for that later.

"I know," was all I said.

With both of us knowing what we had to do, I left my sister in the cave and went home.

CHAPTER 47

I walked back into what had become a house of horrors. What was left of Liz's body was still in the kitchen and a putrid smell permeated the house. I couldn't bring myself to go downstairs where I knew Arianna's body was still tied to the chair in the workshop.

My body screamed as I moved to the second floor. When I got to my room, I retrieved my cell phone for the first time in weeks. It was dead, so I plugged it in lay back on my bed as I waited for it to charge.

After a few minutes, it lit up and I unlocked it, leaving it affixed to the charging cable. A ton of notifications popped up. I had at least twenty missed calls from Arianna as well as too many text messages to count.

They said u left with your mom? Why didn't u tell me?
Why aren't u talking to me?
Brady, I'm worried.
Please call me.
I'm coming over.

A fresh bout of rage washed over me, but I suppressed it. I was sure I'd be making a therapist a lot of money once this was done. Assuming I wasn't going to jail.

That was the thing. I was about to make a call, and I had my story that I was going to tell, but I didn't know if it would hold up. I searched for the number online and put it in the phone, hitting send. After two rings, a voice came over the other end.

"Hillcrest Police Department."

I paused, unable to speak for a minute.

"Hello?"

"Yes," I finally said, my voice cracking. "Detective Wallace please."

***

It took a long time to make my way downstairs. A task that typically took maybe a minute, took me almost ten. I collapsed on the front porch as a battalion of police officers arrived at my house. The uniforms led the way toward me as Detective Wallace followed behind.

"Brady," he said. "Is anyone in the house?"

I nodded.

"Are they armed?"

I shook my head. "My girlfriend and mother. My stepfather killed them."

He looked at me like he knew something like this was coming. He knew something was off with me as soon as we met. But I don't think he quite expected this.

The team swept the house and found Arianna and my mother just as I had said. They transferred me to the hospital where they kept me under armed guard initially. The doctors wrote up a laundry list of my afflictions—broken ribs, a sprained ankle, multiple contusions and lacerations, muscle atrophy and dehydration.

Detective Wallace came by once I'd been treated and settled into a room with an IV going.

"Okay, Brady," he said takin a seat next to my bed. "Tell me what happened."

As in my first conversation with him, I told him as much of the truth as I could without incriminating myself. I told him I overheard my mother and stepfather arguing one night talking about how they were having an affair before my dad died. I told him how my mother implied that my father's death wasn't an accident and that it was Dennis who was responsible.

Wallace took notes as I gave him the details.

I said that we were all shocked when Dennis checked himself out of the hospital, but that was when he went crazy. I told him he knew we found out the truth and that was when he locked up Brandi and me in the basement and beat my mother to death with a hammer in front of us.

Wallace had clearly seen some shit over the years, but

even he looked disturbed by what I was telling him.

The next part was hard for me to recount and I did my best to get everything out without breaking down. I skipped the fact that he took Brandi with him that night. I didn't have to be a detective to know what happened when he'd taken her away, but that was Brandi's trauma and I wasn't going to put it out there for everyone to hear. Dennis had committed enough atrocities that would come to light. That could stay between me and my sister.

I told him how Arianna came to check on us and Dennis brought her down and held her captive too. I told him how Dennis shot Arianna in front of us and left her to bleed out while we watched. I made it through, but just barely, without having had the chance to properly grieve my girlfriend.

The detective was sympathetic. I think he knew my emotion was genuine. He passed me the box of tissues from the table next to the bed. I took one and wiped my eyes. Then I took another and blew my nose. He waited patiently while I let it all out. When I finally had exhausted my tear supply for the time being, I went back to the story.

This next part was a tad fabricated.

I told him that last night, Dennis took Brandi away, but I didn't know where, He was gone for a few hours before he came back for me. I told Wallace he was naked and crazed, holding my shotgun, talking about how he was going to hunt me. I said he took me upstairs and gave me a fifteen-minute head start.

He chased me through the woods, but I got the drop on him, hitting him with a tree branch. With the gun knocked out of his hands, I managed to get it back and I shot him twice. I was shocked that he was able to get up and run away, but I didn't follow him. Instead, I just ran home and called the cops.

"Have you found my sister?" I asked.

"No," Detective Wallace said grimly. "You have any idea where he may have taken her?"

I shook my head solemnly. Now I was lying and I hoped it wouldn't show. I was a little surprised at his next question.

"Do you think Dennis McGill had anything to do with Trevor Wright's disappearance?"

When he asked me that question, it kind of felt like when Michael Strahan broke the single-season sack record. Sack number twenty-two and a half came against the Packers when Brett Favre appeared to just lie down and let him get it in the last game of the season.

Maybe he knew I wasn't a killer or even a bad person, but it felt like he was giving me an out. I took it.

I nodded and said, "Dennis had a weird fixation on my sister. It bordered on creepy. When he found out what Trevor had done, he was really pissed. I thought he was going to find him and hurt him, but he calmed down eventually. At least I thought he had."

Detective Wallace jotted the notes down and stood up.

"Listen, Brady," he said. "We haven't found your sister or your stepfather yet, so we're going to keep an officer here for now."

"Am I in trouble?" I asked.

"There's a lot to sort out here. But, no, you're not being charged with anything at the moment. But that's predicated on you having told me the truth just now."

"I told you everything."

Everything that wouldn't put me in jail.

***

They found Dennis's body the next morning. Detective Wallace came and told me. The spot that they found him in was a few hundred yards from the cave. At least I knew that was where it was. Brandi and I had moved his body as far as we could from what would be Brandi's hiding spot for the next few days. We didn't want the cops to find her until she wasn't going to change for the next month.

The detective said it looked like the animals had got at him pretty good. By the time they found him he was pretty torn up. I figured some of the other woodland creatures had had a go at him over the past twenty-four hours. I didn't have any sympathy.

He confirmed they hadn't found Brandi yet, but they searched the house and Dennis's car. They found the hammer he used to kill my mother, the gun he shot Arianna with and a shovel, axe and a severed pinky finger in his trunk. They were going to run prints and DNA to determine whose it was. I knew what the results would say.

Wallace told me that, based on the evidence they had, there was no reason to doubt my story and that they would not be filing charges against me. I thought I'd be relieved, but I just felt numb.

***

They released me from the hospital the following morning. With my house being an active crime scene, I couldn't go home, but I didn't have anywhere else to go so Detective Wallace drove me to a motel just off the highway. I tried to protest, but he insisted and I felt it better not to put up too much of a fight even though Brandi was my top priority now that the three-day moon cycle had passed. As we drove, Detective Wallace asked if I was going to be okay staying at my house once the forensic team was done with their investigation.

I said I was. I was eighteen and I was pretty sure that I

was about to inherit the house anyway so they couldn't really force me into foster care or anything like that.

He gave me some cash to pay for the room since my debit card and identification were still back at the crime scene. He helped me check in and wished me well.

"Why are you being so nice to me?" I asked, wondering why he wasn't treating me like a suspect.

"Something bad happened to you, Brady," he said. "This doesn't completely add up and I know there's more than you're telling me, but I know bad people. And I don't think you're a bad person. Your stepfather was and he's gone. So I'm helping you now."

"What if you're wrong about me?" I asked, surprised that I would even verbalize that.

"Then you'll be seeing me a lot sooner than you think. I'll be keeping an eye on you."

Fair enough. Although that would certainly complicate my Brandi situation.

I settled into the small motel room and watched out the window as Detective Wallace departed. Once he was gone, I made my way back to the cave. I was still weak, but with the nutrition and medicine I received in the hospital, I was able to move pretty well back to the cave. When I got there, I saw Brandi was gone. So was the collar, removed from the wall.

Before I had left her two days ago to call the cops, I'd given her the key to the chains so she could move freely during the day before locking herself up again at night. I also left her tools to remove the shackles from the cave wall. I was relieved that she pulled it off. Now I just had to confirm that she went were I told her to go once she wasn't going to turn for another month.

I left the cave for the last time without looking back and made my way back to the asylum. For the last time, I navigated the halls to the room and felt immense relief when I found Brandi sitting on the bed in one of the rooms. I ran in and embraced her.

"It's almost over, sis."

After doing what I needed to do, I returned to the motel, took a long, hot shower and passed out on the bed.

I woke up to the sound of my phone ringing. Looking at the caller ID, I saw it was Detective Wallace. I picked up and anxiously said "Hello?"

"Brady, we found your sister."

***

I drove to the hospital and asked the front desk what room Brandi Bennett was in. They told me she was still in the emergency room and escorted me there. Brandi was in one of the bays with Detective Wallace and a uniformed female officer standing by her bed. I ignored them as I ran over and hugged her as tightly as I could.

She returned the gesture, squeezing me tight. Tighter than I would have thought possible.

When we finally broke our embrace. Brandi recounted the story we had come up with. She confirmed everything I said, exactly up until the point where Dennis took her away. She said he'd taken her to the old mental hospital and locked her in a room, saying that he would be back for her after he took care of Brady.

The female officer, Carter her name was, asked if Dennis had assaulted her. Brandi replied with a vehement no, confirming that this was another part of the story that no one but her and I would ever know.

"How did they find you?" I asked like I didn't know.

"We got a call about screams coming from the old hospital," Wallace said. "Anonymous tip."

He gave me a look like he somehow knew it was me who had made the call from a burner phone I'd bought at a gas station three towns away.

"Thank God!" I said.

"Yes, sir," Wallace said. "I guess you both got very lucky here."

CHAPTER 48

Brandi's hospital stay was a short one. It surprised the doctors just how minor her injuries were, considering what she'd been through. Of course, there was a reason for that, but we weren't going to let anyone else in on it. She stayed one night and then came home. Well, home to the motel anyway. We stayed there for three more days until Detective Wallace called and let us know that the forensic team was finished and we could return home when we were ready.

When we got there, we spent a good portion of the day cleaning up as best we could. I'd gotten better than I ever wanted to be at removing bloodstains. I sobbed the entire time as I cleaned the room where we had been held captive. The room where Arianna died.

We finished up, took out the trash and went to bed. The next morning, we talked about what we were going to do next. We were both legal adults so we could stay in the house. We didn't really have much family left since Dad's side had become estranged after he died and Mom didn't have any left after our grandparents died. Dennis pretty much had no one either and, frankly, I had no interest in knowing any of them if he did. We had to figure out how to navigate everything on our own.

Arianna's funeral was the day after Brandi got out of the hospital. We tried to come, but the Kentons would not let us attend. I tried to explain to Ari's uncle at the door that we were victims too, but he firmly told us we were not welcome. Somehow it was like losing her all over again. Still, I couldn't blame her parents for not wanting to see us.

We just hung back until the mourners had dispersed and then we went and placed flowers on her freshly covered grave. We stood there in silence for what felt like hours, just looking at the grave marker where a tombstone would soon carry her name.

Finally, I mustered the strength to go back home.

After a few weeks, the medical examiner's office released the bodies of Liz and Dennis to us. We had them cremated. No obituaries. No services. We didn't even buy an urn for either. When the boxes came home, we dumped Liz's ashes in the woods.

I wanted to flush Dennis's down the toilet but thought better of it, not wanting to have to explain that clog to a plumber. Instead, I drove to a Denny's off the nearest state highway and poured out the ashes in the dumpster.

We found a relatively inexpensive lawyer online, but he actually ended up being very good. For all the fucked-up shit Dennis and my mother did, they had a decent amount of estate planning done. As next of kin, we inherited everything. The house, the bank accounts, their investments, all of which provided a nice chunk of change. They also each had a million-dollar life insurance policy, so we were in pretty good shape financially for a couple of orphans.

***

A few weeks after everything had settled, I saw on the news that they had pulled a dead body out of the river, the victim of an apparent shooting. The body was badly decomposed, but they were able to identify it as a man named David Bixby from Jacksonville, Florida.

Apparently, David was a doctor that had been missing for a few months. He was wanted for questioning in connection with several murders that occurred in Jacksonville right before he went missing. There was also mention of a fatal animal attack at a local trailer park around the same time David went missing. They didn't find the animal but the speculation was that it was a large bear.

Sure. A bear.

I now had an actual name to go with my former pet werewolf. I just hoped he was at peace now because it sounded like that business in Florida was just as nasty as what had happened here.

***

While Brandi and I were dealing with our grief as well as the financial and technical issues around our parents' death, we had another, bigger problem to deal with.

"What are we going to do about my... condition?" she asked as we sat in the living room, the whole house open to us now beyond just our bedrooms.

"We have to make sure you're locked up during those three nights every month when you change," I said. "So you don't hurt anyone."

We decided that the room in the basement was our best option. Dennis's psychopathic plan had actually given us a solution. The door was heavy and the room was soundproof. It should be able to hold her without a problem.

"But, if it doesn't," she told me, "If I get out, you're going to have to kill me. Somehow, I was able to stop myself from attacking you. I don't know if I can do that again."

When the first month had passed, we made our way down to the room in the basement just before sunset. Brandi was wearing a robe. As she walked into the room, I turned my back and she tossed it out before I shut her in.

Once the door was locked, I pulled up a chair and sat there, my shotgun in my lap, loaded with fresh silver slugs. I prayed I wouldn't have to use it.

I didn't. Even though I heard the occasional pounding on the other side of the door, Dennis had done an excellent job of soundproofing the room. It didn't register as more than a normal knock even though I imagine Brandi must have been going crazy in there.

The next morning, once the sun was up, I opened the door and tossed the robe inside. Brandi came out a few minutes later. She looked dejected.

"What's wrong?" I asked. "It worked."

"I'm angry, Brady," she said. "When I woke up, I was myself, but I'm so fucking angry I can feel it in my bones. I have these dark thoughts. It's like I need to feed. To hunt. To kill."

"Brandi," I said, not actually knowing what to say to her.

"What you said the man told you, about the wolf getting into your soul. I think he was right. I feel like I'm going to lose myself."

"No!" I shouted. "That's not going to happen. We're going to make sure of it."

"How? How can we possibly stop it?"

"We'll find a way. We have to."

She didn't look like she believed me.

"I promise."

EPILOGUE

I was standing at the top of the steps when I heard Brandi come in, the dude she was with stumbling in behind her. She had long since let her hair go back to its natural brown color. Tonight, it was neatly straightened and silky in anticipation of her date. She dressed in a tight black minidress with high heels. Her attire was deliberately chosen to garner male attention.

You might say it was bait.

My sister and I had both enrolled in community college. It made sense for us. We had a large house all to ourselves and we didn't have to worry about staying in a dorm where Brandi may have to explain why she disappeared for three consecutive nights every month.

Her date looked like he belonged on the cover of *Douchebag Monthly*. In fact, a lot about him reminded me of Trevor Wright. That was funny: I thought of Arianna every single day since she died, but this was the first time I'd thought about Trevor in a long time. The DNA had confirmed that the pinky in Dennis's car was

382

his, so Liz's husband had posthumously taken the fall for that murder too, leaving me in the clear.

I peered over the railing and saw the dude pawing at Brandi. She giggled like she was into it.

"Slow down, Steve," she said, laying the vocal fry on thick, trying to come off as ditzy . "We have all night."

"What can I say, baby?" the dipshit slurred. "I'm impatient."

"Oh, it'll be worth the wait," she said seductively. "I want another drink. You want one?"

He accepted the offer and she left the room, returning a few moments later with two beers open and ready to go. She handed him one and offered her bottle for a toast.

"To a memorable evening!" she said.

They clinked bottles and Steve downed what must have been half the bottle. He put it down on the coffee table and moved in, lips puckered, trying to kiss Brandi. She leaned back slightly and let him fall forward into her lap.

She put her beer down and shoved him off of her, knocking him onto the floor. He landed on his back and immediately started snoring.

I came down the stairs as she stood and brushed herself off.

"Jesus, that shit works fast," she said.

"Well, he looked pretty fucked up already."

"It's not my fault this prick can't hold his liquor."

"Not many people *can* drink with you these days."

She shrugged, knowing it was true. Since her change last year, she found that her alcohol tolerance was very high.

"Let's move him," I said.

***

Just before sunset the next evening, Brandi and I opened the door to the basement and saw that Steve was now awake, agitated and confused. He was zip-tied at his hands and feet and gagged with duct tape. He started screaming through the gag when he saw us.

"Shut up, Steve," I told him.

He didn't listen, so Brandi slapped him hard. That got him to stop.

I pulled up a chair and sat reverse on it. I pulled my Glock and held it in front of me.

"So, listen, buddy," I said. "My sister is going to remove the gag. When she does, you're not going to say a word until I tell you to. Got it?"

He nodded. I did the same to Brandi and she ripped the tape off his mouth without warning.

"What the fuck?" he exclaimed, ignoring my previous instruction.

Brandi slapped him again.

"I told you not to speak until spoken to," I admonished, giving him a second to compose himself before continuing. "Do you know Heather Turner?"

"Who?"

"Don't play dumb, Steve," Brandi said. "I mean, you *are* dumb, but you know what we're talking about. We already know the answers. We just want to see if you're going to lie to us."

"So," I repeated, showing him the barrel of my gun, "do you know Heather Turner?"

"Yes! I know her!"

"Good. Do you remember raping her?"

"What? I didn't rape that bitch!"

Brandi slapped him again, even harder this time, causing him to bite his tongue. He spit blood on the plastic wrap that covered the entire room.

"My sister told you we already know the truth," I said. "Yet here you are, lying to us."

"I didn't rape her."

"Steve, we went to high school with Heather. She's an old friend of Brandi's. She didn't remember leaving the frat house with you, probably because of the shit you slipped in her drink—the same stuff we gave you, by the way—but she woke up the next morning, in your bed. You told her it was consensual and threatened her if she told anyone otherwise."

"I... I didn't!" he protested weakly, knowing that we had

too many details for him to get away with this.

"But she had to tell somebody, and it all came out to her dear friend Brandi. She begged us not to tell anyone and we promised we wouldn't. But the thing is, Steve, we can't let you get away with this."

"So, what? You're going to shoot me?"

I looked at the gun in my hand and laughed. "This? No. That's just in case you tried anything before we were ready."

I stood up and continued.

"You're a predator, Steve. And Brandi and I unfortunately have some experience with predators. My sister also has certain needs and someone like you is perfect to fill those needs."

He was panicking again.

"What the fuck does that mean? Help! Someone help!"

"Oh, shut the fuck up, Steve. The room's soundproofed, dickhead."

"Please, what do you want?"

"Just you," Brandi said as she started to untie her robe.

The bound man looked more confused than ever.

Brandi turned to me and winked. Her irises were yellow.

"Gonna need a little privacy, bro."

I turned and held my hand out behind me. She handed me the robe and I gathered it and the chair and left the room without looking back.

The last thing I heard as I closed the door were the date rapist's terrified screams as he watched my sister turn.

AFTERWORD

Thank you for reading *My Pet Werewolf.*

Werewolves have always been my favorite monster, but they have also been woefully underrepresented when compared to other mythical monsters. In fact, one of the most lamentable developments in lycanthropy has been their hijacking by the romance genre (Not trying to yuck anyone's yum here, if that's your thing more power to you), but it's long past time to give them back that feral edge and I hope that this book is a worthy step in that direction.

If you want to learn how Dr. David Bixby became the ill-fated "Gunther," you'll be happy to know that a prequel novella entitled...well...*Gunther* is coming very soon! The best part is it will be absolutely free for members of my VIP Readers Club! If you sign up you will also get a free short *Another Day at the Office* (as well as any future free shorts and novellas), updates on new projects and opportunities to participate in contests and giveaways!

Sign up today at www.jameskaine.net

Lastly, if you enjoyed this book and have a few minutes to spare, please consider writing a review. Reviews help indie horror books like this get in the hands of fellow horror fans and are very much appreciated. You can review *My Pet Werewolf* on Amazon, GoodReads, BookBub or anywhere you purchased the book.

Thank you again and I look forward to bringing you more great horror fiction soon!

-James

About the Author

James Kaine is what happens when a 10-year-old gets his hands on a Stephen King book. From the moment he cracked it open, he knew he wanted to be a horror writer. He published his debut novel *Pursuit* in 2022, followed by *My Pet Werewolf* in 2023 with many more to come.

When he's not concocting horrible scenarios to write about, James spends his time with his wife and two children and his loyal Boston Terrier. He loves travelling, heavy music, and New York Giants football which can be terrifying in its own right.

Learn more at www.jameskaine.net

ALSO BY JAMES KAINE

It was supposed to be the time of their life. When their honeymoon is crashed by a maniac on a motorcycle, will they survive the blood-drenched night?

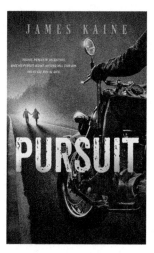

Available in eBook, Paperback, Hardcover and Audio

Printed in Great Britain
by Amazon